For The Weekend

Stone Family Series
Book 4

Sophie Andrews

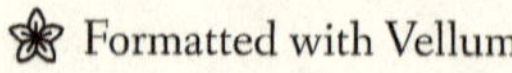 Formatted with Vellum

Content Note

For The Weekend is a steamy grumpy sunshine fake dating romance novel. Roman, the delightedly gruff and grumpy single dad, is a former addict who has had a child with another former addict who is incarcerated during the length of the novel. Eloise, the funny yet chaotic baker, is neurodivergent and plus-sized, and she struggles to deal with family members who disrespect her, including on the page comments that are fat phobic and put her down for being ADHD. If any of these topics are triggering for you, please read with care.

For the readers, especially the ones patiently waiting for me to write one bed and a "it's not gonna fit" scene...

Spoiler: it does.

Chapter 1
Roman

I love Wawa as much as the next guy—the freshly baked bread smell hits every time—but watching my six-year-old daughter sprint from end to end, shouting literal obscenities about how "fucking amazing" it is... Well, it's exhausting.

After driving nearly seven hours from Buffalo, New York, to West Chester, Pennsylvania, I wasn't looking forward to opening the door of our new home to an empty kitchen, and Mazie polished off the last of the food I packed her two hours ago. So I stopped at the regional mini-mart I've been missing for a long time, intent on ordering a ten-inch double meat Italian, but first, I had to wrangle the human equivalent of speed.

"Daddy! They have doughnuts *and* hot dogs!"

"Yep."

"Can I get a milkshake?"

"If you stop running around here like an animal, sure."

She stops in front of me with a can of Pringles. "What about these?"

At this point, she could ask me for a pony, and the answer would be, "Sure."

"Fuck yes!"

Even though the store is almost empty, she's got to stop cursing. A battle I've been fighting for the last year. "Watch your language."

She doesn't acknowledge that she heard me, too busy pressing on one of the order screens.

"First time here?"

It takes me a moment to realize the feminine voice is aimed my way, and I glance to my right before turning back to Mazie, only to do a double take at the woman, her head tilted as she watches my kid with an amused smile on her face.

"Yeah," I say, and the woman laughs as Mazie studies the screen seriously, as if she's actually reading it. Mazie likes to pretend she knows how to read, often making up whole stories from the short paragraphs on the backs of cereal boxes.

"I think she's ordering everything on the menu," the beautiful stranger says, angling her face my way. Her smile reaches sparkling green eyes, lifts up the rosy apples of her cheeks, and it feels like someone twice my size has punched me in the chest.

Flattened me right over.

She moves closer as if waiting for me to answer her, but I can't. Not when she smells like sugar and spice and everything nice and looks like all of my favorite goddamn sins.

There is not an ounce of makeup on her creamy golden skin, and she's tall. Probably only an inch or two under six feet, curvy all over, round in the best places. Her wheat-colored hair is a mix of waves and curls, a halo around her head, and her loose shirt has the word *GORGEOUS* printed across it in all caps. Hot-pink spandex shorts showcase her long and supple legs, and I have a terrible itch to skate my fingers over the dimples of her thighs.

But I don't even know the woman.

Except that, yeah, she's fucking *gorgeous*.

"Good for her," the goddess of a woman says. "I like a girl who knows what she wants."

I nod like a goddamn idiot.

Because I've only just arrived back in my hometown with a daughter who might be purchasing fourteen macaroni and cheeses for all I know, and I never thought I'd run into...*her*.

Whoever she is.

My new favorite fantasy, from the way she licks her lower lip and combs her fingers through her hair. I imagine doing the same thing, wrapping those golden strands around my fist, biting that mouth.

And what the fuck?

I'm with my kid.

In a convenience store.

Not exactly the best time to be picturing this stranger underneath me, but it's been a long damn time, and she is everything I love about the fairer sex, thick and all natural.

"Daddy!" Mazie squeals, drop-kicking me into reality. "I want chicken fingers! They have chicken fingers! Can I get them?"

"Sure."

The laugh the woman lets out next to me is pure delight. "Got you wrapped around her finger, huh?"

"Number 871," a worker calls out at the food counter, and the woman next to me steps forward, glancing over her shoulder in my direction, offering me one last look that I know I'll be using in the future.

Especially when she waves. "See you, *Daddy*."

My mouth goes dry, and she accepts her food with a thanks

then pivots away to pay for it, and I stare at her swaying ass until she's out of sight.

I blink back over to my kid and remember why I'm back home in the first place.

Which is definitely not to fall all over myself in the middle of Wawa because of a flirtatious smile and a well-timed *Daddy*.

It's to be the best father I can be.

"Can I get this pink drink? It has whipped cream and it's pink. My favorite! Can I get it?"

"Sure." I scrub my hand over my face. We have to get out of here.

It's time to go home.

Chapter 2
Roman

"Steve! Steve! Where are youuuuuu?"

I roll my eyes and slump against the counter. All I wanted was a few minutes of quiet with a cup of coffee before I did possibly the hardest thing I've ever had to do.

But *of course* fucking Steve has to go and ruin it.

My daughter races into the kitchen, the pounding of her feet echoing off the hardwood. No wonder why Steve always hides. He's a skittish son of a bitch, and she's basically a wild pony disguised as a little girl.

"Daddy!" She pants as if she's run a marathon. "I looked all over, and I can't find Steve!"

I swallow down a gulp of my coffee, watching her in silence. This game we play always makes her giggle. Her informing me of her latest mystery—she can't find her Elsa Crocs, lost the TV remote, missing her hairbrush—and me staring at her until she confesses that she didn't *really* look.

"I checked under the couch!"

I sip my coffee.

"And under my bed."

With a sigh, I set down my mug. There's no way around it. I gotta get on all fours to find this floppy-eared motherfucker.

Mazie crawls next to me, doing her best to appear as if she's searching for him, but she's merely laughing at me. I check all his favorite hiding spots. In the closet, which is why it needs to stay closed; behind the television stand, which is why I set up the stupid wired gate around it; and in my bedroom, beats the hell out of me why that fur ball likes to hang out in there.

The house is a ranch, so there aren't many places he can hide. And yet it takes me ten minutes to locate him. Behind the toilet, up on his hind legs, cleaning himself by licking his paws and running them down his long ears, tugging them toward his face.

Fucking adorable.

I slowly reach out my hand, holding my breath.

He freezes in profile, studying me with one beady eyeball, nose scrunching up and down.

Prey and predator.

I nab him and bring him to my chest as Mazie throws her hands up, cheering. "You got him, Daddy! Good job!"

Steve nestles against my pec, and I hold him close, stroking my thumb between his ears, dipping my chin to kiss him. Because, yeah, I love the little guy.

Mazie begged me for months to get her a rabbit. The counselor at her last school had an emotional support rabbit, and Mazie spent a lot of time in her office. After hearing about that goddamn rabbit for so long, I finally gave in.

Steve's not the easiest animal to take care of, but he's cute as shit.

And Mazie really does love him.

Plus, he is an excellent emotional support animal. Like right now, with my anxiety bubbling right below the surface, the only things keeping me from completely melting down are my kid and this rabbit.

She tries to pet him, straining her arm up, but I don't stop my trek back to the living room, to his bunny duplex in the corner. "Maze, if you're gonna let him out, you need to watch him." I bend, releasing the rabbit so he can hop back into his home. "If he ever chewed through a wire, Steve wouldn't live with us anymore. He'd live in bunny heaven."

When I shut and latch the door, Mazie presses her face against the cage. "I knoooooow."

"If you know, do it."

She huffs, and I poke her shoulder. "Watch the attitude."

She twirls away from me, a puff of pink in her best dress for meeting her aunt and uncles. I'd started putting my plan in motion over a year ago, waiting until I had everything in order—money in the bank, my job in place, and the house—before I put Mazie and Steve in the car to make the move to a town I haven't seen in over a decade.

But I'm back to begin a new life for Mazie and me.

And now, I have to face everything and everyone I left behind, starting with my siblings. Taryn, Griffin, and Ian agreed to meet me here at ten, and every minute closer spikes my pulse.

I'm not looking forward to seeing them—I mean... I am. They're my brothers and sister, but I'm not looking forward to the conversations we need to have. The questions I'm sure they'll ask. The very possible responses they might have when I give them answers.

My journey back home has been a long time coming, and I understand why they may not accept me with open arms. But as much as it might be a struggle to get back in their good graces, I am here for my daughter. She deserves a life with a family, one that I can only give her with the very people I turned my back on.

I don't expect their forgiveness, yet I am hoping for it.

I sweep my gaze around my home as Mazie dances to a song in her head, and it occurs to me one more time how unbelievable it is that I'm here, in the house my parents once owned. The house my mother used to pace when I cried as a baby. The house that I don't have any visual memories of as a child, but that I remember by the scent—a mixture of Tupperware and watermelon.

I don't know why, but the very vague yet semisweet smell of the fruit always lingered in the back of my mind. Along with plastic. Orange and hard. The feel of my fingers against the accordion lids.

The first thing I did when I received the keys was to search high and low for where the smell came from. I couldn't pinpoint it. Nor could I find any of the vintage Tupperware I assumed my mother used to own, which is why it's always been in my memory. Obviously, it was nowhere to be found, but I needed to search anyway.

To be sure.

I don't have many pieces of my childhood left, and even fewer of them pleasant memories, but what I do have all start and end with Mom. And I knew that if I wanted to give Mazie the life she deserved, I had to come back to where my mother gave me the life I threw away.

The one I always should have had.

I don't realize how much time has passed before the doorbell rings, and I'm stunned into place. I knew it was coming, that they were coming, but now that the moment is here, I can't make myself move.

Fear washes over me, and I briefly wonder if they'd think I'd lost it by carrying Steve around with me.

For The Weekend

"Daddy! They're here!" Mazie screeches from somewhere in the house, probably her bedroom, with the big window that looks out front.

My palms turn clammy and my mouth goes dry as I shuffle toward the front door, my feet heavy, all of my practiced words evaporating from my brain the closer I step to it.

I place my hand on the knob, my heart beating out of my chest, my throat clogged.

I open the door, muscles so tense they're vibrating, and I hold myself very still, bracing for the worst as I take in my siblings.

Ian, with his graying beard and hair, a lot older than the last time I saw him yet somehow even more imposing with his muscles and tattoos. Still the best man I've ever known. Griffin and Taryn are behind him, the Irish twins. I can't see my brother's eyes under the shadow of his ball cap, though his scowl is quite clear, while my sister is staring at me slack-jawed.

I don't know what to do or say, physically unable to move. My organs are barely functioning. My nervous system shut down.

But all at once, Ian has his arms around me, and I'm no longer forty years old. I'm five, hugging my brother after I fell off my bike. I am fifteen when I took Mom's car out for an illegal drive and banged it up. I am twenty-five when he begged me with tears in his eyes to go to rehab.

My exhale is jagged, finally releasing the breath I've been holding so many years, and I hug him back, gripping him hard, my face against his shoulder. Even though I have three inches and quite a few pounds on him, I've never felt smaller.

The nagging fear that they very well could turn me away like I did them fades the longer Ian embraces me, and I make sure the sting in my nose and eyes is gone as I step away from him. Then I shift my gaze beyond his shoulder, ready to greet

Taryn and Griffin, who I know will not have the same enthusiasm as our eldest brother, but before I can say anything, Mazie appears at my side, grinning at all of us.

She has been beyond excited to meet everyone ever since I informed her a few weeks ago that we'd be living here so she could hang out with all of her cousins, aunt, and uncles. She's practically buzzing, and I place my hand on her head, clearing my throat. I look at each of my siblings in turn then back to Mazie. "This is my daughter."

Their stunned gasps are audible and in chorus. "*What the fuck?*"

Mazie, who delights in cursing, props her fists on her hips. "Yeah, Daddy. What the fuck?"

A moment of shock passes, and then all three of them burst out laughing. Even Griffin, who is more stone-faced than I remember.

But my foulmouthed daughter makes for a good icebreaker, and I open the door wider for them all to enter the house we shared when we were younger. The moment they step inside, their amusement clears, voices silent as their gazes drift around the walls, maybe trying to imagine what it used to look like since they have more memories than I do. They had more years here because Ian is twelve years older than me, Griffin four, and Taryn three.

Ian's the first to take a few tentative steps toward the kitchen, his hand brushing along the doorjamb. "Mom used to measure all our heights here," he says, after clearing his throat a few times. "I thought...maybe..."

Although I don't recall her doing that, I had the same thought. Maybe when I opened the door, it would be the same. She would be here.

Taryn crosses the living room, voice quiet. "This used to be carpet." Then she kneels down to Steve's house and sticks her finger through the cage, offering him a sniff. When he doesn't run away, she pets the space between his eyes. "What's this guy's name?"

"Steve." Mazie perks up, skipping to my sister's side. "He's a Holland lop and a little son of a bitch."

Taryn shoots her dark eyes to me, her face so much like Mom's, minus the constant smile. Taryn frowns at me. "I assume she got her mouth from you."

"Like any of us is any different," Ian says in my defense, big block letters on his shirt spelling out *Be Fucking Nice*.

Mazie sits down next to where my sister kneels and tilts her face up. "You're my aunt."

Taryn glances to me before smiling at my daughter. "I am. Aunt Taryn. What's your name?"

"Mazie Violet Stone."

Violet, after our mother.

"Mazie Violet Stone," my sister repeats. "Very pretty."

My kid melts into Taryn's side at the compliment, obviously desperate for female attention. It makes me feel like shit that she's gone without for so long, but Taryn has two kids of her own, and Mazie probably gets a mom vibe from her.

Taryn plucks at Mazie's dress. "I bet pink is your favorite color."

"Yes!" Mazie shouts, and I wince, walking over to where she sits with Taryn.

"Inside voice, Maze."

She ignores me, flapping her hands to make the gauzy skirt flounce. "I love pink so fucking much!"

I roll my head back to my shoulders, taking a deep breath before telling her, "You have to stop cursing."

"You curse," she points out, and true, but...

"You're a kid. You're not allowed to curse."

Mazie eyes me unhappily, but Taryn jumps in. "Cursing is

fun sometimes, isn't it? I know when we get so excited or angry, it feels like there are no other words to use besides curses, *but* —" Taryn holds out her hand, keeping the attention of my six-year-old "—we have to be careful with our words. We don't ever want to hurt other people with our language, right?"

"Right," Mazie says, fully in it.

"I also don't want *you* to be hurt because sometimes people are judgmental and not so nice. I don't want other people hurting your feelings because they judge you for cursing."

"What does judgmental mean?" Mazie asks, and Taryn motions to all of us in answer.

"Some people might look at your dad and think he's not very nice." I assume she's referring to my height, build, hair, tattoos...general demeanor. I don't exactly blend in most places. "They might judge him because of what he looks like, and that's never a good thing. Should we ever judge people or treat them mean because they look different from us?" When Mazie shakes her head, Taryn nods. "You're right. We absolutely should not be mean to people because of how they look or talk, but it still happens. A lot of people will still be mean and judge others. And until you're a little bit older, I think we should work on not cursing, so people don't think mean things about you, okay?"

"Okay," Mazie agrees.

I dip my chin in thanks to Taryn before Ian pumps his fist in the air. "Well fucking said."

I roll my eyes, only to realize I've unconsciously closed the distance, along with Ian. The four of us close together.

Leaving Griffin still standing straight-backed like a soldier at the door. I turn to fully face him, finally meeting his gaze since he's removed his hat. His eyes are the same brown as mine. We all share them, dark brown eyes like Mom.

My brother—the one who I know holds a lot of resentment

toward me...not so undeservedly—makes an assessment of me, top to bottom. Though I would never admit it out loud, Griffin makes me feel worst of all. Because he's the good guy. Former military and current first responder. He literally sacrifices himself every day and always does the right thing.

And I haven't. I've never done the right things. Never made good choices.

At least, until now.

"You don't judge a person by what they look like," Griffin says to no one in particular, his voice steady and low. "You judge them by their actions."

It's a deliberate shot at me. He has every right to be angry, and while my first instinct is to fight back, I don't, because this is all part of the process. Being here in person, listening to what they have to say.

Might as well get started.

"I, uh..." I scratch the back of my head. "I made some coffee."

"Ooh!" Mazie hops up. "Can I have cookies?"

When I nod my answer, she runs to the kitchen, the four of us following. I sold off a lot before moving here, packing only the essentials, including a handful of kitchenware. When Taryn notices the coffee mugs I retrieve from the cabinet, she freezes.

I set three of the ceramic stonewashed cups on the counter. "I bought them from your shop a few years ago."

She picks one up, eyes drifting between it and me. "I... I didn't think..."

Think I knew she made pottery? That I cared she sold it online?

Either answer is shitty, and I don't want to be the person she expects. I want to be better. "You do good work."

Surprise raises her brows, but she accepts my words with a

nod. Then she helps herself to coffee and finding milk in the refrigerator. Mazie asks her for a glass before going on and on about the best way to eat cookies. It's by dunking the whole thing in milk first.

Ian pulls up a chair next to my daughter, easily falling into conversation with her, allowing Mazie to ask him questions about why his hair is gray, if he is as strong as "my daddy," and when she can meet her cousins.

He answers them all patiently. His hair is gray because only the best-looking men have gray hair. He is stronger than her daddy—absolutely not. And she'll be able to meet her cousins soon.

Once she finishes her cookies, I tell her to go into the living room to watch television, and she happily zips off, leaving me to face my brothers and sister alone.

"So..."

They stare at me for a long moment, and then the rapid fire begins all at once.

"What the hell is going on?'

"You bought *this* house?"

"Why didn't you tell us about Mazie?"

"Do you have a job?"

"You think you move back and everything is gonna be fine now?"

"Who is her mother?"

I close my eyes, squeezing them tight as their questions fly so fast I can't keep them all straight. The pinch of my fingernails into my palm centers my awareness enough that I can form some words, stilted as they may be. "I wanted to come home to give Mazie a family." Forcing my eyes open, I look to each of my siblings, swallowing around the rock in my throat. "*I needed my family.*"

They don't respond. Ian, of course, holds nothing but

understanding in his features. I wish he wouldn't be so accepting of me. I spent the last twenty years basically doing nothing but being a thorn in his side. Actually, worse than that. I only realized after I had Mazie what he's probably been feeling. Anxiety, fear, stress, pain, panic, dread. My whole life, I looked up to Ian as if he were my father, and I only ever gave him reason to worry.

Then there's Taryn, eternally suspicious. With good reason. She's had a rough go of it, being the only girl with three brothers. Considering all the things I feel completely out of my depth about with Mazie, I assume it was really difficult for her when our mom passed. I'd taken it pretty hard, but I was so young, I believed I had it the hardest. I thought I was grieving the most. When, really, they all lost her too, and more than my brothers and me, Taryn lost something with Mom that she couldn't replace.

As I figured he would, Griffin appears as if he'd like to leave. I have a lot of work to do, repairing what I broke with my brothers and sister, but I know it'll be more difficult with him. We never saw eye to eye. Although if I really reflect on it, I never really saw eye to eye with any of them because I'm the youngest one. I'm the baby and the fuckup. The bastard who couldn't be bothered to do the most basic of things like return a text. I'm not sure when exactly it happened—if it was my third return to rehab or when I promised to show up to help when his twins were born and his wife died, then I never followed through—but Griffin stopped trusting me. I don't blame him. I've been a shitty brother.

But I want to make it up to them. Or at least try.

"I'm sorry," I start, which is inadequate, but it's all I've got right now.

Griffin crosses his arms and remains silent, though he does jut his chin out, a small acknowledgment.

It's Taryn who gets to the heart of the matter. "Why did you hide your daughter from us?"

"I wasn't hiding her. I was...overwhelmed." I've done a lot of therapy to tackle all of my demons, but the most difficult to overcome has always been the constant feeling of inadequacy.

No one in my life—not my mother or my siblings—ever made me feel that way, but I've never been able to shake the belief that deep down I am simply not good enough.

After all, I am the straw that broke the camel's back. Our father left after I was born. When Mom died, I was the only one never to have visited her in the hospital. And Amy, Mazie's mother, chose drugs instead of the life I tried to give her.

Standing here, with all of my deficiencies on display, I have trouble forcing the words off my tongue. I rub the heels of my hands against my eyes. "I spent most of my life doing shitty things, and I didn't care about who I hurt, but now..." I let my arms flop down to my sides. They weigh one thousand pounds. "I need you."

Then I let go of all the weight I've been carrying for so long and tell them everything.

Chapter 3
Eloise

I ignore the latest text from my mother and toss my phone down, staring at my reflection in the mirror.

"I look terrible." I frown at the hideous bridesmaid dress Lily picked out for me. It's like she intentionally chose the most unflattering color and style for me. I sigh and circle to Clara, who's studying me with a shrewd gaze, and Sloane, who's sitting on my bed, folding the mountain of clean laundry I've been ignoring for the past three days.

"Yep," Clara declares, and I laugh, not at all offended. She has a degree in fashion design and owns a lingerie boutique with her wife, and I asked her to come over to help. "It's not your color."

Cognac, that's what Lily called it. But the reddish-brown-gray color isn't working.

Sloane lifts her gaze and shrugs. "You should tell Lily you don't like it. That it makes you uncomfortable."

I pluck at the single shoulder strap of the satin dress, hating how it cuts across my opposite armpit. "You know I can't do that."

With Sloane's gaze back on my clothes, she mumbles, "God forbid you rock the boat."

"Oh, like you can talk," I snap, even though there's no real heat behind my words.

Sloane and I might not look anything alike—her with dark hair, dark wardrobe, and full sleeves of tattoos, and me with blond hair and a style that she lovingly refers to as unicorn puke—but we *get* each other. We understand each other in ways our respective families never have. Black sheep united.

I glance around my disaster of a bedroom, my closet overflowing and shoes all over the place. "You're a saint for even attempting to clean this."

Sloane's tidy and put together, but she's never minded my ADHD brain and whirlwind of chaos. She's never judged me.

"It's not so bad." She puts away a pile of my underwear. "If only I could make myself tackle my own kids' rooms."

Speak of the devils. Shouts erupt from the living room. Sloane dropped off her two kids, Micah and Livie, this morning so she could run some errands.

"Thanks again for watching them," she says. "Trevor's schedule is..." She shakes her head, and I can see the exhaustion in the slope of her shoulders. Her husband is a big pharmaceutical rep and often travels, so running the household and taking care of their kids falls solely on Sloane's shoulders.

"Anytime. You know I love hanging out with them."

She brushes her hand over her forehead, pushing her long bangs back away from her face. "Yeah. Aunt Ellie's their favorite."

I curtsy and pretend to put on a crown, but Clara stops me from accepting the imaginary prize when she flaps her hand. "Stop moving around and go stand in front of the mirror again so I can pin it."

She opens a bag she brought with her and begins to pinch and pull, pinning the material so she can tailor it. As she works, I stare at myself in the full-length mirror. Objectively, the satin is a nice color, but it's simply not *mine*.

I need bright colors, light ones, and to say nothing of the shape. With the huge bow on the shoulder, it doesn't fit right across my bust, so my armpit roll hangs over the arm hole. The skirt is straight down to the floor and makes me look like a paper bag.

I've always been tall, so I learned long ago how to search for clothes that would fit me well. And after I gained weight, I made sure to buy things that accentuated my figure. I can't say I'm confident every day, all day, but I'm happy with the way I look.

This dress does *not* make me happy.

With the wedding taking place in only a few weeks, I should have tried it on a while ago, but I'm great at avoidance. I've become what some might call an expert.

And there is nothing else I like to avoid more than my family.

Especially when it comes to Lily and the weird competition our mothers have entered us into. I lose every time.

At thirty years old, I should probably be used to it, but every condescending comment cuts like it's the first time, and I'd rather ignore any and all of it than have to face it.

I can already imagine my mother's reaction to how I'll look in the dress and the underlying glee in my aunt's face—or the ongoing put-downs about what I'm doing with my life or any mistake I've ever previously made. Especially when I show up without a date.

The horror.

Though I'm pulled from the start of an anxiety spiral by Clara's gossip.

"Did you hear about Roman?"

Sloane stands to place my now-empty laundry basket in the corner of the room. "Roman Stone?"

Clara nods, but I shake my head. "Stone as in Ian, Griffin, and Taryn?"

"Their brother," Clara says.

"Ian's talked about him before," Sloane adds.

The Stone siblings are well-known in town. Griffin is the fire captain, Taryn manages a popular bed-and-breakfast, and Ian owns the tattoo shop where Sloane works, which is conveniently situated right next door to my bakery. In our little downtown neighborhood, you can't throw a stone without literally hitting a Stone or someone related to one.

While I grew up in West Chester, I'm too young to have gone to school with any of the siblings, but I've become friends with all of them the last few years. Except Roman. The youngest and most mysterious one. "What's the story?"

"He's home," Clara informs me as she fusses with the bow at my shoulder. "Opened up an auto body shop on Union Street, so I've seen him around but haven't officially met him. Taryn's been sort of mum about it."

"I think they're all super protective of him," Sloane says idly as she sorts through the jewelry left out on my dresser.

Taryn Stone's best friend is Marianne, Clara's wife, and with Sloane working with Ian, this gossip is coming almost straight from the source. While I don't like to talk about people behind their backs, I am interested in learning more because rumors have always floated around about him.

"So, what's he like? As mean as they say?"

Sloane moves on to my nightstand, attempting to clear it of the tissues, pill bottles, lotions, 854 hair ties, two empty glasses stacked up, a pencil, and a broken PopSocket. "He doesn't strike me as mean."

Clara places another pin at the seam by my armpit. "Grumpy, though."

I snort a laugh. "All the Stones are grumpy."

Clara and Sloane don't disagree. You can be guaranteed two things with that family: a constant willingness to help their neighbors and a completely surly attitude about it. I love them. "What's this Roman guy look like?"

Sloane shrugs. "A lot like Ian."

"But eighteen feet tall," Clara mumbles around a pin in her mouth. "You can't miss him."

"Tall, you say?" I raise my brows in curiosity. While I don't discriminate dates according to size, I am not a little girl, and sometimes I want to *feel* like one. Which is not an easy task when I'm 5'10" and plus-size.

Sloane holds her arms out at her sides, flexing. "He's huge."

"You have my attention, ma'am."

"Long hair, beard, lots of tattoos. Looks like he can do murder with his hands. Now, spin," Clara directs, circling her finger in the air.

I turn around slowly. "Well, when you're a literal mountain, I think that probably comes with the territory. Maybe I could take him to the wedding."

At the familiar spark in Clara's eyes, I hold my palm up to her. "It's a joke."

Kinda.

I do need a date. But I'm not so desperate that I'd go approach a stranger, begging them to go with me like a total weirdo.

At least, not yet.

"All right, my friend." Clara shuts her bag and steps away from me. "Let me get the dress home, and I'll have it back to you by next week."

"You're a lifesaver."

She tips an imaginary hat, and I shuffle off to the bathroom to change out of the dress and into shorts and a T-shirt. By the time I finish, my two friends are in the living room with Sloane's kids, and Clara says a quick goodbye to everyone before taking off with the garment bag, tossing one last offer over her shoulder, "Let me know if you need help finding a date. I'll find one for you."

"Yeah, thanks. See you later!"

Then it's Sloane's turn. She checks the time. "Okay, munchkins, start cleaning up. We've got to go."

Her kids are spread out on the floor. Micah has a big book open in front of him, while Livie's drawing pictures in a notebook with fat crayons.

"Come on," Sloane prods, poking at both of them with her foot. "We have to get moving, or we're going to be late."

"Where're we going?" Livie asks, rolling to her back, sticking a blue crayon up in the air.

"I told you, you and your brother have swim class tonight."

Micah ignores that and instead stands, showing Sloane and me his book, open to a page with flamingos. It never ceases to amaze me that this kid can read fluently, way above second-grade level. "Crocodiles, alligators, and flamingos live in the Florida Everglades. Did you know that?"

Sloane takes his book to put in the backpack she dropped off with them earlier. "That's pretty interesting."

"And a group of flamingos is called a flamboyance."

I laugh. "Accurate."

Micah shadows his mom, continuing to list off his facts as

she helps Livie clean up her art supplies. "And flamingos can fly, but they usually only do it at night. They migrate to new places with water. Is water an ecosystem?"

"I have no idea, buddy." Sloane eventually hauls Livie to her feet. The girl's a slug.

Micah turns to me as if I'll know. "Is water an ecosystem?"

"I guess. Isn't an ecosystem where animals live?"

"Yeah, it's, like…" He pauses, scratching at his head before he bends over, fists out, visibly frustrated he doesn't know the answer. Micah *needs* to know things and gets upset when he doesn't.

Sloane slings the backpack over her shoulder. "I'll Google it later, okay?"

"When we're in the car," Micah tells her. "You have to Google it when we're in the car—is water an ecosystem?"

I curl my hand around his head, tugging him close for a tight embrace. He's like me and enjoys firm hugs, helps him to calm down. We're both neurodiverse, so I feel for the kid. And for Sloane.

He was only diagnosed with autism and ADHD last year, and it threw her for a loop. No matter how well he's doing or how much he's benefiting from the help he's now receiving, it's been hard on her.

I bend to kiss the top of Micah's head. "Don't worry, you'll find out the answer. Just not right now."

He nods and wraps his arms around my waist for a squeeze.

When Livie hooks on to Sloane like a barnacle, she asks her daughter, "Did you tell Aunt Ellie about school?"

Livie shakes her head.

"What happened?"

Micah answers instead. "She didn't cry yesterday."

I hold my hand out for a high five from Livie. "Nice job! Proud of you."

She's really attached to Sloane and painfully shy around new people, so the start of kindergarten has not gone well. Sloane called me in tears the first day.

And I think I could count the number of times I've witnessed her cry on one hand, so I knew she was going through it this last week. It's why I was happy to give her some alone time today.

"All right, we better get going," Sloane says, and I hug both kids one last time before Sloane herds them out the door. "Thanks, Ellie."

"See ya, Sloanie."

With my apartment empty once again, I'm not sure what I'm supposed to do, and I zone out for a few moments until I spot the bottle of polish I picked out earlier this morning to paint my toenails. I sit on the floor, carefully coating them neon pink as I listen to Chappell Roan on repeat and think about the upcoming wedding.

Allowing myself to really sink into the dread.

It's a no-win situation for me if I go or if I suddenly come down with a Victorian wasting disease.

Because Lily is my only girl cousin, and I'm "supposed" to be in her wedding. That's what "family does," and I always try to do what I'm supposed to because being the family fuckup is tiring.

When I finish with my nails, I let them dry while scrolling social media.

Better than dwelling on the fact that I don't have a date to the most important family event since my grandmother's funeral.

I didn't have a date to that, and people told me how sorry they were I didn't have anyone to help me through the difficult time.

I wonder what they'll say about me at *my* funeral when I don't have a date to that either.

"She died of a wasting disease, surrounded by her cats, enjoying the fruits of her spinsterhood by taking up crocheting and watching *Grace and Frankie* on repeat."

I should be so lucky.

Chapter 4
Roman

West Chester is a college town, close enough to Philadelphia to be considered a suburb, with the feel of a small town. And it never seems as small as when you're the talk of the town.

In the week since we've unpacked, Mazie has started first grade, and I have sort of begun fixing up the house that had fallen into disrepair in the last decade, but I don't have much time, with getting everything up and running at my shop. I've loved cars my entire life, a passion I inherited from Ian. He practically raised me, and I was at his side while he restored a number of cars. It was a skill I picked back up after dropping out of college, but I was never able to hold down a job long enough to make a real living from it until about seven years ago.

A friend of my sober coach hooked me up at a garage, and I never looked back. Especially once word got out that I could restore vintage cars. One thing led to another, and I fell into contact with a film production company, restoring cars for a movie set in the '70s. It earned me a nice little nest egg that I used for this move.

To actually help make my return journey home where I belonged.

But now that I'm here, I've quickly realized I don't have much time to do everything that needs doing with Mazie constantly hovering around me. Which is why I have her buckled into my Tahoe to drive downtown to Ian's tattoo shop on Aster Street.

I hit the dial for music, and without even taking her attention away from her window, she says, "Play 'It's Raining Tacos.'"

I never should have given her access to YouTube.

"No way."

"Come on," she whines. "Please!"

"No."

I tune the stereo to one of my favorite bands, but my perfect angel of a daughter shout-sings over the blazingly fast drumbeat, "It's raining tacos!"

"Fucking song," I mutter, teeth clenched. It's nails on a chalkboard. The stupidest shit I've ever heard, and she loves it.

Instead of fighting her, I shut off the stereo. "Play a game instead."

"What game?"

"Count the stop signs."

I won't play *I Spy* or any other dumb driving games, but make her do something to win a high five? Works every time.

She counts all the stop signs we pass as I make my way through town, tree-lined streets giving way to old stone and brick buildings. We pass cafés and boutiques, a few people walking dogs or sipping coffees at outdoor tables. The spire of the county courthouse comes into view as I turn toward Aster Street, with brick-paved sidewalks and flower baskets hanging from lampposts.

A vinyl record store blasts classic rock tunes next to a pet store, a chalkboard sign out front informing customers they sell homemade dog treats inside. Even though the architecture is old, the downtown has a youthful vibe. Especially because the university isn't too far away.

My new shop is two blocks south, which is perfect for me. I can easily drop Mazie off when I need a babysitter, but right now, I park on Aster, and she immediately pulls me toward the bakery.

I've had to keep Mazie on a leash anytime she's seen it because the place is wall-to-wall pink, and she's been begging me to go. Finally, I give in, letting her drag me to Sweet Cheeks Bakery with its striped pink-and-white awning and curlicue logo on the window. A bell above the door tinkles when I open it, and I feel like a bull in a china shop as soon as I step inside.

Mazie gasps. It's basically her dream. Petal-pink walls with murals of cupcakes and macarons, a gleaming floor of checkered black-and-white tiles, and iron-rod tables and chairs that look so dainty I would most likely break them if I were to sit down.

Mazie beelines for the display case along the left wall, filled with pastries so perfectly arranged they appear fake. She presses her face right up to the glass, leaving smudges from her nose and palms. "Oooooh."

A young Asian girl with a name tag that reads *Mio, she/her* and her hair pulled back in a ponytail smiles down at Mazie. "What looks good to you?"

My daughter then turns to me, finger tapping on the case. "Can I get that? Pleeeeaaaaaaase?"

It's a huge cinnamon bun dripping with thick white icing. The thing is massive. Easily the size of her face.

"You'll be bouncing off the walls."

"Pleeeeaaaaase, Daddy?" She hops up and down, already off the walls.

But she might as well write a list of what she wants when she gives me those goddamn puppy-dog eyes. I heave a sigh as I dig my wallet out of my pocket. "We'll take one of those cinnamon rolls."

"The buns are what we're known for. Eloise is the queen of cinnamon rolls." Mio grins, reaching for a sheet of bakery paper. "Anything else for you today?"

I shake my head. "I'm sure we'll be back."

"Would you like it for here or to go?"

"To go, please," I murmur, tugging Mazie away from the glass. As Mio rings me up, I study the photos covering the wall behind her. Happy customers holding up half-eaten cinnamon buns and other treats. I huff in amusement, realizing every single member of my family is scattered among them. My brothers, sister, and their kids.

When Mio notices what's caught my attention, she eyes me, obviously making some kind of connection. "You know them?"

"Yeah. I'm, uh...Roman Stone."

Her jaw hangs open for a second before she remembers herself. She's clearly heard of me.

"It's so nice to meet you."

Mio smiles and extends the small light-pink box to Mazie, who says a little too loudly, "I'm Mazie. This is my dad! We just moved here!"

"Yeah?" Mio leans over the counter. "You're gonna love living here. Everyone's so nice, and you'll make lots of friends. There are great places to eat including..." She aims her index finger out the window, pointing down the street "See that sushi restaurant? My parents own it."

"It looks like there's a sleeping bag on that sign."

"You're right, it does kinda look like a sleeping bag. But it's a sushi roll. Have you ever had one?"

Mazie shakes her head, busy tearing open the takeaway box. "Nuh-uh."

"You think you'd ever try it?"

"I'll try it, yeah," Mazie says with a suspicious squint, pulling her hand out of the box, her fingers covered in icing. I swipe a bunch of napkins from one of the holders. "Daddy says if I don't like it, I don't have to fucking eat it."

I slap a hand to my face, explaining to a giggling Mio, "She's not— We don't— She doesn't usually curse."

"Yes, I do," Mazie retorts, and I glare at her.

Yeah, the cursing is a fucking problem, and I'm trying to watch my mouth.

"Let's get out of here," I grumble, pushing her toward the door.

Mio waves. "I'll see you around."

With a nod, I head back outside, tugging my tiny trouble-maker with me. "Jesus Christ, Maze, you're gonna get me in trouble."

Mazie shrugs and bites into a piece of the cinnamon roll, smearing it all over her face. I shove one of the napkins at her as we head right next door to Stone Ink.

My brother's tattoo shop is all black and gray. Ironic since it's next to that pink palace and a bookstore on the other side with twinkle lights in the window. I know Ian's girlfriend owns it, and I was informed I'd be meeting her today as well.

I swing open the door, greeted by a B-52's soundtrack and the smiling face of a girl at the desk.

"Hey, I'm Riley," she says, like she's been expecting me, then nods at Mazie. "I see you've been introduced to the bakery, huh?"

My daughter nods, her mouth full.

"So good, right?"

She nods again, attacking that cinnamon bun like she's never eaten in her life.

Riley laughs and walks out from behind the reclaimed wood desk, gesturing for Mazie to sit with her on the gray leather couch.

"Whoa, look who's here," Ian says, and Mazie waves at him, palm covered with icing. He bends, ruffling her hair. "How're you doing?"

"Good," she mumbles.

Ian helps himself to stealing a bit of the cinnamon roll and pops it into his mouth with wide, playful eyes that make her giggle.

Which brings everyone else over.

I was in middle and high school when Ian had his kids, and seeing them now as adults is whiplash.

Jasper, his oldest child, is the first to approach, both of us silently shaking hands. Jaybird, his younger brother, comes in for a laughing hug, slapping my back, telling me, "Good to see you, uncle." Then he introduces me to his best friend, Cash, who is apparently like an adopted Stone. All these guys are tall and muscular, but not close to my 6'5" or 270, though they cut imposing figures themselves.

The genes we inherited from my father. The wannabe professional athlete who threw it all away for alcohol.

Same thing I did. So I can't be too judgmental for *that* fact. Everything else, I sure as shit can and do blame him for.

Sloane brings up the rear, and Ian explains that she is the only female tattoo artist here and specializes in watercolor. Her work is amazing, as evidenced by some of the framed artwork on the walls. She says she has two kids about Mazie's age and would be happy to set up a playdate for them all to meet, an offer I plan to gratefully accept. No matter how much I worried about this move, it was the right decision.

This is exactly what Mazie needs, a big support system. Although I'm not too arrogant to think I don't need it. I did it for myself as much as my daughter.

"There she is," Ian says, gaze focused outside, and a moment later, the door opens, revealing a brunette with big blue eyes, a long dress with a flower pattern, and a smile only for my brother. He greets her with a kiss and an arm around her waist.

When my siblings came over the other day, they all eventually filled me in on their new partners. Griffin was widowed when his twins were born, but now he's with the woman he hired to be their nanny a couple of years ago. Taryn is dating a younger, stand-up guy—from all accounts—and I'm glad. Her ex-husband is a piece of shit, and my sister and her two kids deserve the world. Ian told me he and his bookshop girl started off in some kind of triangle of a relationship while she was still married, but everything worked out for the best, and he actually grins when he says, "Roman, this is Nicole."

She extends her hand to me. "I've heard so much about you. I'm happy to finally meet you."

"You too." I notice a few tattoos on her that I know are Ian's work. His eye for detail is incredible, his art one of a kind. "I appreciate everyone taking the time to meet us."

Ian waves away the thought. "We're all family, right? It's what we do."

And as I sweep my gaze around his girlfriend and kids, biological and not, I suppose we all are. This is what we do.

I'll have to get used to it.

"Where's Juniper?" I ask, and Jaybird blows a raspberry.

"Late, as usual."

As we wait for her, Ian talks about some upcoming fall festival thing at the end of September that apparently closes down the street. All the businesses set up booths outside, and he proudly informs me that Nicole is a new member of the community association and she's put the festival together this year, so I better have my ass there.

I offer him a mock salute as a young woman with long curly brown hair enters from the back. It's Ian's daughter, the youngest of his three kids, and still in college.

She prances in, a backpack on her shoulders. "Hey-oh!" Her gaze skirts over all of us in the front of the shop, and she smiles when she notices me. "Uncle Roman!"

She runs toward me for a hug I don't expect. Her arms wrap around me tight, strength belying her tiny stature, and I recall a time when she was in a car accident with her mother and we thought she wasn't going to make it. But she did, and she's all grown up now.

"Hey, Junie. Good seeing you."

"You too," she says, then kneels on the floor in front of Mazie. "And you must be Mazie."

"Yep!"

Seeing my niece and my daughter next to each other, it's funny how much they look alike, and when I glance over at Ian, he must notice too, his brows up in surprise.

"I love all your pink, and you have a cinnamon bun from next door. Did you meet Eloise?" When Mazie shakes her head, June stage-whispers, "She loves pink too. I think you two will be best friends."

Mazie grins, dimple popping in the same cheek as Juniper's. It's eerie, actually. They both take after Mom so much.

"I'm going to be your new babysitter," June tells Mazie, who cheers.

"And we're cousins!"

June laughs. "Yes, we are."

Riley interrupts, leaning in. "I'm not really your cousin, but you can call me that. I'm June's best friend, and we're together all the time, so I'll be babysitting you too."

Mazie dances in her seat. "Party! Woot Woot!"

Not that I expected this meeting to go badly, but it couldn't have gone any better. Nicole asks me some questions about myself, my business, and if I like to read. She lives in the apartment above the tattoo shop with Ian and says she'd love to have Mazie and me over one night for dinner.

I'm about to answer when I hear an amused "oh god" behind me, and I turn in time to see June point outside. "It's Kyle."

Everyone follows her finger, a few of them snickering at some joke I'm not in on, but I spy a lanky white guy in khakis and a blue button-down crossing in front of Stone Ink. "Who's that?"

"Kyle," Jasper mutters as he pivots toward his tattoo station.

Jaybird curls his hands around his mouth, yelling, "Stop being such a fucking Kyle, Kyle!"

Outside, Kyle stops and throws Jay a middle finger. Jay returns the gesture with both hands.

I glance from person to person for an explanation.

Riley is the one who clues me in. "Kyle works at the bank down the street. He's always going next door. He's obsessed with Eloise."

"And he's a douche," Jay adds.

"He can't take the hint that she doesn't like him, and she's too nice to tell him to fuck off," Sloane says, finishing that last part in a whisper so Mazie doesn't hear. But at this point, it doesn't matter. My kid isn't beating the allegations of being the one to corrupt everyone in her class.

"And who exactly is Eloise?" I ask because I keep hearing her name.

"She owns Sweet Cheeks, and we've been best friends since high school," Sloane explains. "I'm sure you'll meet her soon. She's all over the place."

Chapter 5
Roman

The following week, I feel like I've found my rhythm here. I've had a steady stream of customers, all of them dropping in or calling because I come highly recommended. Sometimes it pays to be a member a big family. Especially when those family members have access to people with big mouths. Including a couple who stopped in days ago to introduce themselves, although Marianne didn't need to. I remembered the pretty Black woman as Taryn's childhood best friend, who is now married to a firecracker of a woman named Clara. Not that I'm much of a talker to begin with, but I couldn't get a word in edgewise as she tossed her blond hair behind her shoulder, giving me the lowdown on everyone in town.

Since then, the marketing sort of took care of itself, and I've been working long hours, attempting to cement my role in the community and to have money for the life Mazie deserves. Books at Nicole's store, so many treats from Sweet Cheeks that I think I'm solely keeping that place in business, as well as the dance lessons she wanted me to sign her up for.

For The Weekend

While I'm still working on repairing my relationships with my siblings, life here has been going pretty well. So, it's funny when I pull up to the back of Stone Ink to find everything going wrong for a woman as she struggles to maneuver through the open door of Sweet Cheeks. I step out of my SUV just as she drops a huge bag of flour on the ground, causing it to split open, sending a cloud of white powder into the air and all over her.

Her surprised yelp melts into a bubbly laugh that sounds vaguely familiar, and I cross the space between us to make sure she's all right.

"Of course this would happen to me," she mutters, wiping flour out of her eyes before blinking them open to me, particles still clinging to her eyelashes, and I know those green eyes. "Oh, hello. This isn't embarrassing at all." She slaps at her clothes, trying to remove the powder, but in the process, yanks the collar of her T-shirt down to reveal her light pink bra and huge tits.

It's *her*.

The woman from Wawa. The first person I met in West Chester. The image I've been using to rub one out in the shower every day.

The twitch of my lips is unexpected yet not unwelcome. "Nope."

She stops when she recognizes me too. "It's you."

I nod, and she smiles. The same one that punched me in the face when I saw it. "The *daddy*."

But, really. No red-blooded straight man would blame me. That sugar-and-spice voice calling me *daddy*?

Straight up spank-bank material.

And I'm positive I know who she is. The famous Eloise.

"Can I help you?" I ask, gesturing to the fifty-pound bag.

"That would be great. Thanks."

I make sure to hold the split end together as I haul it up into my arms, and she sighs. I glance over my shoulder to find her hands on her hips, her head bobbing as she deliberately looks me up and down. "Being as big as a refrigerator has its upsides, huh?"

"I guess."

She motions for me to follow her inside. "You can set it down on the counter."

The kitchen is entirely stainless steel, while the walls are plastered with laminated recipes and stickers, like the one of Strawberry Shortcake and another that could either be a smiling mushroom or a penis. It's hard to tell. After examining it all for a few moments, enjoying the delicious scents coming from the ovens, I pivot to find her wiping her face with a wet cloth at the sink. When she finishes, she turns to me, and I can finally see her clearly.

Her blond hair is pulled up into a ponytail with a stretchy headband, keeping loose strands back from her temples and the nape of her neck. Her cheeks are round and, with a slight turn-up of her nose, she's like something out of a storybook. A princess from a children's fairy tale, and I rock back on my heels, absently catching myself with a hand on the cool metal counter.

She steps toward me, all golden skin and sunshine wrapped in a cute-as-pie package even as her body screams *fuck me*.

"I'm Eloise, by the way," she says, extending her hand.

"Roman." My hand engulfs hers when I shake it, our fingers lingering for a long time. I don't feel like pulling away.

I guess she doesn't either.

She cocks her head in this flirtatious way that I don't think is on purpose, her pink lips pursing in a secretive smile. "Roman Stone. I've heard about you."

I want to tell her that I've heard of her too, and now that she's in front of me, my interest has only piqued.

Her eyes flick over me once again, and I fucking love how she steps closer to me, her head tipping back to meet my gaze. I wouldn't be able to stop looking at her even if horses dragged me away. "What have you heard?"

"You're the prodigal brother returned."

I can't deny it and wag my head side to side.

"You're the mechanic who's eighteen feet tall with the little girl who can't stop cursing but everyone loves."

I draw an imaginary line from the top of my head, measuring myself. "Not quite eighteen feet."

"How tall are you?"

"Six five."

Her eyes brighten at that. "And the little girl?"

"Mazie. She's six, curses like a motherfucker, and everyone loves her more than me. As they should."

Eloise's flirty, closed lips open, revealing a smile that's all teeth and crinkles her nose. It's fucking cute.

She's fucking cute.

And she probably has things to do, but she's not moving. Doesn't care about the destroyed bag of flour sitting two feet away from us.

"I've been in here," I tell her. "But I've never seen you."

She gestures, as if to encompass the room. "I'm usually in the kitchen. I get super focused when I bake."

"My daughter loves your cinnamon rolls."

Eloise crosses her arms, pushing her tits up, practically offering them on a platter for my ogling. I try not to. "Yeah, they're my thing. I make a lot of other pastries, but the buns are what keep the lights on. I had a few videos blow up on social media two years ago, and a regional magazine did an article on me, so people come from all over to buy them. Before that, it was kind of a struggle to survive. But the community's really supportive, you know? We all help each other out. I'm sure you know that. You grew up here. And your family is amazing. I'm always popping in next door. I love Ian and all the guys. Sloane said your kids are going to hang out together, and that's really nice because—I'm sorry."

I lean down, shrinking a bit. "What?"

She flails her hands as if wiping down a whiteboard. "You were smiling...weirdly. I'm sorry, that's really rude of me to say. But it was like you wanted me to stop talking, and I have a tendency to ramble on, sometimes about things people don't care about and—"

"I'm out of practice."

"What?"

"Smiling." I motion to my face. "I don't do it a lot. Maybe that's why it looked weird."

"Oh."

I feel my mouth forming into a semblance of a smile. It probably does look weird. Doesn't feel weird, though. "You can ramble. It's okay."

She releases a loud breath that relaxes her shoulders, and I don't like that she was so tense about it. Like maybe not everyone in her life lets her be herself.

Fuckers.

"Ramble all you want." I shrug. "I'll listen."

She grins, and I have that feeling again. Like the Hulk smashed me.

"What are you doing on October 16th?" she asks, and I can't tell if she's serious or not.

"Uh, I don't know. Do...you...need something?"

She squeezes her eyes shut and waves her hands around by her ears. "No. No. Never mind. Only me being silly. So, uh..." She whacks my left bicep and then sort of pats it, which leads to squeezing. I clear my throat, and she snaps out of her trance-like state.

"Welcome to the neighborhood and all that," she says, overly brightly, and warmth spreads through the hole the Hulk smashed in me. I like her. I like her bubbly yet slightly odd and chaotic energy. Especially when she blushes. "And thanks for helping me with the flour."

"No problem." There's something about this woman that I can't quite put my finger on, but I want to know her better. I should since I've been fucking her every day in my mind.

"Hey, Elle, are you going to make any more fruit tarts this week? Someone's asking about them."

Eloise and I both turn to the interruption. "Oh, um...sure." When the employee's eyes flicker to me, Eloise glances at me like she's been caught with her hand in the cookie jar. "This is Roman. Roman, this is Morgan."

I tip my chin in greeting as I take in Morgan's purple hair, septum piercing, and the name tag like the one I'd seen of Mio's. Morgan's reads *they/them* below their name.

"Hey." Morgan nods at me before looking back to Eloise for her answer.

"Morgan keeps my shop running," she tells me, which earns a vivid red blush from her employee. Then she motions to them. "I'll make the tarts as soon as I can get an order of fruits in. I only have strawberries and blueberries right now. Or, I guess I can always make a berry tart," she muses and looks up to me as if my opinion matters. "People would like that, right?"

I lift a shoulder. "I like berries."

Her answering smile lets me know it was the right answer. She gestures to Morgan. "I'll have berry tarts made tomorrow."

"Got it." They slip back through the curtain, leaving Eloise and me alone once again.

"I should let you go," I say at the same time she says, "You probably have things to do."

She giggles, low and sweet, and I don't want to leave but I do have to pick Mazie up.

"Come with me," she instructs, placing her hand on my arm, steering me through the black curtain toward the front of the bakery.

I feel out of place traipsing through the delicate pink-and-white interior in my heavy boots, torn jeans, and faded Linkin Park T-shirt, but Eloise grins up at me like I'm made of fucking rainbows and glitter, and I think I'd do just about anything to have her always look at me like that.

I don't know her well. Hell, I don't know her at all. Only that she has a sense of humor about herself, tends to ramble, and can pull a smile out of me.

But I have the feeling she can make anyone smile.

Make anyone fall in love with her.

We stop by the front counter, where she waves to a woman with a toddler seated at a table. "Heya, Tabby." She lowers her voice like a monster. "Hello, George."

George, the toddler, shrieks in laughter, waving a piece of a muffin in his chubby hand while his mother attempts to make him sit.

Smiling to herself, Eloise packs up the last cinnamon roll and hands it to me. "For your help earlier."

"You don't have to do that."

"I know." She takes my hand in hers, flipping my palm up to put the box in it. "But I want to. And I hope I'll see you around, Roman."

My name sounds nice coming from her lips. I nod. "You will. Have a good rest of your day, Eloise."

She offers me a wave before disappearing back toward the kitchen, and I stalk out the door, the bell tinkling overhead. Out on the sidewalk, I study the bakery's pretty storefront, a small smile tugging at my mouth. In the reflection of the window, I note that it does indeed look weird, so I immediately drop it. Then I turn and head next door to the tattoo shop, greeted by my daughter, coloring on a big pad of paper in between Juniper and Riley.

"Hi, Daddy," she says, which garners the attention of everyone in the shop.

It's Sloane who eyes the pink box in my hand. "Finally met Eloise."

"Yeah."

She stares at me as if waiting for more information. I don't know what else to tell her, so I shrug. "Helped her carry a big bag of flour into her kitchen."

Jay strips off his gloves and tosses them in the garbage can. "That's what they're calling it nowadays? 'Carrying a big bag of flour.'"

"Exactly how big was it?" Ian asks, a teasing smirk underneath his gray beard.

"Big enough," I say, handing the roll over to Mazie, who tears into it.

"Well," Sloane says, her voice filled with amusement. "Elle does like 'em big."

I really didn't need to know that. My adrenaline's already coursing thick through my veins, simply from talking to the woman. Now I get to think about how true Sloane's statement is?

Fan-fucking-tastic.

"All right, Maze, say goodbye. We gotta get going for your dance class."

My daughter hugs both Riley and June, then hops down from her stool to do the same to the rest of the family, but I stop listening or paying attention when I spot Eloise through the window.

She steps out of Sweet Cheeks, a crossbody bag on, hair up

in a messy knot now, and her headband gone, so a few light strands get trapped in the corner of her mouth with the breeze. She tucks them behind her ear before bending to unlock a retro-looking bicycle with a speckled paint job. Though as I step closer to the window, my nose almost right up on the glass, I can tell it's not the paint. It's rust. And I wonder if it's retro-looking or just fucking old.

Like the thing could fall apart at any moment.

She backs the bike away from the rack and glances over to me.

A wide smile spreads across her face as she waves. I lift a hand in response, like a trained dog. And damn, how I would follow at her feet if she allowed.

She hops onto her bike, pedaling away with practiced grace, and I watch until she's completely out of sight. Only then do I pivot to Mazie, holding out my hand for her to take. But I can't shake the image of Eloise from my head, her laughter ringing in my ears, her smile burned into my memory.

I'm in trouble.

But for the first time in a long time, it's the kind of trouble I don't mind finding myself in.

Chapter 6
Eloise

In the two weeks since I met the refrigerator known as Roman Stone in person, I haven't had any more grain disasters, but I did have an issue with my bike. I only live a few blocks away and like to ride to work whenever possible. The exercise helps clear my head, plus it's a perfect way to start my day with a burst of energy. My ADHD brain loves it.

It was one of those perfect September days with clear skies and a cool breeze, and I happened to ride past his repair shop since it's on my way to Sweet Cheeks, when my bike broke, forcing me to walk while dragging it next to me. Roman saw me and popped right out to come to my rescue.

He insisted he take a look then hoisted the thing up to his

shoulder like it was nothing. I protested—after I wiped the drool from my face—but he told me I'd have it back by the time I finished working.

And there it was. My bike, waiting for me when I stepped outside Sweet Cheeks, chain fixed and back in place.

With his quiet nature and steady gaze, Roman is *enthralling*. Not to mention, he looks like a goddamn Greek god. His long hair is as dark as his brown eyes that don't give anything away, but I've noticed the way they crinkle when he's amused, in that weird estimation of a smile I can't get enough of. He's naturally tanned, darker than me, like he spends all his days out in the sunshine—as Greek gods do—though he's always cooped up in his garage. Quite frankly, I don't know how he does it, ducking all eighteen feet of him down to fix cars, holding itty-bitty wrenches in those oven-mitt hands of his. Of course, there are the tattoos scrawled all over his arms, even on his hands, letters of his daughter's name on his right knuckles and Stone on his left. I'm sure he's inked other places that I've fantasized about only a few dozen times, so I don't have a clear mental picture.

But then he went and fixed my bike like some kind of superhero.

I never stood a chance.

And that's how I found myself marching into Stone Auto Repair a few days ago with a big box of pastries as payment.

"It was nothing," he said, waving his hand dismissively, so I once again forcibly set my gift of gratitude in his bear paws, ignoring the curious stares of the other workers.

As I walked out the door, I heard one of them say, "What'dya got in there?"

To which Roman groused, "Nothing for you."

And I liked him all rough and growly, hoarding my pastries to himself.

Now, it's the last weekend of September, and all of Aster Street is shut down for the fall festival. Every business has its doors open, booths set out front, displaying products or playing games in hopes of finding new customers. People are able to pick up a card from the West Chester Community Association, and if they have it punched by all sixteen businesses, they will be entered into a drawing for something or other.

It's supposed to kick off soon, but of course I'm late getting ready, because of the text reminder from my aunt about the RSVP still sitting on my kitchen counter causing a teensy anxiety spiral. I nearly threw the stupid paper invitation into the recycling bin. I didn't think people sent paper invites in the mail anymore. Let alone any with foil Cinderella shoes on them over the script *She's found her prince!*

I imagine lighting the damn thing on fire to calm my nerves and concentrate on laying out free samples of the cinnamon buns and pumpkin scones. Humming to myself, I step back to take in my booth, not noticing the hulking figure planted there until I smack right into him.

Strong hands grip my arms, and I look up, way up, at Roman "the refrigerator" Stone. And for a moment, I'm stunned. "Hi."

His chest rises on an inhale, and I catch a whiff of his scent that I imagine on his bedsheets, and suddenly, I'm on his mattress in my mind. I hop away from him, cheeks heating. "Sorry about that."

"No problem."

I playfully whack at him. "Guess you need something much bigger than me to move you, huh?"

His dark gaze tracks down the length of me, slow and delicious. He finally meets my eyes again and huffs a sort of offended sound. "Girl, I could throw you over my shoulder like your sacks of flour."

I choke out a laugh with how my throat's suddenly drier than a box of saltines.

"Daddy?"

The name has my focus lowering to the little girl standing next to Roman, her hair braided in two pigtails, her dress full of multicolored tulle with a rainbow across her chest. She has the same brown eyes as Roman, but hers sparkle as brightly as her clothes, a dimple in the center of her right cheek. Adorable.

"Who's this?" I ask, already knowing the answer.

"Eloise, this is Mazie," he says, his hand on the top of her head, and I wonder if he did her hair. My ovaries weep at the thought of his thick fingers plaiting section over section, taking her shopping for those pink glitter shoes, giving her piggyback rides.

Gah!

"Hi!" Mazie bounces on her toes. "Is this your store?" she asks, pointing to Sweet Cheeks behind me.

I nod. "I heard you like my cinnamon rolls."

"I *love* them," she says, hands out and full of sass.

"Do you want one right now?"

Mazie's head bobs, and I glance to Roman for permission before handing her one from the tray. She accepts it but stops with it halfway to her mouth. "What about Daddy?"

I don't let my smile falter and tip my head in his direction. "What about you, *Daddy*? You want one of my buns?"

The tip of his tongue pokes out of his parted lips, resting for a second on his left incisor, and a wild idea about him biting me floats into my lust-fogged brain. Then he very slowly shakes his head, his mouth breaking into a semblance of a smile. "You're trouble."

"I don't know what you mean. I'm always on my best behavior."

He clucks his tongue, gaze raking over me again, and this

time, I know it's him turning the temperature of my skin up a few degrees and not the sun.

Mazie pulls on my apron. "Do you like pink?"

I prop my hands on my hips. "What do you think?"

She giggles. Clearly, I am a lady who likes pink. Between my store, my pink-and-white polka dot apron, and my pink Converse, it's not a question. "It's my favorite color."

"Me too!"

We high-five, and I bend down so we're eye to eye and talk about her dress. Meanwhile, Roman peers down at us, tree trunks folded across his chest, his mouth set in a semi-slanted line like he doesn't want to acknowledge he finds this funny.

After she tells me about her friend Tegan who has a Barbie backpack and how she beat this boy named Boden in a race so he cried—to which Roman murmured "Good"—I ask her, "Who did your hair?"

"Daddy."

That popping sound? Only my eggs spontaneously being fertilized.

"That's pretty impressive that Daddy does your hair so well."

She nods. "He didn't useta. He was real bad at it, always said the hair bands are too fucking small."

"Mazie," he snaps, but she doesn't appear sheepish at all, and I have to slap my palm over my mouth to keep from laughing.

When I pull it together, I say, "Hair bands can be hard to use if they're too small."

Roman huffs. "They always break with one little tug."

I stand to my full height, noticing I could perfectly rest my chin on his shoulder. I mean, I *won't*.

But I *could*.

And because all my brain cells exited my body about the

time he told me he could throw me over those shoulders, I squeeze his biceps. "I would guess one tug from you could easily rip an elastic band. Not exactly dainty."

His eyes dip to my mouth and then lower to where I'm touching him. "No, I'm not."

"Well!" I cackle, high-pitched and frenzied. "I should finish up here."

"Yeah," he agrees, taking Mazie's hand. "We'll let you."

"Wait, I want to stay!"

I smile at the little girl. "We can hang out together later, okay? You come see me in a bit." I wink and put my hand at the corner of my mouth, stage-whispering, "I'll sneak you another cinnamon roll."

She jumps up and down, satisfied, and I finish up with my booth, laying out business cards and coupons for 10% off their next purchase then sneak off to Cuppa Jo's for a coffee before the festival starts.

On my way back, I stop to say hello to Nicole at Chapter and Verse, where she's having a huge sale and activities inside, along with a table out front that has sign-ups for book clubs, author groups, and coloring pages of different classic books. Ian, in all his silver-fox glory, flirts with her, obviously trying to waylay her efforts in setting up. She bats his hand away, keeping it from wandering around her hips, disrupting her answer when I ask if she wants me to drop off any treats.

"We'll take whatever you got, Eloise," Ian answers in her stead, and she rolls her eyes.

"They're for her customers," Nicole says with a shake of her head at him.

He shrugs. "And I'm her best customer." He turns to me. "Am I not?"

I grin. "The absolute best."

He smacks her ass so she yelps, and that's my cue to keep

walking. Jaybird and Cash are posted up outside Stone Ink, ready to pass out flyers and stick-on tattoos, and I steal one before settling behind my table, ready for the crowds, which come in dribs and drabs for the first hour and then suddenly all at once. Mio shows up in time for me to refill our samples, and I spend a lot of time introducing myself to people and grabbing pics and videos for social media.

I've just finished punching some cards for patrons when Mazie plows into my side. "Hiii!"

I laugh. "You on roller skates or what?"

"I don't got roller skates," she says seriously, lifting her feet to show me.

"I'm kidding. You want another treat?"

She nods and claps, her puppy tail practically wagging, and I let her choose if she wants a bun or a scone, and she goes with another roll.

"Your dad is gonna kill me, giving you all this sugar."

"No, he won't." She gestures vaguely behind her, and I glance up to spy Roman talking to Jaybird and Cash, but he looks over as if he can sense me watching him. I smile his way as his daughter confesses, "I think he likes you."

"What?" I shoot my gaze at her. "What'd you say?"

She licks the icing off her fingers, completely unaware she's sent my thoughts careening off the tracks, and shrugs.

With Roman still staring at me, I stutter. "I just... Your dad... I..."

"Look at this!" She thrusts out her arm to show me her stick-on tattoo, and I show off my matching one, which delights her. "Can I stay with you? Daddy has to talk to people about cars. Fuck that!"

I stifle a laugh. "I doubt your daddy wants you cursing like that, but sure, you can stay with me." I lift my attention once again. Roman's still watching me, and I can't help but be pleased. *Can she stay with me?* I mouth, pointing from Mazie to myself, and when he nods, I reach out for a napkin. "You're with me. Come on, you can sit next to Mio."

I set her up at the table and put her in charge of handing everyone a business card because no one can resist how cute she is, and the next time I peek at the tables next door, Roman's speaking with an older gentleman, pointing out something on one of his marketing pamphlets. He doesn't exactly exude suave businessman with his beard, muscles, and tattoos, but he seems to be doing all right for himself, even with all his frowns.

"Is your dad grumpy a lot?" I ask Mazie, absently stacking napkins into a pile.

"Most times. But he likes being with Steve and me. He smiles when we cuddle."

"Oh yeah? Who's Steve?"

She swings her feet. "My bunny rabbit! He's brown and has long ears like this..." She demonstrates how long Steve the bunny's ears are by holding her hands by her shoulders. "Daddy says he doesn't like Steve, but I know he's lying. He loves Steve. Like, *loves* him."

I imagine Roman, Mazie, and Steve all cuddled together, and I need to stop by CVS for a pregnancy test.

"You should come over to play with Steve," Mazie continues. "He's so fast. He goes..." She zips her fingers all over the place. "And sometimes I lose him, but Daddy always finds him, and then he looks at me like this..." She screws her face up in what I assume is an impression of her father. "But that's okay because even when he's mad, he still loves me. That's what he says."

"You have a really good daddy." I place my hand on my lower abdomen, my insides literally weeping. What is it about men who are good fathers that's so sexy?

I don't know, but I'm down bad. So much so that I'm not

even really listening to Mazie as she goes on and on about her loose tooth and playing with Sloane's children.

A familiar voice snaps me out of my daze. "There she is."

I inhale a calming breath and smooth my hand over Mazie's forehead, pushing back a few wisps of her hair before spinning around to face Kyle.

"Hey, Ellie," he says again, flashing me a chummy grin that immediately puts me on edge. Only Sloane, my best friend and sister of my heart, calls me Ellie. To everyone else, I'm Eloise or Elle. Kyle continues smiling, oblivious to my discomfort.

"Hi, Kyle," I reply, keeping my tone light despite my irritation. I glance around, hoping a customer will appear to give me an excuse to ignore him. No such luck.

He leans in, lowering his voice as if sharing a secret. "You've been so busy today, we haven't had a chance to chat. Figured I'd come over and see how my favorite baker is doing."

I force a tight smile, cringing internally. He's been coming to talk to me occasionally for over a year. At first, I thought the guy was lonely. I figured maybe he wasn't good at making friends, but then it didn't stop, and these "chats" kept getting longer and longer. Since I started to understand that he feels more than friendly toward me, I've dodged any and all attempts when he asks me to hang out.

I don't like saying no all the time, but I don't get good vibes from him.

A little bit too Norman Bates for my tastes.

"That's nice of you," I say, trying to sound polite while also giving him an out to leave. "But as you can see, I'm pretty swamped at the moment." I gesture at the customers milling around my booth. It's a blatant hint, but Kyle remains planted in place.

"Yeah, no problem. I can wait."

I bite my tongue in frustration. I hate being outright rude, but I'm losing my patience for all his awkward small talk and habit of getting into my personal space. As I'm debating how to extricate myself from this conversation, Roman steps up right next to Kyle.

"Hi, Daddy!" Mazie jumps from her chair, handing him one of my business cards. "Look it! There are two, four, six, eight, ten, twelve! Twelve cimanin buns!"

"Cinnamon," he corrects gently, "but good counting." He holds his palm out for her to slap even as his eyes trace over me, assessing me silently, before slanting to the man next to him.

Kyle smiles and sticks out his hand. "I'm not sure if we've ever officially met. I'm Kyle."

Roman shakes his hand, and from the sudden streak of red that crosses Kyle's face, I'm assuming it's a hard grip.

From the size difference, it's like watching a black bear against a chihuahua.

"Shouldn't you be selling insurance or something?" Roman asks, voice a tad deeper than usual.

"I work at the bank," Kyle corrects.

Roman merely grunts.

"I'm, uh...just talking to Eloise here about the big turnout today." Even to my ears, Kyle's lighthearted tone sounds brittle.

Roman's gaze flicks to me briefly before returning to Kyle. "Yeah. She has a lot of customers here. A lot of work to do."

His tone is neutral, but the undercurrent of warning is evident. Kyle shifts his weight, clearing his throat. "Well, I should probably get back." He turns to me with a tight smile. "See you around, Ellie."

I resist the urge to shout at him, "Don't call me that!" But he scurries off without another word. Once he's safely out of earshot, I exhale in relief.

"Thank you," I say to Roman. "Sorry about that."

"You have nothing to apologize for. If he keeps bugging you, let me know."

I nod, both surprised and warmed at the idea of having a protector. "Yeah. Okay."

Before I can say anything more, Mazie pulls on his arm. "Are you done working?"

He peers down at her with a softness that makes my chest ache. "Yeah. We can walk around if you want."

"Fu—"

"Mazie."

She redirects her excitement to me. "Wanna come with us?"

I hesitate, not wanting to intrude, but Roman gives me an almost imperceptible nod.

It's Mio who physically pushes me to go. "Morgan'll be here soon. I can take it from here. Go hang out."

I meet Roman's eyes. "Okay. Let's go."

"Your apron," Mio reminds me, and I unknot the bow at my waist, tossing it to her. Mazie places her free hand in mine, and my stomach flip-flops at how this adorable girl has clung to me so quickly. With her between Roman and me, she swings her hands, and for one outrageously improbable second, I think that we make a cute picture, the three of us together.

A merry little trio.

As natural together as cinnamon and sugar.

I push the thought aside as we meander down the street to check out the other stores and vendors. Mazie regales us with random stories and shrieks of glee when she spots a beanbag-toss game.

She and I play, deliberately not following the rules of the game. Instead, trying to outdo the other with silly ways to toss the beanbag. She cracks up when I spin around a few times and aim my throw between my legs.

I think I even earn a half smile from Roman on that one too. It's nice to see how relaxed and happy he is with his daughter. And…maybe me.

Maybe, like she said, he does like me.

We stop for complimentary lemonade outside the furniture store that sells pieces way outside of my price range. But Roman easily agrees when Mazie asks to go inside and test out the couches.

"I like this one! Can we get it?"

Roman sits next to his daughter when she pats the thick purple chaise longue. It belongs on the cover of a romance novel, but Mazie loves it and folds her hands together. "Pleeeeaaaaase."

"No, Maze. We're not getting this. I'm not buying any new furniture until you stop walking all over what we have. So if you keep breaking the fuck—if you keep breaking the springs in our couches, you'll have to sit on the floor to watch your cartoons."

She growls like a tiny animal and takes off again toward the decorative birdcage. Then Roman tilts his head up to me, and for the first time ever, I'm taller than him.

It doesn't last long because he points to the open spot next to him, and I close the space between us like I'm in a trance. He has his arm propped on the top of the chaise, and when I sit, I turn into an eighth grader with her crush's arm around her shoulders.

Butterflies explode in my belly, and all my fingers tingle. I think I might need to run home to rid myself of this energy, but when I finally pull myself together, I face him, hoping my cheeks aren't as pink as they feel. "You've got a really cute kid."

"Sometimes," he teases, watching her as she dances with a pillow.

It takes him a while to turn back to me, so I have enough

time to admire the line of his aquiline nose, the mass of his hair, left loose and long over his shoulders that gives him a wild sort of look. Not to mention the tattoo on the back of his hand that's next to my left shoulder, the way his thumb barely touches my upper arm.

When he does finally meet my gaze, it makes me sweat. "She's really taken to you." He licks his lips and readjusts his position, widening his legs and angling himself so his knee touches mine. "But she's not the only one."

I surreptitiously rub my damp palms on my pants, aiming for a joke. "Yeah, Kyle, he's...something."

Roman doesn't like that, and his hand fully lands on my shoulder like a weight threatening to take me under, buried in his heat and smell and size. He opens his mouth to speak, but Mazie beats him to it.

"Can we go nooooow?"

"Yeah," he answers, gaze still on me. "We'll head back." Then he stands and holds out his hand to me like a gentleman, guiding me up. His fingers linger on mine, until Mazie runs between us and out the door.

On our way back, we stop to pet a dog that Mazie tries to hug, so Roman puts her on his shoulders, and I literally whimper when Roman sets his hand on my lower back, guiding me to the sidewalk.

"We've got to get home," he tells me. "But I'll see you later?"

I nod and tug on Mazie's tulle dress. "Thanks for letting me hang out with you today."

"Can we do it again?" she asks, and I nod. "Absolutely."

Roman agrees, wiggling her leg but talking to me. "Whenever you want."

Chapter 7
Roman

I wipe the sweat from my brow before reaching over to adjust the volume of the stereo playing Rage Against the Machine. It's hot as balls in here. I need to have the air looked at, but I'm trying to keep overhead low, and since I only opened a few weeks ago, I'm not flush with cash to pay somebody to fix it.

After swiping my palm down my pants, I adjust my hold on the wrench and finish tightening up bolts. The owner of this Volkswagen Beetle wanted it restored to its former glory, including a new cherry-red paint job, updated suspension system, and a souped-up engine that would make this bug zip along faster than originally intended.

While Stone Auto Repair is mainly a collision center, I've booked out a few restoration jobs over the coming months. Working on vintage cars requires a special knowledge that is hard to come by, but I've made a name for myself in the industry, and since I'm closer to both Philadelphia and New York City now, I've been able to reach the East Coast population of car lovers.

I don't have any personal social media accounts, but my professional one is filled with post after post of restorations. From Camaros to Corvettes, Vipers to a special 1963 Pontiac Tempest that the owner wanted me to paint so it matched that scene in *My Cousin Vinny* when Marisa Tomei went off on the tangent to prove the kids' innocence.

"Wow. Looks like it came off the sales floor."

I spin around at my sister's voice. "What are you doing here?"

She sweeps her gaze around my shop with a shrug. "Came to see what you're doing since you didn't meet with us yesterday. Are you the only one here?"

I nod, setting my tools down. I currently only have two other people working with me, Luis, a guy not much younger than me, and Shawn, a young kid training on the job, who also does some of the administrative tasks, like answering phones and booking appointments. "They're on lunch."

Taryn slides her hands into her back pockets and closes the distance between us, assessing me with a curious-maternal kind of gaze. "Why didn't you show up yesterday?"

Apparently, my siblings have been meeting for coffee every two weeks, and Ian made sure to invite me in our now-ongoing group text thread, but I didn't respond. After they came to my house and I told them about everything, including how Mazie came to be and why I moved here, it felt good to get it all off my chest. But I didn't think it made it any easier for them to see me as anything more than their fuckup baby brother.

I'm forty years old and hopefully far from that anymore, but having to sit down with them again and hear about how great they're doing, while not having much to say myself, doesn't sound like a real fun time.

I answer with my back to her, moving to the sink in the corner to wash my hands. "Had a lot of work to do."

She follows right behind me, not falling for my excuse. "Or you didn't want it to be awkward?"

I dry my hands off on the towel, still unable to meet her eyes. "Maybe a little of both."

She snorts a half-annoyed, half-amused sound. "You know this is what has always pissed me off about you. Since you're the baby, you get to wait until someone else breaks. Like me here right now. I shouldn't be. I don't have to be, and yet I am, because you got whatever dumbass idea in your head about—" she makes her voice all nasal "—oh, it'll be so weird. No one likes me. Me, me, me, that's all I care about."

I fold my arms across my chest, her attempt at imitation pulling me out of my self-flagellation and straight into irritation. "Is that supposed to be me?"

She widens her eyes. *Obviously.* "It's always been about you. What's best for you. What you need. And you got spoiled. You got used to everyone coming to you and never having to do anything you didn't want. You thought it would be weird or awkward or whatever-the-hell yesterday, so you didn't show up, but did you think about how Griffin or Ian or I would feel if you didn't come?"

She doesn't give me time to answer, going on. "No, you didn't. Because while you're here feeling bad for yourself about all your poor fucking choices for the last twenty years, we're waiting for you to pull your head out of your ass and just be with us. Be our brother. It's not like we ever stopped loving you or waiting for you to come home."

"I—"

"I get that it might be hard for you, but I can guarantee you that it's been just as hard for us too, watching you go through what you did when you were younger, knowing we couldn't do anything about it, and then not knowing anything about you the last few years. It was horrible, so sorry to fucking break it to you, but you owe us this. You owe us goddamn coffee dates."

"I didn't think—"

"And how do you expect Mazie to get to know everyone when you're so afraid to be around us? I know Ian's your safety blanket or whatever, but Griffin and I are here too. We want to be in your life as much as you said you supposedly want us to be. Or was that all a lie? What you said at your house? That you missed all of us? Because there are four of us total, you know?"

"I'm—"

"This isn't a one-way street. You can't keep expecting everyone to come to you when you hide in your corner, because I'm not going to anymore. You are my brother, and I expect you to start acting like it."

"I will—"

"And you better remember to—"

"Jesus fucking Christ, Taryn!"

She silences at my booming shout, and I put my hands on my hips, shaking my head. "Are you done so I can talk, or are you going to keep interrupting me?"

She scoffs. "No, I am not, in fact, done because it is hot as shit in here. I'm in perimenopause, asshole. Turn the air on before I melt."

"Perimenopause," I repeat, forcing myself not to give in to my amusement.

"Yes!" She plucks at her shirt, her skin flushing. "And I'm dying."

"I need someone to look at the HVAC, but I don't have the money to fix it."

She waves her hand with a roll of her eyes. "Why didn't you tell me? I'll ask Dante to see what he can do."

Dante, her construction project manager boyfriend. "He can fix the air?"

She shrugs. "I don't know, but if he can't, he'll know someone who can."

"Just like that?"

She sighs with annoyance. "Yes, just like that. Because that's what family does, you dick. Now, finish up. You're going to buy me a coffee."

The nonchalant transition from tearing me a new asshole to forcing me to take her out throws me for a bit of a loop, but I suspect that's what she wanted. By the time I put everything away, Shawn and Luis have finished their lunches, so Taryn and I take a walk to Aster Street, where we order from Cuppa Jo's.

She tells me about Dante and how they met, rushing over the details of how it was a one-night stand until he showed up at her bed-and-breakfast to work on the renovation, and how she really loved the gift I sent her for her birthday last year, a small *I Love Lucy* vase. She and our mom loved that show, and as soon as I saw it, I bought it. While I may not have always acted like it, my brothers and sister were never far from my mind.

I appreciate how she's doing all the talking now so I don't have to. She's showing me that not every conversation has to be an apology or a list of every bad decision I've ever made. Sometimes, it's this. Fifteen minutes to hang out with my sister, doing nothing special.

Which is really kinda special.

That I have the ability to do it. That I have my family.

Once we're done with our coffees and we're standing at the corner of the block, she tells me seriously, "For a long time, I didn't have the bandwidth to deal with anything outside of my own life, my kids, and my marriage. It was really difficult for me, and that was why I had such a hard time with you. You were drowning, and I wanted to help, but I couldn't. I was drowning too."

"I know." I curve my hand around her elbow. "I never expected you to help because I wasn't ready yet. You don't need to feel bad."

She sniffs and clears her throat of emotion, placing her no-nonsense mask in place. "Oh, I don't."

"Good." I fight the twitch of my lips. So does she.

She punches my arm harder than necessary. "I'm happy you're home."

"I'm happy to be home."

"Start acting like it, huh? Ian's not the only one who wants you here."

I nod, though I suspect it'll be a while before our other brother comes around. As if she can read my mind, she says, "Griffin's still trying to work through everything in his mind. Might go a long way if you actually put on your big-boy pants and went to see him." She arches her brow and aims her index finger at me. "Not like you made me come to you."

"Yeah, okay."

She nods once then takes off in the direction of her B&B a few blocks north. "I'll see you later, Rome. And buy some stickers or something to make your kid stop cursing. Goddamn."

I huff out a laugh. "Look who's talking."

She pivots, walking backward with a shrug. "It's what happens when you're raised with a bunch of feral boys."

I lift my hand in a wave then cross the street, my mind on Mazie and how I really do need to do something about her mouth. Watch my own, to start with. But I'm the first to know bad habits are hard to break.

My mind drifts back to the fall festival, not for the first time today. Spending that too-short time with Eloise on Saturday was the highlight of my weekend. And Mazie's.

My daughter's laughter still echoes in my ears, their conversations on repeat, and I can't help but want to smile, thinking about how they're like two peas in a pod. Eloise slipped right into the dynamic Maze and I had built, especially over this last year. What my daughter needs more than anything is love and fun. Especially from women in her life.

And there was Eloise, providing Mazie with everything she needed, all while dousing us in a kind of addictive chaos, a flurry of energy and sunshine. I could get used to it.

Although my gut dips when I think about being in a relationship again. It isn't only me who could be hurt, but Mazie too. Not that I think Eloise would ever deliberately hurt anyone, but things happen. Good people make bad decisions.

Amy's face flickers in my memory, a reminder of all I have to lose. And while the idea of committing to anyone stalls me out, I'm not averse to daydreaming.

Or indulging in spur-of-the-moment purchases. On our way home from errands yesterday, Mazie spotted a pink cruiser in the window of the bike shop, offhandedly pointing it out, and I pulled a uey.

It had Eloise written all over it. I pictured her riding it, hair flying, smile bright, laughter trailing behind her. So, I bought it. Just because.

I brought it with me today. Right now, I have it in the back of the shop with a big bow on it. I'm not sure when I plan on giving it to her; I didn't think that far ahead, but it's there. Waiting for her.

My imagination conjures up the vision of Eloise seeing it for the first time at the same moment I spot her in real life. Out front of her bakery. With Kyle standing way too fucking close.

Her body language screams discomfort, and I march right over, not quiet about it.

They both pivot toward me, and Eloise's shoulders physically fall as if she's relieved to see me. On the other hand, Kyle is none-too-happy, according to the way his face pinches.

Good.

I jut my chin to Eloise. "What's up, sunshine?"

She shifts closer to me. "I was about to head home."

I tip my head in Kyle's direction. "When this guy came up to talk to you?"

She opens her mouth to answer, but he cuts her off with a stupid laugh that grates like nails on a chalkboard. "I need my daily fill of Ellie."

"He asked me to go out," Eloise explains. "I told him I have plans. *Again*," she murmurs so only I can hear, and I slant my gaze his way, fisting my hands at my sides. This guy is either the dumbest motherfucker on the planet, or he won't take no for an answer. While I don't like either one of those choices, the latter is definitely worse than the former.

"Get the fuck outta here, Kyle," I say, and I'm not sure if she means to do it or not, but Eloise leans into me. Without thinking, I place my hand at the top of her spine, my fingertips wrapping around her neck, catching on loose strands of her hair. The words are out of my mouth before I can help it. "Leave my girl alone."

Kyle's eyes widen, and he takes a step back. "Sorry, man. I..." He gestures between us while tripping backward. "I didn't know you were together. If I'd known, I wouldn't have..."

It's always the pieces of shit who need another man to stake a claim before they'll leave a woman alone, and I roll my eyes at this motherfucker.

Next to me, Eloise tips her head back to meet my gaze, surprise coloring her cheeks, but she doesn't say a word. I don't correct Kyle. I like the sound of it too much. Because I'm a son of a bitch.

Once Kyle's gone, I release my hold on her. "Sorry."

She shakes her head, babbling, "No, it's fine. It's totally cool. Don't worry about it. That was actually really helpful. You were helpful. It's like he never listened to what I told him. He only wants to hear himself talk, I think. So, you saved me. Don't apologize. I should thank you instead."

She lowers her hands from where she'd been flapping them between us. Always in motion, this one. "So, anyway. Thank you. I appreciate you doing the whole scary act thing."

"Scary act thing?" I angle myself so I'm in front of her, looking down at her. "You think it's an act?"

She sets her hands on her hips, trying on an attitude I'm positive I could fuck out of her. "I know it's an act."

I huff and fold my arms across my chest. Her eyes lower, and I let her stare at my ink for a while since she seems to like it, before finally clearing my throat. She zips her attention back up to my face, and I arch my brow. Her cheeks turn pink.

Fucking adorable.

"You done staring?" I tease, and she slaps her hand over her eyes.

"I can't help it! You're like some beautiful bronze statue or something."

"Yeah?"

She drops her hand, her guileless green eyes finding mine immediately. "Yeah. You own a mirror, don't you?"

I nod.

"So you know what you look like."

I nod again.

"Then why are you surprised?"

It's so stupid to think, let alone say out loud, but... "You said I'm beautiful. No one's ever called me that before."

"Oh." She tucks a few strands of hair behind her ear. "Well. You are. I mean, behind all the mean mugging."

I give in to the smile that's been threatening to sneak out since she started rambling, and she grins. Triumphant and wide and all mine.

I know she's proud of herself for being able to make me lose my "mean mug." And that's fine.

It's true, after all.

She should be proud.

Shit. I'm proud of her, and *I'm* the one she's turning inside out.

And I think it's time for her reward. "Give me your bike."

She blinks, confused. "What? Why?"

"Just trust me." I hold out my hand, and she hesitantly wheels her bike over.

"What're you gonna do with it?"

I lift the hunk of scrap metal. "Trash it."

"*What?*" she nearly shrieks.

"How long have you had this bike?"

"I don't know. About a year."

"You've ridden this piece of shit for a year?"

She shrugs. "It was free, and I'm not going far."

"That's not the point." I imagine her falling off the damn thing from the chain breaking again or having a flat tire in the middle of the road and getting into an accident. "This thing is dangerous for you to ride."

"It's not a unicycle," she argues, and I stare at her for a moment, thrown off. The way her mind works. What I wouldn't give to crawl into her brain for an hour or two.

"You've ridden a unicycle before?"

"I tried, and *that's* dangerous. I went face first into the pavement. I had blood—"

"Please stop." I close my eyes, not wanting to picture her bleeding or hurt.

She elbows my side, laughing. "The big guy gets queasy, huh?"

Only from the idea of her injured, but I'm not about to give myself away like that, so I motion for her to follow me around the block and across the street. She chatters away the whole time about nothing in particular. I open the door to my shop to a few curious glances from Luis and Shawn, but I pass by them silently as Eloise waves to them, greeting them happily.

I set down her rusted deathtrap because it's going in the trash as soon as she's gone, and then I tell her to close her eyes. I take her hand in mine to lead her to the back, positioning her so she's facing her new bike.

"Open."

There are a few seconds of silence, and then she lets out a low breath. "Is this...for me?" When she brings her eyes up to mine, I nod, and she covers her mouth. "Oh my god."

I'm not sure if that's a good *Oh my god* or bad, and I rub my hand over my beard and jaw. "Do you like it?"

She circles the bubblegum-pink cruiser, gingerly running her hand over the white leather seat, up the frame to the handlebars with the giant bow, and down to the wicker basket in the front. It's a little girly.

A lot girly.

But I assumed she'd like it.

Yet, she's still not saying anything. I wait patiently until she turns back to me, tears in her eyes. "Roman..."

I lift my eyebrows in question.

"Is this for me?"

"Yeah."

"You bought it for me?"

I nod. "If you don't like it—"

"I love it."

I exhale audibly, my shoulders drooping. "Good, I was worried—"

She throws herself at me. "Thank you." She wraps her arms around my neck. "Thank you so much."

I play it off, even as I loop my arms around her waist, squeezing and lifting her a bit so she's on her tippy-toes and I'm holding all her weight. "It's no big deal."

"It's a huge deal." Her tears wet my cheek. "No one's ever done anything like this for me before."

I don't know what to say, so I stay quiet. I like holding her better than talking anyway. She breathes hot against my neck, and I dig my fingertips into her sides. She giggles, mumbling something that sounds like, "You're strong."

She has no idea, but the idea of lifting her up completely so her legs curl around my waist is too much, and I let her go. Making sure she's on her feet, I keep my hands on her hips, only releasing her to cup her smiling face in my palms. I wipe the wet streaks on her face, allowing myself to drag my thumb over her lips once.

They're plump and perfect and kissable.

"Go on. Lemme see you take it for a spin," I tell her before opening the door for her. She guides it outside and hops on, pedaling it in circles.

She laughs. "This is amazing!"

And my chest opens up, making a hole wide enough for her to ride the damn thing right inside. I'd welcome it. Leave tracks all over me. Evidence of the happiness I feel in this moment.

After a few figure eights and gleeful sounds that I previously only thought came from cartoon characters, Eloise pulls up alongside me. She puts the kickstand down and hugs me again. This time, I stoop lower so she doesn't have to reach so far and duck my face into her neck. She smells of sugar and cinnamon. Feels like everything right in the world.

"I love it, Roman. Thank you. I'll take good care of it. I promise." She leans back so our gazes meet. "You can have free baked goods for life."

A chuckle rumbles in my throat. It's rustier than her old bike, but I suspect it'll get more of a workout with this girl in my life. "I'm just happy you're happy."

Heat laces her answering smile, her emerald eyes going heavy lidded, and my mind races with all the ways I could put that same look on her face again, but the alarm on my phone interrupts my thoughts and this conversation. I release her to silence it, showing her the few daily alarms I have set. "I have to pick Mazie up from school."

"I have, like, a thousand alarms set on my phone too. But they're reminders for me to do basic stuff like take my pills and brush my teeth." Then she realizes what she's said and rolls her eyes at herself. "Awkward."

But the silence that settles between us isn't awkward. It's a good type of quiet. The comfortable kind. Where we don't want to move because we don't want to be anywhere else.

Except I have to be somewhere else.

I pinch her chin between my thumb and forefinger. "See you 'round."

"Bye, Roman." She bites into her lower lip, fighting her growing smile—a tragedy—then hops on her bike. I watch her pedal away before trashing her old bike in the dumpster and settling behind the wheel of my Tahoe. It's not until I check the rearview mirror to back up that I notice I'm smiling.

Chapter 8
Eloise

It was cold. Which was unusual for my kitchen, because it's always a few degrees warmer than everywhere else. But it probably felt that way because I was naked.

And mixing cream cheese icing.

Until a hand landed on my shoulder. Then I was warm all over. Warmer than the icing suddenly melting on the hot cinnamon buns.

Then that hand landed on *my* buns.

I knew who it was before I turned around, but seeing Roman's face made me hot all over.

He was naked too.

Or at least, I think he was. It was sort of hazy below our chests. But either way, I was into it.

He aimed his crooked sort-of smile at me then bent to lick up my throat, growling, "You taste delicious."

He wrapped his huge arm around me, hoisting me up to the counter like I weighed nothing more than a feather, and pressed me down, his hand on my collarbone. He dunked his oven mitt of a hand into the bowl of icing and spread it over my breasts, playing with my nipples. I whined, and he licked his lips like a wolf about to tear apart his dinner.

I wiggled, reaching for him, desperate for him to take his first bite. Then, as he bent over me, mouth moving above my nipple, something blared.

I shoot up in bed and blink into reality.

I'm not in my kitchen, naked with Roman, about to be eaten up whole.

Goddamn it.

Instead of getting up to brush my teeth and take my pills, I lie on my back, staring at the ceiling, thinking about the dream. About Roman and the feel of his hands on me.

Even though it wasn't real, it *felt* real, and I rub my thighs together beneath the covers. Between my legs, I'm tingly and wet, and even though my brain is still foggy, my body is already awake and needy. I keep my petal-pink vibrator in my night-stand and waste no time slipping it and my hand under my pajama shorts. I don't bother with underwear at night, and before I even power the toy on, I slide my fingers through my slit, dragging the moisture up to my clit, and close my eyes, imagining Roman's hands on me.

In my mind, Roman's hot mouth sucks on my nipple, so I pull up my T-shirt to tweak it and spread my legs wider. Enough room for him if he were really here with me. I think of the dirty, growly things he might say to me and arch my back, toes curling as I moan out loud. Pleasure surges through my veins in waves, and the closer I crest, the more my skin pebbles with heat. But right as I'm about to orgasm, the vibrator shuts off.

I kick off the sheet, one hand still on my breast, the other repeatedly pressing the toy like it'll suddenly start up again. It doesn't, and I whimper, tossing it to the side before using my fingers, but it's not the same.

And the fire that had been roiling in my belly dies down to barely a simmer. I come, but it's not close to the satisfaction I need. Rolling to my side, I groan into my pillow, frustrated and tired, before pushing myself up to standing. Then I plug the vibrator in to charge, telling it, "I'll be back for you later."

With a deep breath, I shake off the lingering frustration from my unsatisfying solo session and start my morning routine. I review my schedule for the day while brushing my teeth. I have an app that helps me stay on track with reminders for taking my meds, making to-do lists, and blocking off time for important tasks, because having ADHD means I've had to learn ways to keep myself focused and organized.

After dressing in gray joggers and a light pink T-shirt, I slip into my sneakers and toss a snack and water in my bag before hopping on my new bike. It's perfect. With the basket, big enough to fit my bag, and the color, I love it.

I know some people—my mother—might think it's stupid and immature to love pink as an adult, and some big dudes— like Roman—might be totally turned off by the super-girly things I love, but he went and *bought me a bike.*

Bought me a bike with a woven basket that's the cutest bubblegum pink I've ever seen. Like something out of my Pinterest dreams. If I were any good at taking photos of myself, I could be an influencer on this thing. That's how goddamn cute it is.

And he gave it to me.

Because...

Well, I guess because he is a man who pays attention and he wanted to do something nice for me.

Or maybe, possibly, hopefully this itty-bitty crush I'm harboring on him isn't totally one-sided.

I take the long way to work, drinking in the cool morning air, watching a couple of kids make their way to school. Even though I do most of the baking myself, I hired an assistant to help in the mornings. Leonard is an older, widowed gentleman who's been with me for a while, a man who closed down the bakery he owned with his wife when she died a few years ago. After hearing of the story, and knowing him in passing from stopping at his shop for the best challah I've ever had in my life, I asked if he wanted to come work with me.

He's in before the sun is up, prepping the kitchen, and starting our most popular bakes. When I arrive at Sweet Cheeks, I lock up my bike on the rack and call out a hello to him while tying an apron on.

He greets me with his usual smile as he kneads dough with the heel of his palm. "Morning, Elle."

"How's your back this morning?" I ask with a rub between his shoulder blades.

"All right."

"You haven't bought that pillow yet?" I tsk. "Leonard!"

"Don't you go yelling at me like that. I forgot the name of it," he mumbles, placing the dough into a bowl as I finish putting my hair up.

I wash my hands, speaking over my shoulder. "Your birthday's coming up, right?"

"No, Eloise. You're not going to buy it for my birthday."

"Yes, I am," I say, rinsing away the suds.

"No, you're not."

I toss the kitchen towel over my shoulder after drying my hands with it. "You're impossible."

"That's what my kids say."

"Which is why we get along so well." Leonard's a bit older than my parents, his two adult children in their early forties, and I've met both of his sons. They're great. I even celebrated Passover with the whole family last year.

Though Leonard told me his eldest has been going through some things recently. "Max is still married, right?"

"Yeah."

"But Ezra's single?"

Leonard turns to me, his bushy eyebrows raised. "He started dating somebody. Why?"

I shrug, waving off the question.

"Eloise!"

"Don't you go yelling at me like that."

He puffs out that amused sound I love, straight from his chest, shaking his head at me. "What's going on?"

I paste on a grin and fold my hands in front of my chest. "You wouldn't happen to have plans on October 16th, would you?"

"I don't exactly have much of a social calendar," he intones, and I can't help my laugh.

I love this grumpy guy.

Then again... Do I have a thing for grumpy guys?

I literally shoo the thought away when Leonard elbows me so he can use the sink, my mind having wandered to Roman. Yet again.

"I told you about my cousin's wedding, right?" I ask, pulling out ingredients to start on pumpkin scones. "Her shower is this weekend, and I know I'm gonna get harassed about not having a date, let alone a boyfriend, and I'm just really tired of hearing it. You know?"

Leonard lets me ramble, both of us working, as I unleash ten minutes of pent-up irritation at my cousin, my aunt, my mother, my situation, my waiting too long to remember I need to buy new shoes for the cute jumpsuit I bought to wear on Sunday. It's black with daisies all over, wide-leg, and a perfect fit. Except I don't often wear high heels, and none of my flats look right. I'm in the middle of telling Leonard how I'd really like to find some type of tall black sandal, but I'm not sure if I'd be able to with most stores having switched over to winter, when my cell phone buzzes on the counter.

"Speak of the devil," I murmur and move to tap my pinkie on the screen to ignore the call from my mother, but with my fingers covered in wet dough, I accidentally drop some on the screen, and in my panic about somehow ruining the phone, I swipe the side of my palm on it, answering the damn call instead.

I grit my teeth and flap my hands as Leonard watches me, obviously wondering what the hell I'm doing, as I can hear my mother on the other end of the call. "Eloise? Eloise, are you there?"

"It's my mom!" I whisper-shout at Leonard, and he wipes his hands off on the closest rag.

"Do you want me to talk to her?" he offers in full volume, and I roll my eyes.

"No, Leonard!"

He sighs, muttering something about me being nutty as I fly around the kitchen, washing my hands and wiping off my phone, all the while planning how I'll refute the oncoming lecture on any various topics, from my work to my inability to properly answer a phone call.

"Hey, Mom," I eventually say when I have myself together.

"What are you doing, Eloise?"

"Working."

"Oh yes," she says, dragging it out like it's a chore. "Well, I can never remember. You're always all over the place, bouncing here and there. I never know when I can call you. Since you never call me."

I prop my hand on the counter and mentally count to ten before I answer. "I am not all over. I'm at the same place I am pretty much every morning. In my bakery."

"Well, why don't you call me?" She skims over the fact that she doesn't want to acknowledge she's wrong.

"I don't know. I'm busy."

"Why don't you put it in your calendar?" she suggests and then immediately asks, "What time are you coming on Sunday?"

Confused, I pause to think. I was told I had to be there at noon to help set up the party or whatever. My mother was the one who told me. "Twelve," I say eventually. "I—"

"Why? I told you I need you there earlier. You—"

"You didn't. You didn't tell me I needed to be there earlier."

"I texted you last week."

I close my eyes and bite my lip. She's right. I saw the text, but I was literally elbow-deep in dirty water when it came through on my phone. I told myself I'd put it in my calendar, then evidently forgot all about it until now. "Okay, so I'll be there at eleven."

Though I can't help but poke the bear. If only to prove she really thinks I'm an idiot. "If you knew you told me, why did you call to ask what time I'll be there?"

"Because I don't trust you to be anywhere on time."

"Thanks for that," I say, bending over to put my elbows on the counter. "Really... Feels great knowing you're in my corner."

"Don't be so condescending to me. I know how you are, that's all."

"Yes, and clearly, you hate it."

"I don't hate it, Eloise, but you're always so sensitive about it. I called you because I knew you wouldn't remember, so here I am telling you. I will be there with your aunt at eleven, so I don't have to hear about how I don't help her out ever, and I need you there to prove it."

I nod to myself. Because that's how it always goes.

"But while I have you on the phone, I was thinking about asking Sandy's son to come to the wedding with you."

"Sandy, as in the lawyer you work with?"

"Yes, and—"

"Her son as in Eddie, the kid I used to babysit?"

"Yes, and he's not a kid anymore. He's—"

"A sociopath."

"Don't talk like that. It's not very nice."

I huff. My mother, the queen of nice.

"No. I'm not going to the wedding with Eddie, the kid who karate-kicked the TV onto the floor when I told him it was time for bed and then tried to stab me with a screwdriver."

"He was five. Don't be so dramatic."

"I'm not being dramatic." Irritation makes the skin on the back of my neck prickle with sweat. "That's what happened."

Back then, I also heard that he pushed his sister down the stairs when she was two, and she busted her face in multiple places.

"So what?" Mom asks, and my voice is completely shrill when I parrot her.

"*So what?*" I pivot in a circle. "Am I living in the Upside Down?" Of course she doesn't know what the Upside Down is, and I charge on. "So, at best, he was a brat back then. At worst, a serial killer in the making."

Leonard catches my eye and raises his brow in silent question. I shrug.

"He graduated college now and is working in insurance," my mother tells me. "I figured I can get Sandy to ask him."

What I know of Sandy is that she paves her little boy's way in gold and makes sure she's there to get him out of any trouble he finds himself in. I'm not about to bring this twenty-two-year-old to my cousin's wedding, sociopath or not.

"Do not talk to Sandy. I am not taking him to the wedding."

"Well, who are you taking?" *She* is the condescending one. *She* is the dramatic one. And I'm so tired of being her punching bag, the words are out of my mouth before I've even thought of them.

"I'm taking my boyfriend," I blurt, then immediately slap my hand over my mouth.

"Your boyfriend?" A chair scrapes on her end of the phone call like she's pushed away from a table. "You didn't tell me you have a boyfriend."

I flap my hand at Leonard like he can help me as I flounder to come up with an excuse. He stares at me blankly, so I say, "It's really new."

"Since when?"

"Since...a few days ago," I answer, waving desperately at Leonard.

"Why didn't you tell me?" my mother asks, but before I need to answer, my savior shouts right next to my ear.

"Eloise! I need you!"

I jerk away from Leonard, rubbing at my ringing ear. "Sorry, gotta go, Mom. Talk later."

"You—"

"Bye!" I pocket my cell phone and face Leonard. "Next time, not so close." I stick my finger into my ear. "I think you popped my eardrum."

"Go get some first aid," he says, motioning to the door, and I hug him.

"You're the best."

He grunts, patting my back. "No, but I know meddlesome mothers. Go. When you come back, I'll head out."

Chapter 9
Eloise

I all but sprint out of the bakery's front door and crash into Clara. "I'm so sorry."

She holds her hands up, pretending at being disoriented for a moment before smiling. "God, girl, what are you doing?"

"Panicking."

"Yes, I can see that. About what?"

"I need a date."

"Ohh." She lights up like a Fourth of July firework display and cracks her knuckles. "Yessssss."

"No, it's bad."

"For *you*. Not for *me*. I love this for me."

I sulk and push past her to Stone Ink, throwing the door open. "Sloane!"

"It's too early for you to be screeching," she says, completely undaunted in her work of inking the ribs of a young woman with a bird and flower. At least, that's what it will be. It looks like she's just started, with only the black outline done.

"I'm so sorry," I tell the woman, hands pressed to my heart.

"But I just did something very stupid, and I need to talk to my best friend about it," I finish, motioning to Sloane.

"I totally get it," the woman on the table says with a wince. "Spill it."

"Awesome. You're amazing. Thanks so much." I point at my own side while tipping my chin toward hers. "This is gonna look great, by the way. Sloane's the absolute best." Then I grab a chair and roll up beside the table and officially introduce myself. "I'm Eloise. I own Sweet Cheeks."

"I love Sweet Cheeks."

"Do you? Come over when you're done today. I'll give you a free treat for letting me interrupt your appointment."

"That's really kind of you. Thank you."

I wave. "The least I can do. What's your name?"

Sloane sighs, having lived through my soliloquies for fifteen years. I ignore her, legs crossed, chin in my hand, waiting for my new friend's name.

"April."

"April, it's lovely to meet you. My mother is the worst."

April laughs and then cringes in pain.

Sloane spares a quick glare at me, and I apologize with a shrug. "She is."

Sloane snorts. "I know."

"Worse than my mom?" April asks, entering the game.

"What did she do?"

"Tells me I don't need therapy or medication. Just a cup of tea and a good night's sleep."

I shake my head, laughing. "And they wonder why we need therapy."

But I suddenly stop laughing because it's really *not* funny. Except, if we don't laugh about how our mothers are hurting us, intentionally or not, we'd most likely not be able to roll out of bed in the mornings. I tell April, "My mother and my aunt have been in this never-ending death-match competition, and that's spilled down to me and my cousin."

April listens as I explain how Lily and I have never gotten along because of our mothers and how my mom puts so much pressure on me to live up to whatever stupid standards Lily's mother has placed on her and, therefore, me. I go on and on about what it was like when they'd dress Lily and me up the same at holidays and how my mother constantly compares us. *Why couldn't I go to a better college like Lily? Why don't I have nice hair like Lily? Why don't I try to dress like Lily? Wear clothes to make me look skinnier like Lily? Why can't I find a boyfriend? Lily's been with her guy for years. Why am I wasting the best years of my life?*

I roll the pendant on my necklace between my fingers, my gaze focused on the photo Sloane has taped up on the wall of Micah and Livie. Sloane's an amazing mom, and those kids are so lucky to have her.

"My mom was trying to convince me to take this psychopath to the wedding. I mean, maybe he's not an actual psychopath, but I used to babysit this kid, and it wouldn't surprise me if he killed a few cats back then or something. And she wouldn't leave it alone, so I told her I had a boyfriend and was bringing him to the wedding."

April gasps, and Sloane's tattoo gun pauses.

"I don't know what came over me. The holy spirit, a demon, I don't know, but *now* I have to find a boyfriend by the wedding. Actually!" I throw myself over, bending in half, remembering. "I have the shower this weekend. I'm gonna have to have pictures or something to prove it." I heave myself back up, moaning, "What did I do?"

And that's when I see him.

Roman, The Beautiful Refrigerator, Stone standing by the entrance of Stone Ink.

I force myself to my feet, stuck somewhere between laughing and crying in misery, and meet him halfway. "Tell me you just walked in and didn't hear anything I said for the last five minutes."

He shakes his head. I hang mine. "Clara told me I had to come quick for some emergency here."

Since Clara is nowhere to be found, I can assume *I* am the emergency. Sloane makes the same guess and says, "No emergency. Not a life-threatening one, at least. I'm the only one here right now, so if you two want to..."

She tips her head toward the windows, silently directing us to take it outside, and I remind April of my promise of a free cinnamon bun then shuffle out to the sidewalk with Roman at my heels. He towers over me, blocking out the sun. His eyes are so dark they're almost black, brows slashed down. But when he grips my chin between his thumb and forefinger, there is nothing but tenderness underneath the thrumming current of tension coming off him. "Are you okay?"

"Yeah," I say, but he shakes his head again.

"Don't lie."

"I'm not—"

With a single arch of his brow, I'm silent. And apparently on the verge of tears, by the sting in my eyes and nose.

"I'm embarrassed," I say eventually, and he exhales a long breath, jaw tight under his beard. He's angry, and I'm already so exposed, unable to pretend it's funny anymore, that any negative reaction will send me over the edge. So I do the thing I'm used to when I upset someone. "I'm sorry."

"Why are you apologizing?"

"I don't know. You look..."

"I'm pissed," he says, hands between us like he wants to touch me, but he curls his fingers into fists and drops them to his sides. "Not at you. I...I don't like that you're hurting."

I sniff and clear my throat, but it doesn't do anything to help my blurry vision, and I blink a few times, hoping to stem the tears. "I'm fine. Don't get worked up for me."

"You're not fine, and I'm already fucking worked up," he grates out then grips my wrist, his hand engulfing it. I'm not a small woman, but he makes me feel like I am. Like he could snap my bones as if I were not more than flimsy tissue paper, but he holds me like I'm delicate porcelain, tugging me to him until my hand rests against his chest and my head is tilted back.

"You don't deserve to be bullied by anyone, let alone a parent. Don't ever let anyone make you feel like you need to pretend to be anything other than yourself. You're perfect the way you are."

And I could cry for a whole other reason.

Because I've been trained to hide my eccentricities or apologize for them, I don't know what to do with this man who wants to protect them. Protect *me*.

"I'm used to it," I say, and his voice sinks even lower.

"You shouldn't be."

With his fingers still curled around my wrist, I twist my hand and flatten out my palm on his chest, hard like granite yet moving with every breath he takes, and I don't feel like letting go yet. Except Jaybird sails down the street on a skateboard, calling out to us. "Heyyooooooo!"

Roman and I each take a small step back, putting a few inches between us. I force a smile. He frowns. I'm about to apologize again out of habit, but he lifts his hand. "Don't do it."

I smile for real, watery as it may be. "I won't."

"Good."

Jaybird kicks his board up, catching it. "Uncle, what's up? You meeting Dad or something?"

Roman shakes his head in answer, his focus still on me.

Jay obviously catches on to whatever it is that's happening

between Roman and me and whistles low. "Anywayyyyy. You two have fun out here staring broodily at each other."

I bite back a smile. "I should get back to work."

Before Roman can answer, I speed back to my bakery, where I studiously complete a dozen bakes, locked in on sugar and flour, keeping out my mother's voice and the simmering rage on my behalf in Roman's eyes.

By the time I finish for the day, I realize I missed my lunch and chow down on the cheese sticks and trail mix I packed myself, before stuffing a still-warm mini apple tart into my mouth. I didn't earn these hips and thighs from *not eating* what I make.

I check in with Morgan on my way out, stalling at the door because of the rain coming down outside. My bike is safely tucked away under the awning, but I don't want it to rust, and I don't especially feel like getting drenched today.

With a sigh, I cross my bag over my body and open the door, angling myself away from the raindrops to unlock my bike. As I place my hands on the bars, intent on wheeling it out onto the sidewalk, a car horn beeps, and I lift my head.

A huge black SUV is stopped on the street in front of me, blinkers flashing. A moment later, Roman strolls around the back of the vehicle, uncaring about the raindrops darkening his T-shirt or jeans. "You need a ride?"

I shake my head. "Nah, it's only a few blocks. I'll be fine."

He props his hands on his hips. "You're not riding your bike in the rain."

"I literally live eight blocks away."

"I will literally drive you eight blocks home."

"You don't—"

"Don't be so fucking stubborn," he growls, stomping over to me to manhandle my bike. The same one he gifted me. "Get in the goddamn car, woman."

When I don't move fast enough, he wraps an arm around my waist and hauls me up, carrying me two steps before I shove off him, my annoyance fighting my amusement at how this guy is so offended at my independence. "It's just a little rain."

He huffs and points me to his passenger seat then stuffs my bike into his trunk.

By the time I'm buckled in, he opens the driver's side door and settles behind the wheel, his tree-trunk legs folding up. He combs his hands through his long hair then brushes his palms down his arms, wiping the droplets from his skin, and I'm once again entranced by the art covering him. He leans his right elbow on the console between us as he shuts off his four-ways and drives to the end of the block.

"Which way am I going?"

I shoot my gaze up to the windshield from where I'd been admiring the interlocking skulls with the snake coiled in and around them. "Uh, left at the stop sign. I'm on Chestnut."

He nods and makes the turn before glancing my way. "Warm enough?"

"Yeah. Thanks."

It takes three minutes to arrive at my apartment building, and I can't help but nudge him. "Told you it wasn't that far."

He sends me a flat look, and I giggle. The corners of his mouth dip farther down, and I poke the bear. "So tough. So mean."

"Most people are intimidated by me," he says, his left hand still on the steering wheel, while the other hangs off the side of the console, his fingertips barely touching my knee.

I lean into him, wanting that big hand on my leg, the heat of his palm smoothing up the inside of my thigh. More fodder for my fantasy when I power on my vibrator.

"I'm not most people."

His mouth quirks. "I know."

And I should look into an exorcism or something because the words are out before I even think them. "You want to go to a wedding with me and pretend to be my boyfriend?"

Surprise streaks across his face, and I wave my hands between us. "Never mind. That was dumb."

He clamps both of my hands in one of his. "You always say whatever you're thinking? Or not thinking?"

"Yeah. I'm sorry. That's... My family's always, like, you're so dumb, Eloise."

His fingers grip mine harder. "*What do they say?*"

I'm babbling now. No way to stop it. "I try not to do it, but sometimes my mind goes one hundred miles an hour, and I can't. I really can't stop it. One thought leads to another, and things just come out, I guess." I wiggle my hands out from between his to toy with my necklace. The pendant is a small cylinder with different divots, specifically made to be a nondescript sensory item. "My mom hates—"

"Fuck your mom," he spits, and I cough out a laugh.

"I dare you to say that to her face."

He shrugs. "Okay. When's this wedding?"

"I'm kidding. I don't really need you to come to the wedding."

"Eloise, when?"

I'm like his trained pet. "October 16th."

He tips his head to the side, studying me for a second. "You asked me about that date before."

"I did?" I have no recollection. My brain's Swiss cheese. "When?"

"The day we met in your bakery."

"Really?"

He nods, his gaze sweeping over my face, and somehow I know he's remembering that day. When he carried my bag of flour inside for me.

"You were thinking about this then?"

"No." *Yes.*

"I say random shit all the time." I flail my hands out. "Like asking you to pretend to be my pretend boyfriend. Forget I said anything, all right?"

I make for the door, but he stops me. "I like you, Eloise."

I force a giggle. "Stop."

He shakes his head.

"You can't say random stuff like that to me. I'll believe it."

He stares at me. As if I should believe him.

"You can't come to the wedding with me," I say, thinking of him next to me, all tatted and mean-looking. My mother would *flip*.

My mother would flip!

"Okay, so, don't forget I asked for you to be my pretend boyfriend? But maybe take the night and think about it. Only one of us can blurt out stuff in this relationship."

"I like that you blurt stuff."

"See? Don't say that. Makes it too real." I hike my thumb over my shoulder. "Can you open the trunk so I can get my bike?"

Of course he doesn't answer. Only steps out of the car like it isn't fourteen feet off the ground. Then again, he has no problem reaching it with his redwood legs. I hop down to the pavement and scamper to the back, holding my hand over my head as if that'll keep the rain away.

"I'll take it for you," he says, referring to my bike, and when he stalks off to the entrance, I dutifully follow.

Might as well put a collar on me.

"I appreciate it," I tell him once we're on the sidewalk. I use my keycard to unlock the door and take hold of my bike to walk inside.

Roman stands, watching like a soldier, hands at his sides,

eyes ahead. It's when the door's about to close that he calls out, "Hey." When I turn to look over my shoulder, he tells me, "I don't do anything by accident, and I say what I mean."

I gulp. He's serious.

The beautiful refrigerator *likes* me?

The beautiful refrigerator likes me.

"Just think about it, okay? We can talk tomorrow," I suggest, but he shakes his head.

"I won't be working tomorrow."

"Sunday, I have to go to my cousin's shower." Two days without seeing him suddenly feels like two years.

"So we'll see each other Monday," he says, all cool and calm.

"Okay," I blurt, like it's a date. "We'll talk Monday."

Chapter 10
Roman

I wake up with Eloise on my mind. *Again.*

It's been like this since Thursday, her smile and laughter haunting me in the best way. Her glassy eyes and hurt expression haunting me in the worst way.

Of course I'd wanted to fix it. I'd do fucking violence for her if she needed me to. Without a second thought. Because she's mine.

Or at least, that's how I've started to think of her.

Which is ridiculous.

I've known her for barely a minute, and already I'm possessive over her. But I can't help it. There's something about her that draws me in, makes me want to claim her as my own.

I roll out of bed, my cock hard. Which isn't unusual, especially lately. I think I've beaten off almost every morning since the day I met Eloise, thinking about her.

If she still wants me—hopefully she does, but she seems like the type of woman who might change her mind at the spur of the moment—I know I won't have a problem pretending to be her boyfriend.

Hell, I won't be pretending any kind of attraction to her. It's hot and bright, right there in the middle of my chest. And straining against my underwear every morning.

Mazie's in the living room, watching her favorite cartoon. The theme song drifts down the hallway, and I know I have a few minutes to myself, so I slip into the bathroom, turning on the shower. But before I even step under the spray, I mindlessly wrap my hand around my cock, too keyed up to wait for the water to heat.

I lean against the counter, eyes closed as I stroke myself. I picture Eloise here with me, her green eyes bright with desire, stripping off her clothes to reveal each and every one of her curves, inch by delicious inch. I bet she's soft everywhere, her skin smooth and creamy, from her face to her toes and everywhere in between. I imagine her nipples, big and perfect, hardening under my touch. How they'd feel under my tongue. How she'd moan when I sucked on them.

My hand moves faster, my grip tightening as I think about how she would taste, my mouth on her pussy. Definitely not of sugar and cinnamon, but of something better. Something wholly mind-altering. I know I'd crave her every day if I ever had the chance to lick up her sweet little treat.

I imagine her laid out on my bed, messy blond hair spread across my pillow, her legs open and welcoming. I can almost hear her breathy cries as I sink into her, legs wrapped around my waist, tits pressed up against my chest, fingers in my hair. I'd pound into her until all she could do was scream my name.

I come with a groan, my release spilling over my hand, and I clean up quickly, stepping into the shower to wash away the evidence. But even as I soap up, my mind is still on Eloise. But now I remember how she explained to her best friend and a perfect stranger that her family routinely makes her feel like shit. How Clara marched into my shop, informing me that Ian needed my help with an emergency, only to find my brother wasn't even there. But yes, there was an emergency.

Eloise crying is a travesty.

I've never and would never hit a woman in my life, but I'm not averse to telling her mother, aunt, and cousin to get fucked. It would be my absolute pleasure. Truly give me happiness.

After my shower, I dress and find Mazie still glued to the TV with Steve cuddled in her arms. "Morning, Maze," I say, ruffling her hair and then between the rabbit's ears. "You ready for breakfast?"

She lifts her hands, Steve awkwardly dangling between them, feet out, ears down. "You didn't say good morning to Steve."

I take him from her and hold him against my chest, murmuring a quiet greeting into his fur. This guy's great for stress. I bet Eloise would love him.

Mazie stands on the couch, jumping until I glower at her. She immediately falls to her butt. "Can we go to Sweet Cheeks?"

I shake my head. "You can't eat cinnamon rolls every day."

She pouts, but only for a second. Then she grins up at me, her eyes sparkling with mischief. "I like Eloise."

"Yeah?" I put Steve back in his bunny condo.

"I like her 'cause she likes pink like me and let me stay at the table with her. 'Member that? When she let me hand out those cards? And she makes lots and lots and *lots* of cimanin rolls."

"Cinnamon," I correct, turning back to her.

"And she's pretty and nice and makes you smile," she adds, standing from the couch.

I pause mid-step in reaching for her. Mazie's only six, but sometimes she sees more than I give her credit for. "She does, huh?"

"Uh-huh. You smile at her like you smile at me. Like you're happy."

Her words hit me like a punch to the gut, but I don't have a lot of time to consider just how much I like Eloise because Mazie starts in on where else I might take her for breakfast. Forever trying to convince me take her out.

I've been trying to adjust my schedule to fit Mazie's and take off as many weekends and evenings as possible. It severely cuts into work hours and, therefore, money, but it's more important for me to have time to spend with my kid. We went out to eat yesterday and caught a movie, where we shared a refillable popcorn. My daughter can take down a large popcorn like it's nothing. I refilled that thing twice.

"We're not going out today," I tell her.

"Because we're staying home to play Barbies?"

I blow out a breath. I hate playing Barbies because she always tells me I'm doing it wrong. As if there is a right or wrong way to make plastic dolls sit. Apparently, my Barbie voice is not lifelike enough. And I can't ever get the tiny goddamn clothes on and off them. Most of the time, my doll's naked, like I'm some kind of pervert.

"No, I need to do some things around the house. You said you wanted me to paint your bedroom pink, right?"

"Yes!" She freezes, fist mid-pump. "But Barbies first."

"What? No. I'm not wasting time playing Barbies."

She positions her hands on her hips. "You haven't played with me in soooo long, Daddy. It's rude."

"Rude?" I wrench my head back, a mix of amusement and melancholy settling in my stomach. My kid is so funny—and also really smart. She's curious and inquisitive, always so interested in learning about the world. She reminds me so much of my mom. A person who took genuine interest in everything and everyone around her. The older my daughter gets, the more I wish my mom could have known Mazie. I think they would have been best friends.

It's why I chose Violet as her middle name. I wanted her to have something from the woman who was my world growing up. Now, as my world grows up, I am happy to know she takes very little after me. Even less after her mother.

She is Violet Stone through and through.

"Yeah. Finley in my class taught me that word. It's rude. You're rude for not playing with me all the time."

"I can't play with you all the time. I'm an adult. I need to work so you can be a kid and play."

"But you're supposed to play with me because you're my daddy. Who else am I going to play with?"

It's been only Mazie and me for a long time, and she's used to it, but this was why I moved us here, so she could have more people in her life to play Barbies with. Not solely me.

Still... "You get fifteen minutes of Barbies after breakfast."

"Woo-hoo!" She races off to the kitchen. "Fuck yes! I'm gonna have Cocoa Puffs, and then we'll play Barbie camping."

I heave a sigh and fall onto the couch, my head back and eyes closed.

Is it bedtime yet?

* * *

Before I head into work Monday morning, I stop in at Sweet Cheeks, hoping to catch Eloise.

She's behind the counter, loading trays of fresh pastries behind the bakery case, hair up in a messy bun, stray wisps framing her face, and she's wearing a pink apron dusted with flour. Fuck, she's adorable.

She glances up when the door opens, and I absently rub at

my chest when she hits me with her smile. "Hi! I can't believe you're here so early."

"Morning, sunshine," I reply, even though I don't even think she hears me since she immediately starts up her engine.

"But you know what? I'm glad you're here early. We can get this out of the way." She puts the empty trays aside, not meeting my eyes. "I've been going over and over this all weekend, and I know you said you'd help and you're so sweet for that, but I think it's a really bad idea. The shower was a nightmare. My mom was relentless, asking me questions about my boyfriend, and to be honest, I did consider saying it was you, but I thought that was weird because we don't even really know each other that well, and what would I say? He's twenty-seven feet tall and gorgeous? I mean, she probably wouldn't even believe me."

I shrug, playing it cool with the gorgeous comment. "I don't think she would believe you saying anyone was twenty-seven feet tall, boyfriend or not."

She giggles, sounding a bit nervous, and plays with her necklace. It looks like a mini tire, pink, gold, and black. She rolls it between her fingers as she rounds the counter.

I almost reach for her but shove my hands into my pockets instead while she continues, "My aunt was a complete bitch. Condescended to me about showing up on time then didn't even say thank you to me or anyone else who helped set it all up then stayed to clean. And Lily kept going on and on about her perfect, stupid life and—"

"Lily's your cousin, right?"

She nods. "So, yeah, I think we should forget about you coming with me to the wedding. It's a terrible idea, and I would never force you to hang out with them. Pretend I never even mentioned it or the whole fake boyfriend thing, okay?" She claps, waves her hands back and forth, then snaps like she's performing a magic trick or something and squeezes her eyes shut. "Forgotten."

Unfortunately for her, she can't erase time or my memory, and I'm still standing in front of her when she opens her eyes to me again. Clearly disappointed, she wrinkles her nose.

I rub my palm over my mouth, smothering my smile.

It's too easy to relax with her, enjoy it—her energy and, hell, her silliness. She's beautiful and funny and clever. All I want to do is be around her. Cloak myself in everything she loves, so that I can love it with her.

"I won't forget," I tell her. "And I'll do it."

Her eyes go wide. "Really?"

"Yeah. I'll go to the wedding with you."

Before I even fully have the words out, she squeals and throws her arms around me in a hug, and I not-so-surreptitiously drag my nose over her neck, inhaling the sweet scent of her shampoo mixed with cinnamon.

She pulls back slightly to look up at me, her eyes sparkling. "Are you sure about this? You really don't have to."

I brush a loose strand of hair from her face. "I'm sure."

"It's a terrible idea. You pretending to be my boyfriend."

"Maybe," I agree. Though it's the perfect excuse to spend more time with Eloise and get to know her better, without the pressure of an actual relationship. Because as drawn as I am to her, I'm still not sure I'm ready to dive into anything real. Not with my past still hanging over me like a dark cloud.

"You're going to hate the wedding," she says, and there's no doubt about that.

"Most definitely."

She tosses her head back to laugh, and I barely restrain myself from planting my lips on her throat, tasting her skin over her pulse point. With a pat to my shoulders, she steps away from me, but I let my hands linger on her sides.

"Do I have permission to tell your family to go to hell?"

She tips her head to the side. "To do that, you'd have to talk to them. You really want to do that?"

"Not particularly. Unless it's to tell them to go to hell."

She thinks on this for a moment. "No, no telling anyone to go to hell, but that's a good idea. We should go over the rules or permissions or whatever."

"Rules?"

"Yeah." She vaguely gestures between us. "What we can say, if or where we can touch each other, you know?"

I have no rules, and she has all my permissions. Matter of fact, if she could start at my chest and make her way down to my dick, that'd be great.

"Maybe we should go out," she says and then immediately backtracks. "No, never mind. I'm already asking so much of you—"

"Dinner?"

She stills. "Hmm?"

"Let's go to dinner and talk about your rules or permissions or whatever."

She playfully smacks at my arm when I parrot her words back to her, as if she thinks I'm kidding. I step toward her, crowding her against the glass counter. I'm careful not to touch it and leave handprints she would need to clean up, though I'm all but crushing her. I can feel each of her inhales and exhales against my neck, her tits brushing my chest with every breath. Reaching around her, I snag her cell phone from the top of the case and enter my phone number into her contacts before setting it back down.

"Text me a night that's good for you. I'll find a babysitter for Mazie," I tell her, and she nods, a bit like a bobblehead.

I allow myself one last touch, a pinch of her chin, and then I force myself to leave.

Because my feelings for and attraction to Eloise are anything but fake.

Chapter 11

Eloise

Roman and I decided to go out on the following Friday, but in the meantime, I wrote out and deleted multiple texts to him of random thoughts I had during the day, including but not limited to:

Scale of 1 to 10: how bad do you think it would be if I wore sweatpants to the wedding?

Been thinking about naming the new bike Betsy. What's your opinion? Also, does that make you the father?

If you want to, we can have a big, dramatic breakup at the wedding. I think it would piss-off and delight to my mother because I can't be DRAMA, but I'd also steal the spotlight away from Lily.

What are your thoughts on wedding cakes that are not cake? Like imagine nine tiers of cinnamon rolls or three layers of pie.

But I didn't want him to think I was a total weirdo and kept those questions to myself. Even if I was still desperate to know his answers.

Now, I check myself over in the mirror, aiming for cute but not over the top. Sure, I have the hots for him, but I don't want him assuming I'm thinking of him every day. Even if it's the truth.

Wearing my most flattering jeans, white tank top, and a cute cardigan with flowers all over it, I loop my purse over my shoulder and head outside. Roman's beast of a car rolls up right as I step onto the sidewalk, and I'm there before he's even closed his door.

"Wait." He huffs, rounding the hood. "Woman, will you wait? Goddamn it."

"What?"

He doesn't think it's funny like I do and shoots me a glare as he opens the passenger side door for me.

"Such a gentleman," I tease, and he rolls his eyes.

"Wait for me next time."

I salute him and buckle myself in as he stalks back over to the driver's side and settles in his seat.

"I made reservations at Tabby Cat," he says. "Hope that's okay."

"We could have walked there after work. Probably would've been easier for you."

Tabby Cat is right across the street from my bakery and only a few blocks from his shop. He didn't need to drive to my house to pick me up, but he shrugs.

"I wanted to."

"Like a real date," I say absent-mindedly then feel my cheeks flush, though he either didn't hear or doesn't care. He merely looks me over, from top to bottom, his eyes stumbling on my chest, before pulling out onto the road.

He clears his throat. "You look good."

"Thanks. So do you." His dark hair is pulled back in a bun at the nape of his neck, and his usual black T-shirt has been replaced by a black button-down, rolled up his forearms. His muscles test the stitching, and I can't help but drag my finger over the seam on his shoulder. "So, are you a body builder or what?"

He glances at me, that hesitant quirk to his lips—like he's still trying to remember how to smile—lifting the corner of his mouth. "Not a body builder."

"But you're massive."

He doesn't disagree with me. He also doesn't reply.

"You're a gym rat, huh?"

"A bit," he says, and fifteen questions immediately come to mind.

"How many push-ups can you do?"

I swear he's about to laugh, but he rubs his hand over his mouth and beard. "I don't know. A lot. I usually do sets to failure."

"What's your squat?"

He exhales audibly. "Heaviest I ever squatted was four-ten."

"Four-ten," I repeat, amazed. "I think my heaviest squat was about two hundred."

"You a gym rat too?"

"I used to be. I played volleyball growing up, but after I quit, I sort of lost my desire to be in the gym."

He eyes me at the stoplight. "You're not wearing any pink."

I gasp when I realize I forgot and dig into my purse as he hooks a left to park the car. Using the mirror on the visor, I apply my bright-pink lipstick, blotting on a tissue. When Roman opens the door for me, I don't know what to do with it, and he holds out his hand. "Give it to me."

I stick the tissue in his palm and hop down, holding his

other hand. With the sun setting, the sky is a watercolor painting, and it's funny to be downtown but not going into my bakery. I wave to Mio's parents as we walk by the window of their sushi place. Roman places his palm on my back, ushering me across the street to Tabby Cat, a wine bar and bistro with tables outside that are filled up. Directly across from us, I spy Morgan cleaning up Sweet Cheeks, about to close down, while Stone Ink is lit up and open, with people milling about inside. Through the windows of Chapter and Verse, I can see Nicole organizing books while Ian holds a cat so a toddler and their parent can pet it.

It makes me wonder about Roman's daughter.

"Who's with Mazie tonight?" I ask as he opens the door for me.

"June and Riley. They're having a girls' night."

I cluck my tongue. "And I'm missing it for you."

"Sorry," he says flatly. "Being my fake girlfriend really fucks up your social calendar, I guess."

"I'm glad my fake boyfriend has a sense of humor to go along with all the muscle. You're not just brawn. You've got brains too."

"Too bad it's fake though, hm?" His dark eyes tilt at the corners, playful. "Won't see how big your fake boyfriend's dick is."

I choke on my tongue. "Is it? Big, I mean." I wave away the question. "That was inappropriate. But you were the one who brought it up. Look at what you've done to me! Now I won't be able to stop wondering about your dick."

As we approach the check-in stand, he lowers his head, his mouth against my ear. "You won't have to wonder. I'm telling you it's big."

My brain goes static and then shuts down, so I'm unable to do anything but follow when Roman gives his name to the host, who leads us to a table near the bar. But with my mind back by the entrance, I can't pay attention to what the man is saying. Something about our server and the wine list.

I blink over at Roman, who's staring at me like he knows he's scrambled my mind. "All right?"

"Uh-huh. Yep. Definitely."

"Good." He lowers his attention to the menu, but with how long his legs are, his knees butt up against mine, and I'm completely useless. Thank god, Nate strolls over.

He's wearing his baby in a carrier on his chest and a big grin. "Eloise, hey. How are ya?"

"I'm good." I pinch George's foot, lowering my voice to the monster gravel he loves so much. "Georgie!" He shrieks in laughter, kicking, and I keep going. "I'm gonna eat you up, I love you so."

"Hey, I never had the chance to thank you for his birthday gifts," Nate says, and I wave him off.

For George's first birthday a few weeks ago, I'd given them a *Wild Things*-themed basket, including the book, some stuffed Wild Things, and a T-shirt with the characters on it.

"I know you're really busy with this place." I wiggle George's foot. "And this big guy."

Nate nods. "My best boy. Helping Daddy out, right?"

George claps a few times, cooing "Dada" a few times and then "Mama."

"I know, I know, Mama's coming to pick you up soon," he says, smoothing his palm over his son's head. Then he informs me, "Tabby's working late."

"That's what she gets for being so smart," I say, and he laughs.

"Got that right." He turns toward Roman. "What's up, man? Roman, right?"

Roman nods, and they shake hands.

"How's your daughter?"

"Good."

When Roman doesn't say anything else, Nate smiles, nodding along like he expected as much. "Well, I'll let you two enjoy your dinner."

I wave as he retreats then turn to Roman. "You two know each other?"

"In passing."

Nate co-owns Tabby Cat with the chef, but he ran a bar for a long time, a neighborhood spot I used to love going to. Now, he's married with a kid, and Tabby, his wife, often stops into Sweet Cheeks with the baby. So I know them pretty well, but I have no idea how Roman does. I wait for him to explain, and when he doesn't, I shake my head. "Like pulling teeth with you. How'd you meet in passing?"

"I don't know," he says almost defensively. "We see each other around, and Mazie and I went to check out some place with...dress-up or something. He was there with a bunch of other dads."

"Oh yeah." I tap my fingers on the table, remembering Nate and his best friends are all dads. "You should hook up with them, set up some playdates."

"I don't know if you could tell, but I'm not exactly a play-date kinda guy."

"You went out with Sloane and her kids."

"That's different." He focuses on the menu, as if that'll make me drop this line of questioning.

"How?"

"I know her."

I snort. "You know Nate."

"Not like I know Sloane."

"Yeah, but if you hung out with him, you'd get to know him better."

He sighs, slowly drawing his eyes up to mine. "I have five friends. I don't want any more."

I bite back a smile. "Five? That's it?"

He nods seriously.

"Am I one of them?"

He stares at me for a long moment, his tongue poking out to wet his lower lip before he finally answers, "Yeah."

I press my hand to my heart. "I'm touched."

His focus follows and lingers on my cleavage. My boobs are huge. No matter what I wear, I can't hide them, so I've learned to ignore the stares. But I *want* Roman to stare at me.

I want him to lick his bottom lip again as his pupils expand. I want his shoulders to lift on a deep breath like he's controlling himself, and I want him to like what he sees so much, it makes him uncomfortable.

All those things happen, and when he shifts in his seat, I can't help but smile. I check out the long list of wines, specialty cocktails, and few beers on draft. "What are you going to get to drink?"

"I'm good with water."

I tip my head up. "Just water? You don't look like a wine guy, but this *is* a wine bar."

He scrubs his hand over his head, messing up his hair further then tugs on his shirt, eyes skirting around the place behind me. "I don't drink."

Of course he doesn't. I'd heard the rumors, but it's impossible to know what's true and what's not.

He sets his elbows on the table, hands clasped together, and doesn't equivocate when he says, "I've had some addiction issues in the past. I'm sober for about seven years."

I imagine he must have had to have this conversation a few times before—maybe more than a few, from how he's so calm—but I'm embarrassed. Not for him, but because I feel so stupid for teasing him about the wine. I don't know what to say.

"It's fine, though," he says quickly, leaning forward to place his hand over mine. "Order whatever you want."

I shake my head. "I'm such an asshole."

"No, you're not."

"I am. I—"

"Did nothing wrong. Don't be weird about it."

His monotone delivery pulls a laugh out of me. "I'm really sorry."

"Don't stress about it." He rubs the pad of his thumb over the length of my pinkie, and he could probably crush every bone in my hand if he wanted to. Yet, he's gentle. Like I'm blown glass.

"You fascinate me," I confess quietly, and he dips his chin an inch, his mouth curling into what I can only describe as a smirk sinful enough to make a nun drop her robes.

"Yeah. I'd say the same about you."

I wouldn't normally fish for compliments, but this feels too good. Being with him is too good, and I need to know it's real. "You think I'm fascinating?"

"If I tell you the truth, you'll think I'm a creep."

I'm on the edge of my seat. "Why?"

"Because I'm worse than Kyle." When I frown, not understanding, he slides his hand from mine and sits back in his chair, putting as much space between us as the table and chairs will allow. "Since that night in Wawa... If you knew how often I thought about you, you'd hire someone bigger than me to kick the shit out of me."

Well...

"First of all, there is no one bigger than you," I say, earning an amused glint of his eyes. "And I think you might be surprised with how much I would enjoy being obsessed over."

He arches one brow, deliberately raking his dark gaze over me then clucks his tongue. It is deliciously filthy. "Don't make promises you can't keep."

"Try me."

Chapter 12
Roman

Eloise might as well have shot off a starter pistol for how adrenaline rushes through my veins, my heart beating hard against my rib cage. I feel like I'm running, trying to catch up to her, barely clinging to my sanity.

First, she hooked me with her outfit. The tight jeans hugging her ass and that even tighter top, with her tits spilling out. Then she went and put on her hot-pink lipstick, like a neon sign, hypnotizing me. I spent more than a few minutes trying not to think about what her mouth might look like stretched around my cock. How that pink would smear and her lips would puff up more than they already are.

Worse was her dare. *Try me.*

She doesn't want to know how obsessed with her I am. Because that would require me stripping her naked and eating her out on this table instead of our dinner.

I breathe a sigh of relief when our server arrives at our table, so I can stop holding my breath that I'll make a goddamn fool of myself. I let Eloise order first, and she asks for an iced tea even though I remind her she can drink whatever she wants. She merely shakes her head and offers me a kind smile that eats away at the darkness that has settled over me the last two decades.

After I tell the server I'll stick with my water, we give her our dinner orders right away and then she's gone, leaving Eloise and me alone again. I lean back in my chair, trying to stretch out my legs as much as possible in the tight space. The restaurant is cozy, intimate even, but not exactly built for a guy my size. Eloise fits just fine, though, her pink lips curved in a smile as she watches me try to get comfortable.

When I finally settle, I ask, "How long have you and Sloane known each other?"

"Since high school." Eloise smiles. "She's like my sister. I love her." Then because I love hearing her talk, I wait, knowing she will. And she does. She goes on about the day they met in gym class freshman year. Sloane, in all black, stayed in the back when they had to run the track, and Eloise, in what I assume had to be all pink, hung back with her.

"No one who looks at us would think we belong together, but we've always clicked," she says, snapping her fingers. "Neither one of us fits in with our families, and I think we saw that in each other." Then she shrugs, adding more quietly, "Sometimes the people who are supposed to see us the clearest, don't. You know?"

That felt a little more honest than she might have meant to be, and it seems like maybe Eloise needs someone to see her clearly.

And fuck, if that doesn't break my heart.

I have the impulse to do violence again, but since it's mostly frowned upon by society at large, I try for a different topic.

"Do you have siblings?"

"One, a brother, but we're not like you and your siblings. I've always wished I had a family like yours. All together and..." She has a faraway look in her eyes, and there is something in her desire to be wanted that makes me want to spill everything. Tell her about my whole life so she knows she's not alone. That I see her. And even though my family is great, *I* haven't always been great. I don't deserve my family, but she does. She deserves the world.

I scrub a hand over my face then fold my arms over my chest. "I, uh..." I shrug. "I don't know if..." When she tips her head to the side, curiosity and concern written across her features, I spit it out. "I'm not sure what you heard about me, but it wasn't only alcohol. It was pills too. Mostly pills, actually. For about fifteen years of my life, I swallowed anything that would take the pain away."

She sits quietly for a few moments, which may as well be hours in Eloise time. Then she sets her hand on the table, palm up. "Do you... Will you tell me about it?"

Anything. Everything she wants to know. I'll tell her.

I take a deep breath and shift forward in my seat to place my palm on hers, her dainty fingers folding over mine.

I don't really know where to start, so I go all the way back to the beginning. "I don't have memories of my father at all. For all intents and purposes, Ian is my dad. Ours left when I was two, so my brothers and sister know and remember more about him than I do, but to me, he's...a shadow. He's nothing except half my genes, and I guess I got stuck with the addiction half."

"What about your mom?" Eloise asks, and I let my attention drift to her fingernails, the round tips, her thumb brushing back and forth across the back of my hand.

"She was everything. Mother, father, friend, confidante... angel. I can appreciate now as a parent what it must have taken for her to keep four kids fed and clothed and happy, but I didn't understand back then. In my memory, she was perfect, and whatever attention I didn't receive from her, I had from Ian. I never wanted for anything. Until it fell apart."

I lift my gaze to the wall directly across from me, lost in the past. "I had a full ride to Penn State for football, and my mom would come to as many games as she could. I was on track to be drafted. That was the goal. I was the number one defensive end in the country, but I tore my quad and needed surgery. I called Mom right away, and she came out to stay with me for a few days. I lived off campus with a bunch of guys, and there was my mom in the middle, cooking dinner for all of us, making sure I was doing my PT."

Across from me, Eloise laughs softly, drawing my gaze back to her, and I allow myself a semblance of a smile, a few moments to sit with the happy memory. Before I permit the sad ones to invade. "She went home, and a few weeks later, she was gone, and I never even saw her. She was in the hospital for three days, and I never went. I wasn't there."

Eloise frowns, brows together, head shaking, as if I shouldn't be upset about that. As if it wasn't my fault. And while her death wasn't my fault, my not being there was. I should have been with her. I should have held her hand. I should have told her I loved her. Every day.

Because she gave up so much for me, and I couldn't even give up a weekend to drive down there.

"You were in college," Eloise says in my defense, but there is none. There is nothing I regret more in my life than not being there when my mother needed me.

"She never asked anything of me," I go on, voice like tissue paper. "And I couldn't do one basic thing for her and be there in the hospital." I clear my throat of the emotion there. "I never had to face hard things, and I didn't want to go and face what I knew what be the *hardest* thing I ever had to do."

Eloise squeezes my hand in support, but I shake my head, feeling unworthy of it. "It's my biggest regret. I ran away from it and I kept running."

Eloise folds both of her hands around mine, tugging slightly, as if she can will me to accept her words. "You have to forgive yourself."

I shrug.

"Your mother would want you to. She'd never blame you."

I fix my gaze on the condensation of my water glass.

"If you were in the position your mother was in, would you blame Mazie?"

"That's not..." I trail off, my mind coming to a stop. No one has ever asked me that question before.

"You wouldn't blame her. I know you wouldn't. You're an amazing parent, like Ian. Like your mother. And you know deep down your mom wouldn't want you still blaming yourself about this."

I shut my eyes to the sting, her words sinking in, and a long moment passes before I can meet her gaze. When I do, I find her features full of understanding. "No wonder you've struggled for so long. You've been holding on to this since you were in college? Of course you self-medicated."

I lick my lips and lay out the rest. "After the funeral, I went back to school and gave up. On classes, on football, on my friends. The only ones I kept around me were the ones who never said anything to me about how much I was drinking or how many pills I was taking. Who offered me names and numbers of people who could get me more. I dropped out and slept on couches. I stopped answering calls and texts and got jobs fixing cars when I needed money so I could buy more drugs. If it came in pill form, I took it. Something to sleep. To stay up. For my pain, real or phantom. And chased it all with a bottle of whatever was closest."

Eloise doesn't physically react, save for tightening her grip on my hand. "You went to rehab?"

"A few times, although it never stuck. Ian paid for it every time."

"He's a good man."

I dip my chin. "The best. My best friend."

"One of your five," she says, and I raise my gaze to her, her soft smile unraveling the tension in my chest.

"Yeah." I huff a sort of laugh.

"Not many spots left."

"Lucky you already have one," I say, and she agrees, dragging her thumb back and forth over my knuckles.

"So you haven't talked to your dad at all?" she asks, and when I shake my head, she quirks her brow, thinking for a second. "None of you have?" I shrug as she tips her head to the side. "None of you care to find out about him? He's your dad."

"So? He's our dad, but that doesn't automatically make him worthy of our respect. Is that why you let your mom talk down to you?"

I know I've made a mistake the moment she rips her hand away from mine, and I lean forward.

"I'm sorry, Eloise. I shouldn't have said that."

She bites into her lip, and I'm about to apologize again when the server sets down our food. I thank her then turn back to my date. Her green eyes have a glassy sheen. *Fuck me.*

"I'm so sorry, sunshine. I'm an asshole. Please, don't—"

"You're right," she interrupts, barely a whisper, and I nearly dive across the table to hear it. "I don't know how to talk to her. I don't know what to say to any of them. I'm not a confrontational person, and I don't..." She peers up at me with watery eyes, and yeah, I might commit a felony.

"Don't cry. It kills me to see you cry."

She blinks a few times and dabs at the corners of her eyes with her napkin before sniffling and taking a gulp of her iced tea. "I'm thirty years old, and I don't know how to tell my mother that she hurts my feelings. It's pathetic, right? I'm pathetic."

"You're not pathetic." It's her mother who's pathetic. Everyone else in her life who's ever made her feel this way. When she still doesn't brighten, I make an attempt. "I don't think I've ever talked this much in my life at one time. Might have said more words to you tonight than I have all year."

"Yeah?"

When I nod, she smiles, and I breathe a sigh of relief, gesturing for her to eat. She picks up her fork to stab a few vegetables next to her salmon. I dig into my steak frites, and we eat silently for a few minutes before she asks me to go on. "So, how'd you end up here?"

"Mazie."

"You moved back for Mazie?"

I swallow a bite of food and wipe my mouth, using the time to consider how much I should tell her about Amy, if anything at all. It's been so nice talking about all of this with Eloise, but I feel like that might be a step in the wrong direction. "When I found out I was having a child, it was like a switch was flipped inside me. All the years of falling into and out of sobriety, it all suddenly coalesced. I thought about my mom and how much I loved her. I knew I could never be as perfect as she was, but I needed to try. So I spent the last few years trying to give Mazie the kind of life my mother gave me, but I needed my family to do it, so..."

"So here you are," Eloise fills in, grinning like she's actually proud of me.

"Here I am," I repeat.

"With me."

"With you," I confirm, and she takes a deep breath that I feel in my lungs too.

It's as if my whole life has led up to this moment, to this woman, the opportunity to make her happy, win her smiles, and, if given the chance, protect her from anything that might hurt her.

So that makes it all worth it. That I can be the man here with her.

While we finish our dinner and a shared creme brûlée for dessert, she takes over the conversation, telling me more about Sloane, and Eloise's theory about how every relationship—romantic or platonic—has to have a grumpy or sunshine person. I don't get it, but then she points out that I'm her grumpy, and I like that, so I don't argue.

Anytime I can be her anything is okay with me.

I pay the bill, even though she tries to argue, but quiets when I grumble her name, and we walk out of Tabby Cat with my hand on her lower back. At my SUV, she waits for me to open the door for her, but before I close it, she holds out her hand. "We never got to talk about the rules."

"The rules?"

"About...touching or kissing," she finishes, cheeks flaming.

"You can touch me anywhere," I say without hesitation, and she giggles. I take her hand in mine and put it on the center of my chest then let my hand fall to my side, testing her. Seeing what she'll do.

When she understands the silent challenge, she slowly skims her palm up to my throat and splays it along the back of my neck, fingers sinking into the hair at the base of my skull.

"This okay?" she asks, and I close the distance between us. She turns in her seat, feet on the edge of the running board, and I place my hands on her knees, holding them open to make room for me between them and lower my head to hers.

"It's good."

"Maybe we should kiss to make sure it looks real," she whispers, and I don't need to be told twice.

My lips are on hers less than a second later, brushing and prodding at the plump pillows until she parts them, allowing my tongue to find hers. She tastes like sugar, and I have to mentally tell myself to relax my grip on her thighs. But then she makes this needy little sound in the back of her throat, and I forget all about what I'm supposed to do and drag her closer to me, gripping the sides of her thighs as tight as I want, pressing my fingertips into the softness of her hips.

She's all heat and sighs, and it's the best kind of torture, knowing she is as desperate for my tongue as I am for hers. She licks into my mouth like I'm her favorite ice cream, and my cock grows semi-hard because I know that's how she'd lick my dick.

Fuck.

I pull away to find her breathing as raggedly as I am. I drag my hands over the sides of her face, pushing her hair away without an ounce of gentility. I'm a wild animal pawing over her, but she's in my car and had her tongue in my mouth a moment ago.

She is mine.

At least for this goddamn family wedding of hers.

"How was that?" I ask, and she sways toward me as if drunk, biting into her bottom lip.

"Mm-hmm."

I raise my brow, needing more of an answer.

She pats my pecs before swiveling in her seat to face forward. Then she giggles. "Yep. That'll, uh...really show my family what's what."

That pulls a laugh from me. It sounds raspy, even to my ears. "Right. For your family."

Still refusing to look at me again, she inhales audibly. "Just get in the car, Roman, before you make me blurt out something else neither one of us is ready to hear."

I'm not so sure about that, but I do as she commands. "Whatever you say, sunshine."

Chapter 13
Roman

I'm in the middle of filling out some paperwork for a car I inspected after an accident. I was told the driver is fine, but the car is not. It needs a lot of work, from the axle to the frame rails, a total safety system rebuild, as well as a complete replacement of the left side panels. It's gonna run north of six grand, and I'd be surprised if the insurance adjuster doesn't declare it a total loss.

This part of the job is necessary yet boring, and I'm so grateful for the reprieve of my cell phone ringing that I barely even look at my screen before hitting the button to answer.

Then it hits me all at once who it is when I hear the white noise.

Amy.

An automated voice fills my ear. "You have a collect call from an inmate at Champlain Valley Rehabilitation Facility for Women. This call may be monitored and recorded. To accept the charges for this call, press one. To decline, press two or hang up."

I let out a breath and hit the number one.

"You may now begin your fifteen-minute call," the voice tells me, and I sit on the edge of the seat, the usual anger and hurt twisting up my gut.

Then Amy comes on the line. "Hey, Roman."

"Hi."

"How are you doing?" she asks too brightly, and it annoys me.

"Fine."

"That's good."

I should probably be more supportive. She is the mother of my child, and yet I don't have it in me, so we sit in silence for a minute until I lose my cool.

"What do you want, Amy? I'm getting charged for this."

"Oh, sorry my *imprisonment* is fucking up *your* life."

I rub at my forehead. "What do you want?"

"I want to talk," she says, sounding like she might cry. "I want to hear about Mazie. Does she miss me?"

Here again, I should feel some sympathy for her, but I don't because she fucked up her life and ours—Mazie's and mine. *She* did this. But I'm not that much of an asshole to tell her the truth.

"Yeah," I answer but don't elaborate. "What do you want to know?"

"How is she?"

"Mazie is..." *Better than she's ever been.* "Doing really well."

"Yeah? How about school? Does she like it?"

"She loves it. She started dance class too."

"Oh my god," Amy says, voice breaking. "You have to send me pictures."

I sigh. "Yeah. Okay."

"And the bunny. What's his name?"

"Steve."

"Right. Steve. How is he?"

"Good." And because I'm tired of answering her questions and because I did love her at one time, I ask, "How are you?"

"I'm...okay."

I don't respond. I have no idea how to fucking respond to this situation. Ever.

I met Amy at the lowest point in my life, and we fed into each other's worst tendencies. I don't know who dragged whom down, but I was the one to stay clean when we said we would get clean. The day she told me she was pregnant was the day I had my last drink, gulped down my last pill. Amy managed to be sober through her pregnancy and a few weeks after, but it didn't take long for her to backslide, using postpartum depression as an excuse. Maybe it was too hard for her, I don't know, but from where I stood, it didn't seem like she tried all that hard. I was the one taking Amy to her doctor's appointments. I was the one offering to go in with her. I was the one telling her to take a walk because she seemed like she needed a break.

But it was all, *I'm fine* or *I don't need you* or *Just for half an hour*.

It wasn't long before I found her stash. Coke to stay up, pills to sleep. Then there were the few glasses of wine to relax.

I didn't want Mazie growing up in the shadow of an addicted parent like I did, so I knew what I had to do. I told Amy she needed to clean herself up or I was taking Mazie and leaving.

It worked. For a few months. But then she slipped.

The older Mazie grew, the harder it was to hide what was going on, and while I wanted my daughter to have two parents, it wasn't going to be at her expense. Because I stopped trusting Amy with our daughter.

I packed up Mazie and moved out, to Amy's crying. She begged me to stay, apologized, made the usual promises, but when it became obvious it wasn't going to work, she called me a bastard for taking her child, a motherfucking asshole for leaving her alone.

But I made it clear I wasn't going to keep Mazie from her; all she needed to do was clean up her life. I did it and knew she was capable of doing it too. Although I also knew how difficult it was to stay sober.

Amy hadn't been very present in our daughter's life, but when she was, she was a good mom. So when she called a few months later, telling me she'd turned her life around and wanted to see Mazie, I agreed.

We went over to her new apartment, decked out with brand-new furniture and electronics. She bought Mazie a bunch of toys and dresses, ordered more food than we could finish, and topped it all off with ice cream and popcorn while we watched a movie. I was impressed, and we all had a great time. It almost felt like it was back to normal. Until someone banged on her door.

It was multiple cops. There to arrest her.

Mazie didn't understand what was going on, but she knew enough that seeing her mother in handcuffs was bad. She was hysterical, which only made *me* hysterical. Especially when they separated us, interrogating me about who I was and what I was doing there.

It was traumatizing, to say the least. Seeing my baby carried away as she screamed and cried, her hands reaching out for me. It wasn't long before I was reunited with her—in the back of a police car—but the damage had been done.

Mazie didn't want to leave my side for weeks, had outbursts in school and crying fits in the middle of the night. She already had trouble understanding why we lived separately from her mom, so attempting to explain that she was in prison...it was a nightmare.

Arraigned on multiple charges of theft and fraud, Amy was entangled in a web of her own making. She had been stealing prescription pads from the medical office where she worked, forging scripts to feed her escalating addiction. She had also siphoned off money from the practice, masquerading her theft as legitimate expenses while pocketing the funds for her own use. Instead of seeking sobriety, she had merely learned to hide her addiction behind a facade of lavish purchases. Her case was open-and-shut.

I didn't attend the trial. Didn't bring Mazie to see her like she asked. She was fucking lucky I didn't revoke her parental rights. After thinking about it, I came to the realization that it was my job to keep Mazie safe, but that I should leave it up to her to decide if she wanted a relationship with her mother once she's released from prison.

So, Amy would continue to receive updates every few weeks in the form of a phone call or an occasional picture for the next four years. The only positive out of all this was that she had to dry out while behind bars.

"Do you need anything? More money in your account?" For as much as movies and television shows are fiction, they're still pretty accurate at portraying what it's like to be in a cellblock.

I visited Amy once after sentencing, and she was in a rough way. She told me how the inmates barter and trade their commissary goods, and I didn't know what else to do besides promise that I'd keep money in her account. I didn't feel bad that she'd been caught breaking the law, that she was paying for what she'd done, but I had loved her at one point. It broke my heart to see her like that, physically a mess. Worse off than when she came home from a bender.

"No, I'm okay. I'm just..." Amy sniffles on the phone with

me now. "I'm trying, Roman. I'm really trying to take this day by day, but it's hard."

"You're still doing counseling in there, right? How's that going?"

"A fucking joke."

"What about your job?" Last we talked, she'd started working in the kitchen.

Amy's sad tone flips to ire. "This skinny little bitch got me kicked out. Thinks she runs this place. She doesn't run shit. I—"

"You have one minute remaining on this call," the automated voice tells us.

"I'll talk to you next time, Amy."

"No, wait, Roman. Wait." When I don't hang up, she rushes out her request. "I was thinking you could bring Mazie to visit me."

"No." I stand up. "Absolutely not."

"Why not?"

"Because I'm not bringing our six-year-old to a prison. She doesn't need to see you in there, and I don't even know why you'd want her to see you like that."

"Because I love her."

I pace the office. "Yeah, you really have a great way of showing it."

"Fuck you. You have no idea what I'm going through in here."

"And you have no idea what I'm going through out here. I'm not putting Mazie through that. End of fucking story."

"Well, when I get out—"

"When you get out, we can talk about your relationship with her," I interrupt. "But not now. Not like this."

"What relationship?" Amy's voice rises, a hint of desperation creeping in. "You won't let me have one with her. You won't let me be her mom."

I barely keep my voice restrained, not wanting my coworkers to overhear me. "How can you? You're in prison. You can't be her mother. At least not right now."

"You're a son of a bitch, you know that? You—"

Her sentence is cut off abruptly, and then the automated voice tells me, "This call has ended."

"Fuck." I grit my teeth and toss my phone on my desk, my fists clenching with the need to relieve this pent-up stress.

This is so fucked up.

I may have thrown away a lot in life because of my addiction, but I refuse to give up anything else because of it. I made it out, and like my mother, I won't let my child suffer because they have a parent who continues to let it rule their life. I'm not above taking Mazie away from Amy. I don't want to.

But I will if I have to.

I slump into my chair, elbows on my knees, head in my hands.

That call, it's a reminder.

Of why I won't get into another serious relationship. Why I can't let myself fall for someone, why I can't let Mazie become attached. Because even though Eloise is obviously not Amy, even though she's sunshine and warmth and everything good in this world, I can't risk it. I can't risk Mazie being hurt again when she's doing so well. I can't risk myself when I moved for a fresh start.

It's been a few days since Eloise and I went to dinner, since that kiss that left me reeling. We've texted, flirted, talked about the wedding weekend. But it's not enough. I want more. I want her. And that scares the shit out of me.

Not only for Mazie and me, but for Eloise too.

I'm a mess. A fucked-up, broken mess with baggage, a past, and a daughter who needs me to be strong, to be stable. I can't afford to lose my head or my heart. Not even to Eloise, who I fear has already taken a much-too-large piece of it.

I'm so fucking screwed.

I glance at my phone and the photo of Mazie smiling with a Rocket Pop in her hand, blue popsicle juice smeared all over her mouth. I'll do anything to protect her joy and innocence. She deserves to remain a happy child as long as possible.

But even as I know I need to protect her, it's impossible to keep my distance from Eloise. I'm already in too deep.

I have been since I first laid eyes on her.

That was it. I was done.

And I fear I've fucked everything up. Without thinking, I type out a text to my brother to see where he is, and I thankfully don't need to wait long for his response. Even though it's not my lunchtime yet, I pocket my phone and head out with a few directions to Shawn and Luis. Then I drive to Griffin's house.

He's waiting for me by the door of his suburban Colonial with flower beds, an American flag flying, and a *Feminists Live Here* doormat. He opens the door for me, brows pinched together, and I'm not sure exactly what to say to him now that two of us are finally alone.

Thanks for letting me stop by.

Sorry I'm a dick.

I'm surprised you have so many houseplants.

So, channeling Eloise, I blurt out the thing that's been plaguing my mind. "How do I know I'm doing the right thing?"

Griffin doesn't answer, merely studies me from top to bottom. "Take your shoes off. Don't want you fucking up my carpet with oil."

I shuck off my boots as I hear soft footfalls before seeing a young woman coming toward us in ripped jeans and a sweater falling off her shoulder. She smiles at Griffin and then at me, her voice edged with a Southern twang when she says, "Hi, you must be Roman."

I nod and take her outstretched hand.

"I'm Andi. I was about to make lunch. Would you like to stay?"

I glance at Griffin to answer, but he's as stoic as ever, so I turn back to her with a shrug, and she reaches out to my arm, squeezing. "It's leftover pulled pork. I hope that's okay."

"Of course it is," Griffin answers for me, watching her like a hawk, though it's less predatory and more like security. Like he wants to make sure she's safe at all times, even in their own home.

I know the feeling.

"Sounds great," I say.

"Good. Why don't you two have a chat? It'll be ready in about twenty minutes." Andi's smile has yet to drop. She's a petite thing, and, if I had to guess, about thirty years old. Same as Eloise. I'd heard they were friends, but I imagine Eloise is friends with everyone. She could charm the devil.

She's charmed me after all.

Before Andi pivots away from us, she shoots Griffin a look and whispers something that sounds like "Be nice, Captain," but I can't be sure because I'm too busy witnessing my soldier brother transform into a puppy dog at her orders.

Know that feeling too.

"Come on," he says, waving me to follow him to the living room with big comfy couches and lots of framed photos everywhere of the twins—Logan and Grace—or the four of them all together. We take a seat on opposite ends of the sofa, neither one of us relaxing back, and it's a long time before we speak.

At the same time.

"So why did you come here?"

"I need to talk to you."

Then we both stop and grunt in amusement. My brother lifts his hand, silently directing me to go first, so I rub my palms on my pants and start again.

"I need to talk to you. Get your perspective."

He nods once, his gaze steady. It's intimidating how he can stare for so long without blinking. I don't know if it's a SEALs thing or a Griffin thing, but it freaks me out, and I set my focus on the fireplace across from us. The television above is playing football highlights on mute, Camden Long catching a pass. "How do you know you're doing the right thing?"

"I don't understand the question," he says, and I absently remove my cell phone from my pocket, clicking on the call log and then showing him that I spoke with Amy.

I'd told all my siblings about Amy and what had happened when they came to my house that first day. Expectedly, Griffin didn't have much to say, the tension around him palpable. He didn't need to speak. I knew he was disappointed in me, in my choices, the situation.

But that's why I'm here now. Because he always does the right thing, and if there is anyone I can ask about my choices, it's him.

"Am I doing the right thing by keeping Mazie away from Amy? I think I am, but then I have a conversation with her, and I second-guess myself. All of it. Am I doing any of this right? Being here? Buying the house? I don't know what the hell I'm doing. I don't know what's right. If I ever did."

It's a long time before I can meet his gaze, my throat thick, my stomach tight as I wait for him to answer. He doesn't, and I swallow down my nerves. As much as I'd like to ignore the lingering need for his approval, I can't. I'm forty years old and a fuckup. I need him, the one who always does what's right, to tell me it'll be okay.

But he doesn't.

What he does do is shift, leaning forward to place his elbows on his knees and clasp his hands together. He takes a deep breath and then another. I think a whole minute passes before he speaks.

"You've gotten yourself into a lot of messy situations, and I think we all have a right to be upset with you about that. How you basically removed yourself from our family for a long time. It was fucked up."

I swallow the reflexive need to defend myself. Because he has every right to feel whatever it is he feels, and it's true. I've made a lot of fucked-up decisions.

He goes on, "But I understand the innate desire to run away from hard times. Because I did it too. You did it with drugs. I did it with the military. Mine may have been the acceptable choice to society, but I still chose to bury everything. I just did it in a uniform."

Then he angles his head to me, eyes on mine. Unblinking. "Part of the reason I was always so angry with you actually had nothing to do with you. I was angry at myself. Because that thing in me, telling me to run as far away as possible, to hide all the pain and bullshit we had to deal with, I knew that thing was in you too. But I didn't want to face it. I didn't want to admit that I was afraid, and if I allowed you that space to be afraid, that meant I'd have to face it myself."

I'm not sure how to feel about this confession. From the most stand-up guy I know. A literal hero. Admitting his fears.

His Adam's apple bobs a few times before he continues. "I am a fixer, and I couldn't fix you. I couldn't even fix myself. So I took my anger out on you, and I'm sorry. You needed my support, and I didn't always give it to you."

To say I am floored would be an understatement, but he doesn't let me respond. He holds up his palm. "And I don't want to hear another goddamn apology from you, all right?

You're here, and you're trying to do better. That's apology enough. So, to answer your question about if you're doing the right thing... I don't know." He rubs his palm over his mouth a few times. "I don't know what the right thing is."

But that can't be correct. That's why I came here, to him. Because he should know. He's a retired Navy SEAL and works as a fire captain. He's noble and virtuous and Captain fucking America. But he doesn't know what the right thing is?

I shake my head. "That's it? You don't have any advice?"

He sits back, tossing a glance in the direction of the kitchen, where we can hear Andi singing softly, running water, and clanging dishes. "I might have acted like an asshole to you about your past, but I don't have all the answers. Life isn't objective. While I might have made different decisions than you, had different outcomes, I told you...it came from the same place. Some people will say drug addiction is bad. Others will say what I did in the military is worse."

He settles his gaze back on me, and even though I doubt he'll ever tell me anything about what he's got locked up tight inside him, I suspect he fights his own demons. On that level, we understand each other. He lifts a shoulder, telling me, "All I know is that I would rather die before I let anything bad happen to my family. That's how I make my decisions—with my kids and Andi at the forefront of every choice. Would it cause them pain? Or bring them happiness? Everything else... it's all white noise."

I suppose on that spectrum, I am doing the right thing. Because Mazie has never been happier, and being around Amy right now would only bring her pain.

Griffin claps his hand on my back. "You're doing good, kid. Keep it up."

Chapter 14
Eloise

We've been driving for almost two hours, from West Chester to a ski lodge in the Poconos for Lily's wedding, and Roman keeps my mind off the mile markers by answering any and every question I throw his way. I learn more about his childhood and his mother, who was a beloved teacher and friend to the community. He tells me how each of his siblings takes after her in some way—Ian, an ability to create art, Griffin, his love of reading, and Taryn, her fierce yet loving personality. When I ask Roman what he inherited, he shrugs and mumbles, "I think I'm more like my dad than anyone would like to admit." Then he quickly moves on to how all four Stone siblings have tattoos in Violet's honor and tugs up the sleeve of his T-shirt to reveal the single balloon with his mother's name on it, floating up to the sky on his right triceps. It's both sad and sweet, yet I ruin the moment by asking how far down his tattoos go.

The man merely tosses me a delicious curl of his mouth before asking what tattoos I have. When I tell him none because I'm afraid of needles, he murmurs, "All that pretty skin. A beautiful canvas."

It takes me about two and a half minutes to recover.

We talk a lot about Mazie and Steve, the bunny rabbit, but we don't touch on Mazie's mother at all. Roman doesn't seem to purposely avoid talking about her, but he also carefully sidesteps mentioning her. I don't know if there is drama or if it was a contentious divorce, but since Roman seemingly has full custody, I assume there's some type of bad blood there. And if so, I don't want to accidentally bring it up, so as curious as I am, I keep my mouth shut about it.

"I'm tired of answering questions," Roman says, cutting me off before I can ask about why he chose to be a mechanic. "Your turn."

"But you're so much more interesting than me."

He silently replies by motioning outside of my window. We're in the mountains now, the trees a colorful blend of orange, yellow, and red, but that's not what he's showing me.

It's the sign.

We're fifteen miles away.

I let out a whiny sigh, and he clamps his bear paw on my thigh. "It'll be all right."

"If you say so," I pout, and he squeezes my leg.

"I won't let anybody say anything to you. Don't worry about that."

I study his profile, so stark and rugged, yet somehow gentle. Or maybe that's me projecting what I want on to him.

Then again, he's always been soft with me. I couldn't be scared of him if I tried.

"I can feel you stressing," he says, rubbing his thumb back and forth on my inner thigh. "Tell me who everybody is so I know when to run interference."

I take a deep breath. "Okay. So. My mom's tall with bleach

blond hair, but even without that, you'll be able to tell who she is because she'll be the one yelling at me."

He turns to me. "She doesn't really yell at you, does she?"

"No. Well... I don't know. She doesn't talk to me like an adult, I'll say."

Roman doesn't like that, and he grumbles something I don't quite catch, so I go on.

"My aunt Beverly has short, dark hair with this... *No more wire hangers* vibe."

"What?" When I hold up my hand, pretending to wave around a hanger, he frowns. "Am I supposed to know what that means?"

"You've never seen *Mommie Dearest*?"

He shakes his head and exits off the turnpike.

"Well, maybe you're better off without watching it. Sloane and I had a weird obsession with it when we were kids. Probably because of the controlling mothers... We were working out our trauma."

"I still don't get it."

"Never mind. The point is, between my aunt and my mother, you need to play it cool. They'll sniff you right out if they know something's up, so be cool."

He huffs. "I'm always cool, sunshine."

I bite the inside of my cheek to keep from grinning. He's called me that before. *Sunshine*. Because I'm his sunshine?

Not that we're in a relationship. Or, I mean, a *real* one. We're in a fake one for this weekend, but I suppose it still proves my theory correct.

"What about your cousin?" he asks, dragging me out of my *sunshine* haze.

"Oh. Uh, she's..." I flit my hand around. "She's mostly harmless. A spoiled princess who always gets what she wants."

"And what about you? What do you want?"

I tilt my head back, watching as he rolls to a stop at the red light and turns on his left blinker. "What do you think I want, Roman?"

He slants his gaze to me, answering only after his eyes skate from my face down my throat to my chest and back up. "I have a few ideas."

I immediately lower the window for some air. "You better put that...charm away. We have a wedding to survive."

When the light turns green, he makes the left as he swipes his palm over his mouth. "No one's ever accused me of being charming before."

"Well, there's a first time for everything, isn't there? Save it for the audience. But not too much in front of my dad, okay? We actually get along, and I want to keep it that way."

"You a daddy's girl?"

I shrug, unapologetic. "A little, yeah. He's a doctor and a lot more understanding of my ADHD."

"You have ADHD?"

"Yeah, you couldn't tell?" I ask with a laugh, but he narrows his brows in my direction.

"No. It's an invisible disability. Why would I be able to tell?"

I'm about to make an excuse, explain away how I'm flighty and inattentive and constantly interrupting others. Because that's what's been drilled into me—that I should hide my eccentricities so as not to make others uncomfortable.

Even as I feel nauseated about spending the weekend with my family, where I'll be made to feel bad about how different I am, I feel the need to apologize. Make myself smaller.

It's sick.

When I don't answer, he juts his chin toward me. "That why you're always playing with your necklace?"

I release said necklace. "You noticed that?"

"I notice everything about you." At the next stoplight, while I'm still reeling from his *I notice everything about you*, he reaches for the round pendant, rolling it between his fingers like I do before dropping it back into place. "What's it like for you?"

"My ADHD?" When he nods, I tip my head side to side. "When I was young, I was always in trouble for talking in class. My grades were okay, but it was a struggle. It didn't come easy, not like my brother."

"What's his name?"

"Alex. He's finishing up his residency to be an orthopedic surgeon. He's two years younger than me and kind of a douche."

"Kind of a douche?" Roman purses his lips, muffling the distinct sound of laughter coming from the back of his throat, and I'm determined to make him really laugh this weekend. I'm dying to hear it.

"Okay," I acquiesce. "He's a big douche. Twenty-eight and knows everything about everything. I can't stand these young kids."

"Young kids? Twenty-eight isn't young."

I hold out my palm like it should make sense. "But he's in a whole different decade than me."

"You're only thirty," Roman says, and when I nod like *duh*, he says, "Did you know I'm forty?"

I gasp, playing at horror. "I'm fake-dating an older man!"

That earns me a quirk of his brow. "How old did you think I was?"

"I don't know. I figured in your forties because of your siblings, but to be honest, it's really hard to tell with you. You look anywhere from twenty-five to fifty-five. You're ageless like The Rock."

"The Rock is not ageless. I'm pretty sure he's, like, fifty."

I hike my shoulders up to my ears, dropping them heavily. "Well, you could tell me he's thirty, and I'd believe you."

He places his hand back on my thigh. "It bother you that I'm a decade older than you are?"

"No," I answer immediately and honestly.

"Good." He nods. "Now, tell me when you were diagnosed."

"In college. I played volleyball all through high school and was really active in clubs, always out with friends. I was *that* girl...you know, the super-talkative one, friends with everybody? It never occurred to me or my parents that the reason I was always on the go or my mind wandered was because I had ADHD. But then I went to college and..." I mime an explosion with my hands. "Everything fell apart. I didn't have my safety net. I didn't have a daily schedule with places to be and things to do and people telling me where to go. I had low executive functioning skills... I didn't even know what executive functioning skills were then. Only that I couldn't figure out how to plan my day. I couldn't figure out what the most important thing to do was. I didn't want to go out or do anything because I couldn't even think about getting up to get dressed. It was too overwhelming."

Roman runs his palm up and down my leg, soothing me, but I doubt he's even consciously thinking about it. It doesn't feel like it's a decision. It feels like he's mindlessly touching me because he likes it. Because he's already realized *I* like it.

I continue with the rest of my story, feeling more emotionally safe than I have in a long time. "I ended up failing out of school and went home. Mommy dearest was pissed at me, but after a few weeks, it was my dad who took me to an appointment to see a psychologist and then a psychiatrist. I was diagnosed with ADHD and depression. They put me on some antianxiety and depression meds, which turned everything around with help from a therapist so I could understand coping mechanisms—and why I could function in high school, but suddenly not in college. It took about a year, but in that time, I became obsessed with baking. So, I went back to school and got a degree in business to learn how to open my own bakery, and fast-forward a few years, here I am."

"With me," he says, an echo of what I said during our dinner.

"With you," I agree.

And it's with that calming thought that he makes a turn onto the long drive leading up to the lodge.

It's huge and luxurious, set back against the trees at sunset, like a Bob Ross painting. Happy little trees and happy little people, but all I feel is anxiety.

Until Roman opens my door and takes my hand. "I got you."

It's all I need to hear to take those steps up the small slope and enter the foyer of the stone building, all rustic beauty and expensive crystal. With a duffel on his back, and the rest of our bags in his right hand, he threads the fingers of his left hand with mine, a silent reminder that he's got me.

At the check-in desk, he lets me take the lead but stands behind me, caging me in, almost like he's protecting me from whatever enemy is lurking in the lobby, which has me giggling as I accept our room keys. He tosses me a curious look as he holds my hand once again, but I merely shake my head and point to the elevator.

Our room is up on the third floor, and when I offer to carry my bags, he rolls his eyes at me, gently smacking my ass with one of them as I lead us up to our room. I open the door, allowing Roman in first, but he freezes only a few steps inside.

"What's wrong?" I stand on my toes, trying to peek over his

giant frame, but only make out the door across from us, which leads to a balcony. "My mom booked the room. Is it all right?"

"Yeah. Fine by me, but..." He shifts, allowing me to scoot past him and see the bed.

The bed.

One. Bed.

I let out a breath and squeeze my eyes shut. "She was worried I wouldn't book in time and told me she'd do it. I didn't think... I should've..." I spin to face him. "I'm sorry."

"Why are you sorry?"

"Because..." I gesture behind me to the lone bed. Granted, it's enormous, but still. "I don't want to make you uncomfortable."

He tosses the bags on the floor and sprawls out on the bed, hands behind his head. "This might actually be the most comfortable I've been in a long time."

I flop next to him. "Don't find many beds that fit a refrigerator, huh?"

"Nope."

"You aren't mad?"

He angles his head to me, his face set in annoyance. "No. I'm not mad." His dark eyes make a circuit of my face. "There are very few things that will make me mad. One of them happens to be anyone who's made you feel so self-conscious."

I roll onto my side, suddenly wanting nothing more than to curl up next to him. Fall asleep with my head on his shoulder. Name my firstborn after him...the usual.

He brushes a few wisps of hair from my temple before exhaling audibly and studying the room, a fireplace below the flat-screen television and the small table for two tucked into the corner next to the window. Everything is decorated in muted blues and greens, lots of dark wood and plush white bedding.

"Gotta admit, though, this is a nice fucking room."

I cackle. "Yeah. Yeah, it is."

His mouth tugs up at the corners in a smile, obviously finding amusement in my maniacal, slightly delirious laughter, all this nervous energy with nowhere to go. "You wanna go take a walk?" he asks. "Explore the rest of this dump?"

"Yeah. Let's see what awful amenities they have."

"Probably nothing." He stands and holds out his hand for me, lacing our fingers together again as we head out the door. His fingers are long and thick, callused on his palm, but gentle in his touch, and I don't think twice about leaning into his side or wrapping my other hand around his forearm, as if I could ever keep him in place. Though he doesn't seem like he wants to go anywhere.

Inside the elevator, he pulls me closer to make room for a handful of other guests and ducks his head down to mine. I can't be sure, but I swear he kisses my hair. Before I can question it, the doors open to the main floor, and he guides me out to the patio, the ski slopes in the not-so-far-off distance. The air is crisp and clean and a touch cold.

Roman loops his arm around my shoulders, immediately warming me up. "Can't say I've ever stayed anywhere this nice before."

I burrow into him as close as possible, hands fisting his T-shirt, and I press my nose into his chest, inhaling his scent, comfy like clean cotton and spicy like cardamom. Intoxicating.

I inhale deeply and absent-mindedly rub my cheek against him like a cat. I don't realize what I'm doing until his hands are on the back of my head, guiding it up. When I meet his gaze, I blink a few times, embarrassed. "Sorry about that." I pat his chest. "You'd be surprised how soft these hard-packed muscles are."

For how big I am, he dwarfs me. With his hands on either side of my face and the breadth of his body blocking out anything else, I can only see him. "Don't ever apologize for touching me."

I swallow at the command, at the pure lust in his voice, lowering it a few registers, deep enough to send a shiver down my spine. Of course, I reach for a joke. "Because you're worse than Kyle?"

He nods solemnly. "So much fucking worse."

Then he closes the last few inches between us and kisses me.

It's slow and sweet and makes my toes curl, a bare hint of his tongue along my bottom lip. And over all too quickly when I'm abruptly hit with reality.

"Well, I see you've finally arrived."

I hop back, startled, and find myself face-to-face with my mother. Her eyes are wide, her lips pinched, and I wipe my hand over my mouth as if I could wipe away the evidence of the kiss.

She stays silent, eyes darting back and forth between me and the real-life mountain next to me. I wrap my arm around his waist. "Mom, this is my boyfriend, Roman."

She is tall, but only about 5'8", and she has to tilt her head back to take in all of him. All 6'5" and 200-some pounds of him. The tattoos and long, dark hair. Tawny skin and unyielding gaze.

For the first time in her life, I think my mom isn't the one to judge first. She is being judged.

And maybe found wanting.

"Roman," she says eventually in greeting.

"Nice to meet you, Mrs. Thorne."

"You can call me Katherine."

"Katherine," he repeats, and Mom clears her throat, obviously not knowing what to make of him.

I fucking love it.

Until she turns her gaze to me. "I was worried you weren't going to make it in time."

I roll my eyes. "Why wouldn't I?"

"Why *would* you?" She checks the slender silver watch on her wrist. "It's almost time for the rehearsal, and you're not even dressed."

I glance down at my leggings and Barbie sweatshirt. "It'll take me five minutes to change."

She hums dubiously, and I sigh. "I will see you there."

She arches her brow in warning then turns to Roman once more. "I suppose we...can chat later."

He doesn't verbally answer, only nods, and I don't miss the way she eyes him, a little nervously.

"Don't be late," she singsongs as she trots off, and I heave a sigh, sagging into Roman's side.

"Say the word, and I'll tell her to fuck right off with her bullshit."

"Kind of you to offer, but no. You can't do that."

"What can I do?" he asks, tugging me to face him, settling his hands on my waist.

"Being here with me is enough."

He murmurs a quiet assent then kisses me again, though it's not slow and sweet like before. This kiss is demanding, possessive. I moan, fisting my hands in his shirt, pulling him closer so I can feel the heat of his body against mine, the hard muscles beneath his shirt. And I'm more interested in climbing him like a tree than I am in going to this rehearsal and dinner.

He moves his hand to the back of my neck, holding me in place, and I melt into him, forgetting about anything else but him and the groan he makes when I slide my tongue along his lips, searching for his. He tastes faintly of coffee and the apple-cinnamon muffin I brought for him to snack on while we drove, and he lowers his head, dragging me further into him with his magnetic pull. I press up onto my toes, desperate for more. I drape my arms around his neck, aiming to show him how much I've been thinking about this since our dinner, but he breaks the kiss, evidently much more responsible than me.

"We can't do this right now," he says against my lips, and I wonder... Does that mean there is another time to do it?

"What was that for?" I place my hands on his shoulders to steady myself since I'm dizzy. "There's no show to put on."

"Because I wanted to," he rasps, voice like sandpaper. "Not because someone was watching. Not because I'm supposed to." He strokes my cheek with his thumb, his eyes never leaving mine. "I kissed you because I wanted to."

Chapter 15
Roman

I stick out like a sore thumb, and I couldn't give two fucks about it. Besides my physical stature, my tattoos and hair set me apart. And probably my face.

I must be frowning—probably have been all night—because Eloise playfully frowns at me before breaking up into giggles, elbowing me about how she didn't need me to scare anyone away. While I'm not doing it on purpose, my glower does seem to be doing the trick to keep anyone from saying any shit to her.

After the pleasant introduction to her mother and that too-short kiss by the lake, we headed back to our room to change for this rehearsal and dinner. When I asked Eloise if I needed to pack anything special for this weekend, she said a suit for the wedding but everything else was casual.

Well, casual apparently means a fuck of a lot different to me, because while I'm in jeans and a plain gray T-shirt, all the other men are in polo shirts and pants with creases, the women in nice dresses. Even Eloise changed into some flowery number with fluffy sleeves and these boots that hit her knees. Sexy as hell.

But I don't give a shit about fitting in. I'm not here to impress anyone.

I'm only here for Eloise.

She wanted me to stay with her during the rehearsal, and even though it seemed like the bride and groom didn't want me there, no one said anything to me about taking a seat in the back. As soon as it was over, I met her at the top of the aisle, put my hand at the small of her back, and guided her into me, kissing her forehead. Her cousin, Lily, a woman who appeared to have the personality of a two-by-four with the body of one as well, watched the whole thing.

I know Eloise's mother gives her shit about her appearance, but my girl's beautiful. Those lively green eyes and full lips. Her smile—pure joy. Not to mention her bangin' body. Tall and luscious with thighs I have trouble not touching. Sweet and sexy and undeserving of the shit her family puts her through.

After the rehearsal, we were herded into this restaurant on the other side of the lodge, where Eloise introduced me to her father, Robert, her cocky son of a bitch brother, Alex, and a few other in-laws. Of course, there was also her aunt Beverly, a real viper, and the groom, Nick, who seemed to be more interested in drinking than doing whatever it was he was supposed to with Lily.

The lot of them have no idea what an amazing person Eloise is, either dismissing her outright or putting her down, and I quickly realized the best way to shield her is to keep her at my side with my hands or lips on her at all times.

A real chore, to be sure.

If I felt her getting tense during any conversation, I simply curled my arm around her shoulders and kissed her temple or held on to the back of her neck to bring her closer to me. Each time, whoever it was making her feel bad—her mom, aunt, cousin, or that old woman who smelled like a mix of rubbing alcohol and some god-awful perfume that made me sneeze—usually turned tail pretty quick, evidently put off by the very mild PDA. Or maybe it's because I'm the one with my hands all over her.

Me with my big hands and tattoos and worn denim. How dare I?

Although, it's not like they protected her otherwise. Treat her like shit, cool. Have her bring a guy like me home, horror.

Fuck 'em.

Fuck 'em all.

"What time does this thing end?" I whisper into Eloise's ear, where we sit alone at a table in the corner, her father having vacated the seat across from us.

Robert Thorne is an okay guy. He doesn't make Eloise nervous, so he automatically receives a pass from me, although he would've earned it anyway because he's the only one here who's tried to engage me in conversation. Not that I'm a great conversationalist, but he at least asked how Eloise and I met—when I carried in a bag of flour for her, not a lie—and how long we've been together—about three months, definite lie.

Coulda fooled me for how easy it feels to be with her, though.

She's mine. For now. Even if it's pretend. Even if it's only for the weekend.

"I think we can sneak out soon," she answers, meeting my gaze. "I'm going to run to the bathroom and make another lap around the room so it doesn't look so suspicious, and then we'll go. 'Kay?"

I nod and help to scoot her chair back, dragging my hand over the back of her thigh, the hem of her dress dusting my forearm. I'd like to flip it up and bend her over, see if I could make her skin flush as pink as the cotton.

I play out that fantasy in my mind for about ten minutes,

only stopping when I start to get hard behind my zipper. That's when I realize she still hasn't returned from the bathroom and coast my gaze around, searching for her. There're about thirty people here, and she's not one of them. I stalk over to the door I saw her exit from and immediately spot the signs for the restrooms. Except I don't need to go any farther than a few more steps because Katherine Thorne has Eloise cornered, her voice no more than a low hiss.

"...constantly touching and kissing you. It's completely inappropriate."

Eloise's hands are balled into fists at her sides, her cheeks red from anger. "How is it inappropriate? He's holding my hand and kissing my cheek. It's not like he's sticking his tongue down my throat."

"It's more than that, and you know it."

"I don't know it," Eloise says, her voice rising, which earns a stern finger pointed at her.

I move to take a step forward when Katherine says, "He looks at you like he's going to strip you down and have sex with you right in the middle of the room."

I freeze.

'Cause she's not wrong.

That is what I want to do.

Eloise rolls her lips over her teeth, obviously fighting a laugh, which pisses Katherine off more.

"He's my boyfriend, Mom," she says, and that sets me back on my heels. She's introduced me as her boyfriend all day, but hearing her say it in that voice, like she's fighting for me—for us —it feels real.

"So?" Katherine throws her hands up. "Doesn't mean you two have to act like that."

Eloise lets her head fall back to her shoulders, her eyes on the ceiling as she breathes a few times. When she speaks to her mother again, it's much quieter, more defeated. I know before I hear the first word that it'll make me rage.

"If I didn't come with a date, you'd be disappointed. I come with a date, and you're disappointed. Is there anything I can do that doesn't make me a disappointment?"

Her words gut me.

And I charge ahead, speaking before I even fully form the words in my brain. "You're not a disappointment," I growl out, standing between her and her mother. I take her face in my hands. "You hear me? You are not a disappointment. You're gorgeous and funny and smart and sweet." I lower my forehead to hers, breathing life into my words. "So fucking sweet, my Eloise. Don't let anyone make you feel any different."

When I lift my head and find her eyes, she's blinking rapidly, chin trembling. Almost like she doesn't hear it enough.

Fuck that.

I twine our hands together and pivot, effectively blocking Eloise from her mother. If Beverly's a viper, Katherine is a fucking vulture, shredding her own daughter to pieces.

I glare at the woman, and she visibly shrinks away. "You have anything to say to me? To my face?"

She purses her lips, trying to view Eloise behind me, but she can't. I won't allow it.

"You've had enough time ripping her apart, don't you think?" I say, keeping my voice as even as possible. "Making her feel like a *disappointment*."

"She's not..." Katherine stands on her toes, peering around my side. "You're not, Eloise."

I scoff. "Why don't you try it with some feeling next time, huh? Maybe it'll sound more believable." I pull Eloise behind me, angling my body to shield her as we pass Mrs. Thorne, not bothering to lower my voice as I wrap my arm around her, pulling her into my side. "Is this what you've had to put up with all these years?"

Eloise sniffles once and then shakes her head like she has water in her ears. "It's fine. I'm fine."

"It's not fine, and you're not fine." I tug her into an alcove and push her back against the wall, skating my hands over her as if searching for bullet wounds.

Might as well be, for how her mother so easily cut her down.

When I'm satisfied Eloise is all right for the moment, I slide one hand around her neck and the other around her waist. "Your mother's full of shit, you know that, right?"

She nods, but it's not good enough.

"Say it."

"She's full of shit."

"I know it's hard, but don't let her make you feel bad. She's taking out her unhappiness on you, but it's bullshit. Whatever she says, it's wrong."

"I know," Eloise eventually replies, too weakly for me.

I want my confident girl back.

"Tell me what you're good at."

She wrenches her head back. "What?"

"Tell me what you're good at." I bend my neck, placing a kiss against the corner of her mouth. "Tell me something you're good at, and I'll show you what I'm good at."

Her exhale is ragged, and she sways slightly, her hands clinging to my T-shirt. "I, um, I'm really good at baking."

"Yeah, you are." I kiss her lips but don't linger. "What else?"

"I...am good at..." She tilts her head up when I skim my nose along her jaw. "Riding a bike."

I nip her earlobe. "I think you can do better than that. What else are you good at?"

She swallows. "Being a friend."

I hum in agreement and leave a wet kiss on her throat. "You're a really great friend."

Her tits brush my torso with each of her breaths. "I'm pretty good at sports. Volleyball, basketball, even golf."

I picture her in a tiny golf skirt, her thick thighs and ass on display, and lower my mouth to her collarbone, licking the divot there. "What else are you good at?"

"Making people laugh."

I pull down the neckline of her dress and drag my teeth over the soft and pillowy mounds of her breasts. If I knew where to find the zipper, I'd take the goddamn thing off, but the light is too low and I'm not that patient. Instead, I let my hand drift from her waist to her thigh and glide it back up to her ass, taking the bottom of her dress with it. I squeeze her cheek, gripping it tightly, and she inhales sharply. "Roman."

"Tell me one more thing you're good at, and I'll show you," I say, slipping my fingers under her thin lace panties. "One more, sunshine. Tell me."

She rolls her hips like the needy thing she is, and I push her harder against the wall, grinding my cock against the sweet heat of her pussy, hidden only by a mere scrap of material. With her hands on the back of my head and neck, she forces my mouth to hers as she murmurs, "I'm good at making you smile."

I grin into a kiss. "Fucking right, you are."

Then I give her what she wants and pull her underwear to the side to slide two fingers up and down her slit before circling her clit. She responds by sighing into my mouth, biting and pulling at my lip, surprising the shit out of me.

Sunshine likes it a little rough, eh?

I grunt and clutch her hair in my fist, tugging, forcing her head back until she's staring at the ceiling. "Now you get to learn what I'm good at. Let's see how quick I can make you come all over my fingers. How long you think it'll take?" I suck on her pulse point at the same time I thrust my fingers into her wet heat, barely holding back a possessive growl. I own this pussy. It's mine now. "Come on, sunshine. Show me how you like it."

She mewls, attempting to straighten her head, but I don't let her. At least not until I've sucked a red mark into her skin, claiming her as mine. Then I let go of her hair, and she immediately yanks me to her, kissing me. It's sloppy, all tongue, and I fucking love it.

I continue to pump my fingers in and out of her, swallowing her moans. She's so wet, so responsive, swiveling her hips, panting out her breaths, fingernails sinking into my skin.

When I feel her start to coil with tension, knees becoming looser, I wrap my arm around her waist to keep her up and double down on my efforts, rubbing my thumb against her clit. She bucks in my hold, brushing against my stiff cock, and I feel like a fourteen-year-old kid again, ready to come in my pants.

I know I'll have a wet spot on my Hanes, but I'll deal with that later. For now, this is all Eloise.

My good and perfect Eloise.

"That's it," I praise against her lips since she's incapable of kissing me anymore, too tied up in her pleasure to focus. Makes pride swell in my chest, that I can make her like this.

I can make her forget about anything else but us. I doubt she'd even know her name right now.

"Let go for me."

And she does. She comes apart in my arms, her body shaking as she rides out her orgasm on my hand. I slow my movements, easing her down, then slip my fingers out of her. When I bring my fingers to my mouth, sucking her tangy taste off them, her eyes widen, her cheeks flushing pink.

She doesn't drop her gaze, but she does shift her weight and clear her throat. "You are pretty good at that."

I let my hand settle at my side. "And you told me a bunch of things you're good at, a bunch of things that prove your mother is full of shit. Next time you need a reminder of your confidence, you let me know."

Her eyes shine with gratitude, and she throws her arms around my neck, stilling when she feels my cock against her stomach. "You...want me to...?"

I shake my head, placing one last kiss on her neck. "Not tonight. Let's get you cleaned up and into something comfy. We'll watch a movie or something."

She jerks back. "Really?"

I don't know what's so confusing about that and arch my brow. "Yeah."

"You don't want to...?"

I'm not sure what the end of that question is... Get down on my knees and eat her out? Rip her panties off her and fuck her into next week? Take off my shirt and tattoo the divots her fingernails made into my skin?

I want to do it all, but not after what happened with her mom. Not when I know she has to be up early tomorrow for this wedding. And especially not when I don't have the time I want to explore every inch of her delicious body and act out every depraved fantasy I've had about her.

So... "I do, Eloise, I really fucking want to, but not now. Let me take care of you in other ways tonight."

Her answering smile is slow-growing and a little shy. It burrows under my skin, knocks my heart right out. Stomps that organ into submission until she takes the whole damn thing in her hands. Steals it out of my chest.

But that's okay. My heart is hers now. To do with what she will.

She offers me her hand, laces our fingers together, brings it up to her mouth, and kisses the back of mine like *I'm* the special one. Like *I* am the one *she* is grateful for. "Thanks, Roman."

I don't deserve her appreciation, but I take it anyway. Tuck it away for when this will all inevitably end and I won't be able to make her smile anymore. Because even with that knowledge, I still want her. I still want to take advantage of this time when I can pretend that won't happen.

"Anytime, sunshine. Anytime."

Chapter 16
Eloise

When I roll over to quiet my alarm, I accidentally knock my foot into the hot mountain next to me. *Literally* hot.

After we came back to our room last night—to the room with only one bed—we did exactly what Roman said. We changed into something more comfortable and watched a movie, some action flick on cable about the White House being blown up...or something. I didn't pay much attention because Roman lay next to me in only black boxer briefs.

He told me he ran hot, and usually only slept in underwear, then asked if I would mind.

Would I mind?

I proceeded to laugh maniacally. Because who in the hell would mind?

The man is a walking side of beef. Pure muscle. Every part of him is huge. If I didn't find it adorable that he sometimes has trouble making it through doors and has to turn sideways, I'd say it was too much. But this man is just enough for me. Even with barbells through his nipples.

Especially with barbells through his nipples.

The thing in his pants, on the other hand?

It's a goddamn anaconda.

It's all well and good in rap songs, until it's right there, next to you, outlined in cotton. I'm not exactly a nature girlie, and the thought of trying to tame that monster is intimidating.

Not to say I would be the one to do it.

Roman was a perfect gentleman last night, surprising even when he asked if I wanted to snuggle.

My heart wept at his actual words, "You need a cuddle, sunshine?"

Fuck yeah, I did.

I always need a cuddle.

And his arm was so heavy, it felt wonderful. Immediate sensory relief.

We talked a lot, not about my mom or family, but more about my ADHD. He was so interested in learning about things that helped, praising me for my daily adaptations as if I were solving world hunger and not simply living my life. We talked a lot about Mazie, flipped through the hundreds of pictures on his phone of her and then the posts of cars on his social media. He told me how he grew up working on cars with Ian, and when he was old enough, it was the only thing that interested him. The only thing that he felt kept him connected to his family that was so far away, not necessarily physically but certainly emotionally. He explained how he'd lived in a few different places, going wherever the next high took him, but that he'd been in upstate New York for the last ten years or so, and that's where he'd met Mazie's mom. Since he gave me that in, I asked about her, but all the answer I got was, "That's a long story. For another time, maybe."

It was almost two in the morning by then, so I agreed and burrowed under the covers. He reminded me to set my alarm because I'd asked him to earlier, and he kissed my forehead. Then the living heat box threw his arm over his head and fell asleep instantaneously.

I laughed, thinking it was a joke.

But, no. The man closed his eyes and went to sleep like a magic trick. Look, folks—now, he's awake. And now, he's asleep.

I ended up scrolling on my phone for another forty-five minutes before I closed my eyes, so I'm not super energetic after less than five hours of sleep.

But I was told in no uncertain terms that I would *ruin* Lily's big day if I didn't meet the bridal party in the salon at seven thirty this morning.

Before I creep out of bed, a seventy-five-pound weight bands around my waist, a face against my neck. "Morning, sunshine."

"Morning," I say through a yawn.

He pulls me right up against him, my back against his chest, my ass against the steel rod in his underwear. He's clearly not embarrassed—nor should he be. Though he might want to call a doctor about giant syndrome. Could a person only have it in their penis? Not that the rest of him is all that small. I'd have to Google it to know for sure.

"You're so soft," he murmurs, hand snaking up under my pajama top to spread over my belly, and I start to tug it away. He doesn't budge, but he does raise his head. "What?"

"That's my pooch."

He doesn't respond. Doesn't move except for his fingertips pressing into my skin. I curl my legs up as if I can make myself smaller, but he isn't having it and tightens his hold, angling his elbow to force me to straighten out.

"I like your pooch," he says, grinding himself against me as if to prove the point.

And yeah, okay. I *get* it.

But as I'm about to put on the ugliest dress known to man and stand up next to a bunch of women who are half my size, I'm not particularly excited about it.

I can already hear my mother's fatphobic comments about me eating the wedding cake tonight.

"I can hear you thinking," Roman says, lips moving against the nape of my neck. "What's wrong?"

"I don't feel like getting up."

Another squeeze of his arm. "So don't."

"I can't be late. I'm sure I'll get shit about last night."

"Well then, come on." He pats my thighs and hops out of bed, absently adjusting himself before digging through his duffel to pull out a pair of athletic shorts. When he catches me watching him, he raises his brow in question.

"What are you doing?" I ask, still in bed.

"Getting dressed." He pulls on a T-shirt. "You have to be down there in half an hour, right?" When I nod, he shrugs. "I'm goin' with you."

"For your makeup?"

"You think I need it?" he deadpans, and I crawl to the edge of the bed.

"No. I think you're beautiful the way you are."

He meets me, pushing my rat's nest back from my face, holding me so I'm peering up at him, me on my knees, him looming over me. I like it. I like feeling how big he is, strong yet tender, embracing me so softly. Better yet, I know he can be rough.

He shows me again by gripping my hair, tugging tightly. "Don't let the sons of bitches get you down."

I stifle a laugh. "Okay."

"Okay," he repeats and presses a kiss to my mouth before releasing me so I can take a quick shower and throw on some clothes. Once we're both dressed and brushed, we head down to the salon hand in hand, and it fills me with giddy joy to see all the bridesmaids' eyes become dinner plates when we enter the room.

The man can make an entrance.

"Roman," Aunt Beverly says with a barely concealed grimace. "Nice to see you again."

He answers with a grunt then turns to me, yanking me close to lay a kiss on me.

With tongue.

The squeeze to my ass earns a few murmurs, and I can feel them all watching when he brushes his lips over my ear. "You don't owe anybody anything. Not your smile and definitely not your tears."

I nod and realize I have to uncurl my fists from his T-shirt so he can leave. When I do, he pinches my chin. "Text me if you need anything."

"Okay," I croak, dying inside. I have to lean against the wall as all 6'5" of him stalks out of the overtly feminine salon like he owns the place.

"Well done," one of the bridesmaids whispers to me as she fills up a champagne flute with a mimosa mixture to pass to me.

I gulp it down before finally replying, "Thanks. He's pretty great."

The morning is a flurry of brushes and wands, steam and curlers, but my aunt stays away, mostly fussing over Lily. I don't even see my mother until we're all dressed for pictures. Besides a curt, "Hello, Eloise," she stays quiet.

All because Roman stood up for me last night, and while my first instinct is to apologize, I remind myself of what he said.

You don't owe anybody anything. Not your smile and definitely not your tears.

I don't need to feel bad about anything. I don't need to slap on a smile when I don't want to, and I certainly don't need to apologize when I never did anything wrong. My mother is the one who owes *me* an apology.

The ceremony is held outside with a backdrop of fall foliage and white linen, and I immediately spot Roman, seated on one of the chairs toward the back. He's in head to toe black, but I don't get a good look at him until I'm positioned with the other bridesmaids at the makeshift dais. That's when I notice he has his hair slicked back in a bun, a newly trimmed beard, and the top few buttons on his shirt undone.

I'm toast.

But it's his unshakable gaze that truly does me in. My anchor amid this sea of floral prints and forced joy. It's the way his eyes soften when he looks at me and how his mouth quirks to the side. His weird little smile that's only for me.

The moment the ceremony wraps, I practically run to him and his waiting arms. But he doesn't pull me to him as he's been doing since we arrived yesterday. Instead, he holds me out, inspecting me from the top of my breezy curls to my heels. He whistles, and it's as ridiculous as it is thrilling, and I bat at his chest. He responds by wrapping his arms around my waist and kissing my throat. "You're beautiful."

"I'm the swamp thing."

"A beautiful swamp thing," he says, and I snort-laugh.

"This swamp thing needs a drink."

He takes my hand in his, and we follow the rest of the guests inside to the banquet hall, where I snag a glass of champagne. With our pictures already taken, my bridesmaid duties are essentially fulfilled, so Roman and I find our seats so we can watch the newlyweds enjoy their carefully choreographed first dance.

Leaning into my fake boyfriend's side, I quietly tell him, "It's going to be real laid-back when I get married. No first dances or assigned seats." He angles his head so he can meet my gaze, though he stays quiet, and I go on. "It'll be outside with comfort food, and there'll be disposable cameras everywhere for everyone to take pictures. Nothing formal. I want the exact opposite."

"Sounds like fun," he says eventually. "Will I be invited?"

I shoot him my sassiest smirk. "Yes, but you have to bring a date."

He huffs an amused sound and drapes his arm around my shoulders. "I'll see what I can do."

The reception is a blur of pleasantries and stilted conversations, most people not bothering to even approach us.

"I think you scared everyone away," I tease, tracing the melting skulls and dark flowers that make up the sleeve of his tattoo that's on display since he ditched his suit jacket during dinner and he rolled his shirt sleeves to his elbows because he's actively trying to kill me. Last night, he'd told me he's had a lot of work redone because of "stupid shit" he had inked when he was younger. Including the portrait of SpongeBob, which he got one night while he was high. I laughed about that for five minutes straight.

He certainly doesn't seem like someone who'd have a SpongeBob tattoo. What he does seem like is someone who might commit murder. And he's proud of it. "Good. It's working."

"The mean mugging?"

He hits me with his mean mug, and I giggle. His features thaw, and he cups my cheek, brushing his thumb over my mouth. "You're missing your pink."

I scrunch up my nose. "Had to be demure today."

"Fuck demure. I want you to be pink."

"Between Mazie and me, you're surrounded with it."

"I don't mind," he says with a shrug, dragging his knuckles

across my jaw and down my throat, plucking at the neckline of my dress. "Pink might be my new favorite color."

I feel the flush rise from my chest—his new favorite color—and with the way his pupils blaze with heat, I suddenly have a hard time breathing.

"You okay?" he asks, skimming his fingertips over the side of my breast, knowing *exactly* what he's doing to me.

"Fine." To put some room between us, I scoot my chair back. "But I want to dance."

He doesn't budge. "Dance?"

"Yeah." I tug on his arm. "It's a wedding. People dance at weddings."

"I'm not much of a dancer."

"Everyone can dance," I say, pulling him toward the dance floor. "Just follow my lead."

He grumbles a few curses but lets me drag him to the dance floor, where other couples sway to a slow song. I pull him close, wrapping my arms around his neck, and he hesitantly places his hands on my waist. I can feel the warmth of his palms even through the fabric of my dress, and I lean my head against his chest.

"See? This isn't so bad," I murmur.

He doesn't reply, save for a kiss to my head, an answer all its own, and the song ends after, like, forty-seven seconds, moving right into Guns N' Roses. I pout, but Roman's already shaking his head. "That's all you get from me, sunshine."

"It wasn't even a whole song."

"More than anyone else has ever had."

"Really?" I tip my head, curious. "You never danced at your own wedding or attended homecoming or something?"

"Do I look like I attended homecoming?" My laugh cuts off when he says, "And I was never married."

"Oh."

"So, no, I've never willingly danced with anybody except for you."

I press my hand to my heart. "I'm honored to pop your slow-dancing cherry."

He fights a growing smile. "You're something else."

"Something good?"

"Something amazing." He curls his hand around my neck, pressing his forehead to mine, in a singularly possessive yet romantic move that has me melting into him. Our noses touch, skate along each other until our mouths barely meet. It's more of a shared breath. Something infinitely better than a kiss.

Something offered and accepted.

And my heart's in my throat when he says, "Let's get out of here."

So, I can only nod and place my hand in his.

Chapter 17
Roman

I can't keep my hands off Eloise. It was torture being with her all night, allowed to touch her but not the way I wanted to.

Thank fuck I can remedy that now.

My hands are on her ass as soon as the doors of the elevator close, and with her fingers digging into my hair, I lick down her throat, sucking over her pulse, biting on the slope of her shoulder.

I know she hated the dress, complained a lot about it, but I didn't think it was *that* bad. Until I tried to pick her up and couldn't since it trapped her legs. Growling, I bend and throw her over my shoulder to carry her out of the elevator and down the hall to our room as she wails in protest. "Roman!"

"That's good practice," I say, unlocking the door, "screaming my name."

I'm not at all delicate when I toss her on the bed, and she stares up at me with huge, surprised eyes, mouth quiet. A rare occurrence. After throwing my suit jacket on the chair in the corner, I start to unbutton my shirt. "You done with that dress? Need to wear it again?"

She shakes her head. "Why?"

"I'm gonna rip it off you."

Her laugh breaks off. "You're serious."

"As soon as I'm done taking off my shirt."

She scrambles up, hands flying to the hidden zipper on her side and pulls it halfway down, but she tumbles off the bed to the floor by the time I'm done with my shirt. I'm on her before it even lands on top of my jacket, and as I promised, I rip that fucking thing off her. All it takes is two hands on either side of the seam and one good yank.

"Oh my god," she shrieks, staring down at herself, the satin in tatters, still clinging to her left shoulder with a gigantic bow. When I move, my intent clear, she holds up her hand. "Wait. Wait. You've done enough, Conan the Destroyer."

In only a strapless bra and underwear, she lets what's left of the dress fall off her, and I stand back to admire all that's mine. For the night, at least.

We hadn't bothered turning on all the lights, just the small one by the door, and it bathes Eloise in a golden hue, high-lighting all my favorite things—her full tits, the roundness of her belly, her thick thighs—while the darkness shadows all the places I have yet to explore.

"I want to fuck you," I state plainly, and a beat passes before she nods.

"I want that too."

"But I don't have any condoms. I didn't plan for this to happen."

She searches the room, as if some might appear. Even opens the nightstand, coming up empty, save for a notepad and pen. When she faces me again, she drags her gaze over me. "I don't know how you feel about it, but I have an IUD and that's more than 99% effective. At least, that's what the brochure said, and you know what they say, if it's printed on a brochure..." She giggles, shaking her head. "I mean... That was weird. I'm nervous. Are you nervous? You don't look nervous. Like, at all. Which is great. One of us should be confident. But it's been a while since I had sex, more than a year, and quite frankly, I'm nervous you're going to tear me in two. But since we don't have condoms, we don't have to do it—P in V, I mean. We could do other things. Other things are good, but also, I'm okay with—" she pushes her palms together then motions to my cock, sticking straight up in my boxer briefs, the head poking out above the elastic "—as long as you don't pierce my uterus with that thing. And, of course, if it's okay with you, and you're healthy, we don't have to use a condom. I trust you. I—"

I don't need to hear any more and silence her with my mouth, one hand on her neck, the other against her spine, my tongue finding hers, silencing her rambling until she's panting and rubbing up against me. When I back away, I tell her my truth. "I love hearing your tangents, but I can't concentrate when you're barely clothed and I'm hard as a fucking rock."

"Oh yeah. Okay. Right."

I roll my forehead against hers. "I haven't had sex in a long time either. Almost two years. I was tested after, and all clear."

"Me too," she says against my mouth. And then, "Two years? Wow. I feel like you should be having a lot more sex. You're depriving the population. You could probably make good money doing OnlyFans or—"

"Eloise." I hold her at arm's length, and she stops.

"Hm?"

"I mean it, I love when you talk, but I plan on fucking you so hard, you can't."

She opens her mouth, I suspect to let another train of thoughts loose, but she nods instead, stuttering, "Uh-huh. Yep. Okay. Got it. Good."

"Good." I wipe my hand over my mouth, biting back my laugh.

This girl. Drives me wild.

With nothing left to say, I flick her bra off her, releasing those big beauties and immediately lower my mouth to suck on each one. They're heavy in my hands, with big pink nipples, and I lick at them until she's digging her fingernails into me, hips restless and searching, and I can't leave my girl wanting. So I drop her underwear to the floor and grip her ass in both my hands, pulling her fully against me, and she rubs herself on me like a cat.

Practically purring in my hands.

I grunt my approval and roughly nip at her bottom lip, tugging on it, and she hisses but doesn't back down or back away. No, she wraps one of her legs around my thigh, and I can't help myself. I need to feel her, remind myself of how sweet she is.

I glide my hand between her legs, dipping my middle finger into her, only up to my first knuckle, teasing her. She exhales a soft, "Please, daddy."

Fuck. She can blow me away with those two words. Yeah, I'll take care of her. Yeah, I'll be her daddy.

"You want to come?" I grate out against her chin. "You want to come on my fingers like a good little girl?"

She nods, whimpering, and I spin her around, facing the mirror, both of us in the reflection. I take in all of her, every single one of her curves illuminated by the soft glow. She's a vision, all silky skin and warm shadows, her breath coming in quick pants. Standing behind her, I band my left arm around her torso, playing with her nipples, and loop my right arm around her hips to give her what she wants.

This time, I slide two fingers over her clit and curl them into her, finding her wet and hot and already gripping me tight. When I do finally fuck her, I'm gonna explode. And fast.

For now, I concentrate on making her feel good, on enjoying the show.

"Look at you," I murmur, my voice a low rumble against her ear, and her pupils are so big, there is almost no green left in her irises as she watches us. As she watches me fuck her with my fingers.

I lick the shell of her ear, and she shivers, her skin pebbling. I twist her nipple hard, and she bucks her hips back, grinding against my cock. "Yeah, you like that. You're gonna look so good riding me."

She lolls her head back to my shoulder, but I shrug, forcing it up. "Look, Eloise."

She licks her lips, and when she dutifully focuses on my fingers thrusting in and out of her, I leave a wet kiss on the nape of her neck before skimming my hand up between her breasts to lightly wrap around her throat. "You look good with my hands on you." I stroke the swollen spot inside her, and she cries out, squirming in my hold, so I tighten my grip, keeping her eyes on mine, my hand angling her head up. The tattoos on my fingers spelling out my last name are on full display, like it's hers too, and I like that idea.

Love that idea.

"You look so pretty with ink," I murmur into her ear, hitting that spot again, her pussy clenching my fingers like a vise. "You think so too, huh? You like my hand around your throat. Maybe your first tattoo should be my name here."

She shudders, her breath hitching, close to coming, and she has trouble not closing her eyes, so I squeeze. "Open. Watch."

She does. She keeps her eyes open and watches as she comes, heaving out a sound that's completely untamed. Unself-conscious.

There is no worrying when she's with me. No thinking. No anxiety about not being good enough.

Because she's perfect. She's beautiful and bright and pure sunshine.

I turn her around, wasting no time, kissing her, my tongue in her mouth, my wet fingers gliding all over her. She's as voracious as I am, no time needed to rebound. She wants more.

She wants it all, her arms around my neck, stretched up on her toes, her naked body completely aligned with mine, and my cock aches.

Though it's not time yet. Not nearly.

I break away from Eloise and gesture to the bed, but when she doesn't move fast enough, I lay a sharp slap to her ass that makes her gasp. I do it again to watch her flesh jiggle, to see the pink bloom on her skin. "On your back," I tell her. "Hold your pussy open. I want to see what I'm about to eat."

She half laughs, half moans. "For a man who doesn't talk all that much, you're pretty good at dirty talk."

I place one knee on the edge of the bed and jut my chin in a silent command for her to shift back, spread her legs. She complies. "For a woman who never stops talking, you're pretty good at staying quiet. Now, show me."

She skates her hands down her sides, over the patch of light brown hair between her legs and spreads her lips, revealing my real favorite kind of pink. She's glistening, her arousal evident, and I swallow a moan. I ditch my pants and underwear, kicking them off somewhere behind me to absently run my hand over my cock. It's wet at the tip, and I'm dying to be inside her. So much so that I need to verbally remind myself to wait. "Soon," I say, more to myself than her. "I'll be inside. But first, I have to make you good and ready."

I dive down, spreading her thighs with my hands, able to use both since she's so good, so perfect, holding herself open for me. I kiss her clit, tease it with quick licks before dragging the flat of my tongue up her slit, tasting her essence straight from the source, and there has never been a better way to drink her sweetness down.

She quickly loses control, writhing and wriggling all over, including her hands, so I bat them out of the way. She fists the sheets, and I take over, working two fingers inside her pussy. I stroke her slowly, gently, curling my knuckles until I find that spot that makes her cry out, and I don't let up. I suck on her clit, flicking it with my tongue, listening to how her sounds change and build, letting me know what she likes and needs to get her there. And when she does eventually come, her body convulsing, I am rewarded with an echoing cry through the room.

But I still don't stop. I keep going, my fingers pumping in and out of her, using three instead of two. I stretch her open, swiftly taking her to the edge again with my mouth. I won't stop —can't stop—until she's dripping. She needs this, needs to be soft and pliant to be able to take me, but she's fighting me reflexively. Shaking her head back and forth, mumbling my name over and over, thighs squeezing. She's trembling so badly, scooting up the mattress so far that I need to clamp my arm around her, holding her down, and my cock grows even harder. Having to restrain her even this little bit is hot. Her unconscious and wild lack of inhibition is a thing of beauty. Makes me work harder because I want more of it.

I want all of her.

Frantic and irresistible.

Unruly and absolutely flawless.

That's what she is when she comes again, body shaking and voice breaking like she can't take it anymore.

I kneel between her legs, slipping my fingers out of her. They're drenched in her arousal, and I pet her thighs, bringing her back to me as I lick my digits clean. She blinks up at me, long eyelashes fluttering, her makeup still on, and the sudden image of it smearing intrudes on my thoughts. So, I don't argue when Eloise draws herself up and says, "I want to taste you."

I flip us, landing on my back with her straddling me as she bites into her lower lip, containing her growing smile. "Go ahead," I urge. "Put your mouth on me."

She is all too happy to oblige and leans down, her tongue tracing the lines of the tattoos on my chest to my pierced nipples. She flicks each of the barbells with her tongue, her teeth grazing the sensitive flesh. I hiss, my hips involuntarily rising, and I comb my fingers into her hair, pulling out the pins keeping it up.

The honey locks drape over my hands, and I clench them as she moves lower, licking over the indents of my abs, her hands exploring the ladder of my ribs. She places kisses on my hip bones but stops to hover over my straining cock. She tilts her head, the whites of her eyes huge. "I swear this is even bigger than ones I've seen in porn."

I grip the roots of her hair. "You watch a lot of porn?"

She grins, cheeks flushing. "I'm a casual observer. Ya know…"

This girl. She's something else.

I let a laugh loose, my chest rumbling with the sound, and she gasps, darting up straight. "I did it!" She points at my face. "I made you laugh! I did it! I knew I could. You—"

I haul her to me, slamming her lips to mine, nipping and licking at her until she wiggles away from me, crawling backward to fist my cock. Her manicured fingers don't touch, but I love the picture it makes, her pale hand wrapped around my cock, red from the blood flowing to it. She leans down, tongue flicking out to the head, swiping away the dot of moisture before following the vein.

Then she opens wide, taking me into her mouth, and I fix the pillow behind my head so I can watch her. She hollows her cheeks, sucking, but she can't take all of me, not even close, though the sight of her trying, her lips stretched wide around my cock, it's enough to make me lose control. I shut my eyes, muscles contracting as I concentrate on how good the wet heat feels instead of how badly I want to come down her throat, and when I finally have control of myself, I snap my eyes open to see her head bobbing in time with her hand, working her spit down my length.

I let her suck on me for another minute or two then pull her off and roll us so she's on the bottom and her legs are open for me. "Stay relaxed," I say, holding her thighs up in a wide V, her pussy on full display, my cock bobbing between us. "Stay just like that."

I spit on her, rubbing it against her clit and down her slit before spitting into my hand to stroke my cock, using it as lubricant. She whines when I press the wide head against her entrance and push in. She's tight, so fucking tight, and I blow out a breath as I slide in an inch.

Eloise whimpers, and I take hold of her chin, our gazes locking. "You okay?"

"It's never going to fit," she whispers.

"We'll make it fit," I promise, my voice a low growl. I spit on my fingers again and circle her clit. She responds with a long sigh, and I slip out of her, only to slide right back in, one inch and then another, going deeper each time.

"That's it," I praise. "Taking it like a fucking champ."

She breathes a laugh that turns into a moan. "It feels... I feel so full. Are you all the way in?"

"Not even close, sunshine."

"Oh, fuck me," she groans, throwing her hands over her eyes.

"Yeah. That's the idea."

"Don't joke," she whines. "You're going to impale me."

"Not quite," I grunt then stop once she has a few inches of me. I curl my hands around her calves. "How's that? You still with me?"

She nods. "Make me come, Roman."

What my woman wants, my woman gets.

Careful to stay at this depth, I thrust in and out of her, mesmerized by the way her tits bounce and jiggle, how her skin turns a pretty pink to match her nipples. Even her belly goes splotchy.

Her inner walls twitch, grasping for me, and I grind my teeth, keeping my own orgasm at bay as she falls off the edge, shouting *yes* and *please* and *Roman, please, please, please* over and over again.

That's when I lose control. Of their own accord, my hips move faster, my cock driving in and out of her. She feels so good, so fucking good, her tight little pussy taking me, her moans filling the room.

I can't hold back, can't slow down. I fuck her hard, my body slamming into hers, filling her completely. She screams, convulsing, another orgasm ripping through her, and I follow, my cock pulsing with my release.

I collapse on top of her, our bodies slick with sweat, breaths coming in uneven pants, but when I try to roll off her, Eloise wraps her arms around me, keeping me in place. "Don't," she says against my temple. "Not yet."

Exhaling a ragged breath, I give in and lie on top of her, my heart beating against my rib cage. An echo of hers. I place a kiss on her throat and collarbone, waiting until both of us relax, and then I turn, wrapping my arms around her, in no hurry to extract myself from her.

She lays her head down, humming contentedly, and without permission, my eyes close, my mind shuts down. The last conscious thought I have before I fall asleep is that this weekend wasn't long enough.

I'm not ready to give her up yet.

To stop pretending.

Chapter 18
Eloise

"You don't have to come in with me," I say. *Again*.

Roman ignores me *again* and holds the door open, gesturing for me to enter my apartment building. I heave a sigh, like I'm the one put out, when he's the one who's carrying my bags after driving home two hours while I slept.

"Thanks," I mumble, passing him, my shoulder skimming his chest on the way. I don't apologize, and he doesn't move.

And the tiny touch is enough to set off a reel of memories from last night.

Of his arms holding me, one hand on my throat, the other making me delirious with pleasure.

Of his mouth on the most sensitive part of my body and his delicious growl when he licked his wet lips after making me come.

Of the almost painful fullness and his pounding hips.

I exhale and blink into reality, forcing myself to step forward and hit the button for the elevator. Which is a terrible idea, because once the two of us are stuck in the metal box, his fresh cotton and spicy cardamom scent envelops me, and I'm lost.

I can't even remember how to walk when the doors open. I'm stuck staring at him.

This mountain of a man.

The guy who protected me all weekend, who reminded me to keep my head up and fuck anybody who tries to bring me down.

My fake boyfriend.

Our pretend relationship may have started as a ruse, but these few days with Roman felt anything but fake, and I'm not ready for this to be over. I don't want to lose this connection we've found.

He nudges me with my bags, prodding me out, and I lead him to my door, feeling his eyes on me the whole way. Once my door is unlocked, I don't think twice. Whirling around, I ask, "Do you want to come in for a bit?"

He nods. "I have some time."

Inside, I'm finally able to take my bags from him so I can toss them on the floor. The door clicks shut behind him, and then he's on me. His lips find mine but don't stay there long, trekking down my neck.

"Bedroom's this way," I say, curling my fingers into his shirt, pulling him in the direction, and he follows willingly.

"Nice place," he murmurs against my skin, clearly not having seen a single detail of my apartment. I smile, tilting my head to give him better access, breath hitching when he nips me.

"You haven't even looked."

He hums, the vibration sending shivers down my spine. "Show me later."

My back hits the wall, and my breath hisses at the cool contact. Roman pulls away, dark eyes filled with heat. He's so tall, so broad, so...everything. I want him even as my body aches from last night's activities.

As if reading my mind, he cups my face gently, thumbs brushing over my cheeks. "You sore?"

"No."

"Don't lie to me."

A hot blush creeps up my neck. "A little."

He slides his hand down, over my chest, stomach, and settles between my legs, squeezing my pussy like he owns it. After last night, I suppose he does.

"I should probably say sorry—"

I interrupt with rushed words. "No, you shouldn't—"

"But I'm not going to," he finishes, and I huff out a laugh. "Good."

"I'm a bastard," he says, and I shake my head, but he goes on. "I should kiss you goodbye and leave, but I don't want to. I'm not going to. That makes me a bastard."

"Okay." I twist my fist in the neckline of his T-shirt, dragging him down to me, speaking my words into his mouth. "So fuck me like the bastard you are."

His grunt is downright sinful, and he bends, clamping his hands around the backs of my thighs, hoisting me up so I can wrap my legs around his waist. He carries me to the bed, where we lie down on my mattress. With his tongue in my mouth and my hands in his hair, I'm not sure who's pushing and pulling, but we roll back and forth until his T-shirt is off and I'm down to my bra and underwear.

He raises himself up above me. "Where do you keep your vibrator?"

"That's presumptuous of you to think I have one."

"I bet you have more than one," he says, finally taking a peek around my bedroom that's ultra girly with fluffy rugs and a bunch of fake plants everywhere because I'd be damned if I could keep a real one alive. He tips his chin back to me, hitting me with a knowing glint in his eyes. "I bet they're all pink, and I bet you use one every night because an orgasm helps you fall asleep."

I pout. He's exactly right. "How do you know that?"

"You couldn't keep your eyes open last night."

"That's because you made me come, like, eighteen times."

He squints at me. "Like I'm eighteen feet tall?"

"It's a good number for you, obviously."

"Obviously," he deadpans before sitting on the edge of the mattress to rummage through my bedside table drawer. When he finds my stash, he inspects the three before deciding on the dark pink rose.

"Lie back, sunshine," he orders softly, climbing onto the bed next to me. I comply, my heart pounding with anticipation, skin rippling with goose bumps, all because he's staring at me. That's all it takes for my nipples to pebble and my stomach to flip.

"Please, daddy," I beg, earning a growl of approval, and I cup my breasts with my hands, searching for relief.

"I'll take care of my good girl," he says and draws a line with his tongue from my lips to my breastbone before lifting his head, taking in my pose—the cups of my bra pushed down, my thumbs and index fingers pinching my nipples, knees bent and parted, totally wanton. "You're so pretty like this. Like a painting." He leans away another few inches, palming my stomach. "You should be memorialized like that. Hung in a museum so everyone can see your beauty."

"Roman," I whine, desperate for his hands on me but also because I don't feel like I deserve his words.

He bends, scratching my lower belly with his beard, raking his blunt nails over my hips when he drags my underwear down my legs. Then he's there, mouth and nose buried, inhaling deeply, like I'm some lavish meal. I arch my back when he licks along my aching flesh, and he slips his fingers inside, stroking me gently, carefully. I want more, digging my fingers into his hair, fighting for control, which he refuses to give up. I'm already wet, ready for him, but he takes his time, building me up slowly, dropping kisses on my thighs and hips and stomach.

"This isn't fucking me like a bastard," I grit out, and hot air wafts over my sensitive skin when he huffs.

"You're right. This is me fucking you as much as you can handle right now."

"Bastard."

He murmurs his agreement then turns on the vibrator, the low hum filling the room. I jolt at the sudden intensity when he presses it against my clit, and he keeps his hand on my stomach, holding me down, as I mindlessly squirm beneath him.

Pleasure courses through me, and I have trouble keeping my eyes open, but when I can, I see him nodding as if to himself, lips moving in quiet praise. "Good girl. Let go."

He eases his fingers back inside me, and that's all it takes. I'm all light and sensation, crying out, shuddering with my release, and I need a few deep breaths before I can pry my eyelids open. The shades on my windows are up, afternoon light filling the room, highlighting Roman's large form like some religious tableau. He does make me speak in tongues like the Holy Spirit, so it's not far off.

He sets the vibrator aside, his eyes never leaving mine, then shifts to his knees, running his hands up and down my thighs, in no rush to move. Though the bulge behind his jeans is evidence of his arousal. He's right in that I really don't think I could take his cock inside me, but I want to help him, offer him the same mind-bending orgasm he's blessed me with.

When I reach for him, he catches my hand, brings it to his lips, and kisses my fingers. My palm. My inner wrist.

"This is about you," he says, his voice rough, like he hasn't used it in ten years. Or used it too much in the last day.

Maybe he has. He said so himself on our date at Tabby Cat; he's given me more words than he's given anyone else this whole year.

I aim for his zipper again, but he knocks my hand out of the way. "Just lie there. Let me look at you."

I rid myself of my bra and relax against my pillows, which I think Roman likes if his audible exhale or the way he licks his lips is any indication. He unbuttons his jeans, pushing them down enough to free his erection from his boxer briefs, the elastic fitting beneath his heavy sac, his thick length aimed straight at me.

Last time, I didn't have enough light to really admire him, but now I can study every detail. The slight flush of his golden skin with those deep, even lines of his abs that a person could float a boat on. He has birds tattooed above each of his indented hip bones that seem almost too romantic to be on this masculine of a man with veins on his flat, lower stomach pointing to that monster cock of his.

"Touch yourself," he orders as he takes himself in hand, stroking slowly, his eyes locked on mine, and I don't hesitate. I slip my fingers down my slit, circling my already oversensitized clit, and I let loose a sigh that's one-part needy sex machine and one-part overused sex doll.

His chest rises and falls, mouth pulling as if in pain, but I can tell he's already close to coming and I stroke myself faster, matching the rhythm of his fist, tugging hard on his cock, a pearl of moisture pooling on the thick head. The sight of him, the sound of his harsh breaths, the knowledge that he's doing this for me, *because* of me, pushes me over the edge.

"Roman," I moan, muscles tensing as another orgasm rips through me. He groans, hunching over as his release hits my stomach in warm lines. He shudders and places his left hand on the bed next to my hip, his right hand pulling whatever is left out of him, a few drops landing on my thigh.

A tattoo of a different kind.

He collapses next to me, and we both lie together for a minute, soaking in the aftereffects of this intimacy that is as hot as it is a fantasy.

It's never felt like this before. I've never had this immediate connection and desire for someone, and I don't know what to do now that our weekend of faking it is over.

But I don't have too much time to think about it because my cell phone buzzes with a message, and I roll over to find my jeans, retrieving it from the pocket. Behind me, I feel and hear slight shuffling as Roman dresses, knowing he'll be leaving. And I won't have his protection anymore.

I'll have to fend for myself against my mother's text message.

MOM

> You and I need to have a conversation about this weekend. I am disgusted at your disrespect. To say nothing of how your "boyfriend" treated me.

My jaw tenses, my shoulders up by my ears, and it's a few seconds until I remember to tell myself to relax. I set my phone down and wipe a tissue over my stomach and legs before finding one of my sleep T-shirts to throw on. It just about covers my ass.

"You okay?" Roman asks, rounding the bed to take my face in his hands. When I merely nod, he narrows his brows. "What's wrong?"

I can't lie to the man. I'm physically incapable of not telling him the truth. He should probably work for the CIA.

"My mom. She texted me."

"What did she say?"

"She's mad."

His nostrils flare slightly, and he's got that angry bull thing going on, but he's not my real boyfriend and he can't continue to fight my battles for me.

"It's fine." I tap his forearms, signaling him to let me go. Which he does. Eventually.

"I don't believe you," he says, stepping back. "But I have to get home to Mazie."

"Of course." I paste on a smile. Not convincing enough, I guess, because he frowns.

Though I don't give him another chance to show me how he knows me better than almost everyone else in my life after only a few weeks, as I pull him to the front door. And I do mean *pull*. This motherfucker is a tank, and he doesn't travel easily.

"I don't like leaving you to deal with this alone," he says as I try to shove him out the door.

"It's okay," I pant. He doesn't budge. "I'm used to handling my mom."

He's rock solid, unmoving. "You shouldn't have to be used to it."

"Maybe not, but I am." I wrap my arms around him and drive. Finally, he shifts, too easily. Not because of my tremendous tackling form but because he stepped back, taking me with him. I tilt my head up. "Anyway, I'll be fine. I promise."

He smooths his hands down my back, still unconvinced and evidently unimpressed by my athleticism.

"Text me later," he says, and I acquiesce with a nod. Then

he dips his head to press a kiss to my lips. "Take care of yourself, Eloise."

"You too."

After another few moments, during which I consider begging him to stay or take me with him, Roman finally pivots and heads down the hall to the elevator. I watch until he disappears inside, then close my door.

Leaning against it, I take a deep breath. I already miss him, miss the safety and comfort I felt all weekend. But I meant what I said—I'm used to handling my mom. As unpleasant as it is, this is nothing new.

Squaring my shoulders, I march back to the bedroom. Time to call her and get this over with. The sooner I let her vent, the sooner we can move on.

At least, I hope so. Knowing my mom, she'll probably drag this out as long as possible.

But I have my memories of my weekend with Roman to keep me warm. No matter what she says, she can't take those away.

Chapter 19
Roman

It's not until a little after eight o'clock that Eloise finally texts me. Mazie's in the bathroom with bubbles up to her eyeballs, but since she always requires me to stay close in case she needs help, I lounge in the hall on my back with Steve sniffing around my ear.

SUNSHINE

What do you call an angry baker?

?

SUNSHINE

A sourdough!

Was that a joke?

SUNSHINE

Don't be rude.

It was a terrible joke.

SUNSHINE

No. This is a terrible joke...

SUNSHINE

Want to hear a joke about pizza? Never mind, it's too cheesy!

Don't quit your day job.

SUNSHINE

Speaking of, I owe you a lifetime of cinnamon rolls for coming with me this weekend.

You don't owe me anything.

SUNSHINE

Stop being a gentleman and just say "You're welcome, Eloise. I'd like my first batch delivered tomorrow morning."

What did your mom have to say?

SUNSHINE

Way to bring down the party.

SUNSHINE

She said I should be ashamed of myself.

I sit up so quickly, Steve startles, darting into the bathroom, Mazie shrieking in delight. But I can't concentrate on them with the blood rushing in my ears.

You should be ashamed of yourself?

It's a while before she finally replies. A long enough time that I complete a couple laps of the hallway.

SUNSHINE

She said I was acting like a hussy. I didn't even know people still used that word. Maybe she's been watching too many old Westerns or something, but either way, I don't think I was a hussy. Right? I'm not a hussy. I was acting like your girlfriend. You were acting like my boyfriend. Granted, a possibly overattentive one BUT STILL. I didn't do anything wrong. We didn't do anything wrong, but she went on and on and on about how I made a fool of myself in front of the entire family and how disappointed she is in me.

It takes me a few tries to type out a response that makes any sense because my brain is on overdrive, imagining telling her mother off once and for all. It's not very good, but it is the truth.

She fucking sucks.

SUNSHINE

LOLOLOLOLOLOLOLOLOLOLOL

SUNSHINE

Yes.

I really wish you would've let me tell her off. Tell them all off.

SUNSHINE

No. She already doesn't like you.

SUNSHINE

Shit. No.

SUNSHINE

I didn't mean that.

Of course she doesn't like me. I never expected her to.

I don't want her to.

SUNSHINE

Why wouldn't you want her to like you?

Because I don't need her approval. Or anyone else's. If I gave a shit about what every person thought of me, I'd still have my head stuck in a bottle.

SUNSHINE

But you're my boyfriend. She should like you.

SUNSHINE

Fake boyfriend, I mean. IF THIS WERE A REAL RELATIONSHIP I WOULD WANT HER TO LIKE YOU I KNOW YOU ARE NOT MY REAL BOYFRIEND IT WAS NOT A FREUDIAN SLIP JUST FORGET IT

I stop pacing at her all-caps message and sit back down on the floor, holding my left hand out for Steve to come back to me as I type out the text with my right hand.

You think you have some magical abilities? You can't make me forget anything you say.

SUNSHINE

I'm not delulu. I know you're not my real boyfriend. I just have fat thumbs and my mind's going too fast for my fingers to catch up when I text.

The idea of being Eloise's boyfriend doesn't freak me out. After this weekend, I know anyone would be lucky to have the privilege of being hers. But *I* am not delusional enough to think a woman would want to be strapped down with my baggage. Let alone making my sunshine girl carry the weight.

Nah.

I couldn't—wouldn't—do that to her.

But instead of ending the conversation here, like I should, I text her back.

> What are you doing right now?

She sends a picture of a full laundry basket.

SUNSHINE

Ignoring this. What are you doing?

I send her a photo of Steve cradled in the crook of my left elbow, burrowed against my bare chest.

SUNSHINE

OH MY GOD MY HEART YOU HAVE TO WARN A WOMAN DID YOU KNOW THE NUMBER ONE KILLER OF WOMEN IS HEART DISEASE AND HERE YOU ARE TRYING TO GET ME TO HAVE A HEART ATTACK AT HOW SWEET THIS IS OMGGGGGGGGGGG

SUNSHINE

Also. I never got to tell you, but I think your nipple piercings are super hot.

> LOL

SUNSHINE

Shut up. Did you literally laugh out loud?

> No.

SUNSHINE

Then why did you say LOL?

> Isn't that what people do when they think something's funny?

SUNSHINE

Yeah, but I've only seen you laugh one time.

> But I do think you're funny.

She sends me another picture. This one of her face, her hand covering half of it, a pink blush on her skin.

> Goddamn, you're pretty.

SUNSHINE

> Okay. I seriously am putting my phone down now because you're going to make me fall in love with you, and I know you don't want that to happen. So goodnight, Conan. See you tomorrow with your pastry!

I toss my phone down to pet Steve, shifting him up higher so I can breathe into his soft fur, nuzzle his tiny flank.

She is right. I don't want her falling in love with me.

I...

Fuck.

* * *

I'm not surprised by much, but receiving a phone call from Camden Long manages that. He's the starting tight end for the Philadelphia Founders and recently signed one of the biggest contracts in the league, and he apparently likes classic cars. That can race.

If I were in his position, I wouldn't be risking it all with fucking drag racing. But then again, I wasted my chance in the bottom of bottles. So what do I know? I'm just the mechanic who agreed to soup up his Camaro ZL1.

By the time I hang up, I hear Luis call out, "My queen" and glance over my shoulder in time to see Eloise sashaying toward me, a burst of sunshine even on this gray October afternoon. My heart does that thing it always does when I see her, like it's trying to leap out of my chest and into her hands. It's ridiculous, really, how smitten I am.

She's carrying another one of her pink boxes from Sweet Cheeks, like she has been every day this last week. I truly didn't need to be repaid for the wedding weekend. Not like fucking her into another universe was a hardship. But she insists, and since I can't eat a pound of pastries a day, Luis and Shawn have been benefiting.

Luis intercepts her, taking the box from her hands, even as she playfully pushes him, jokingly calling him an asshole for stealing my treats. He merely winks and takes the box over to Shawn's corner, where they both help themselves to my payment.

I check the time on my phone and note her visit is later than usual. She's been coming in around lunch, but it's after four.

"Hey, Roman," she says, approaching me with a smile like I'm the best thing she's seen all day. I want to kiss her right here, right now, but I hold back. We're not alone, and I don't want to make her uncomfortable.

"Hey, sunshine," I reply, straightening up. My eyes drift down to her lips, then back up to her sparkling green eyes. "You're late."

"I didn't know I was on the clock." She plays it off like she doesn't understand my meaning. Like we haven't fallen into a pattern where she comes to see me at the same time every day and where we don't text each other every night. "I came to see my favorite munchkin," she says before spinning around to Mazie, who's doodling on coloring pages. "There you are!"

My daughter tackles her with a hug, and Eloise lets herself be bowled over then listens intently as Mazie prattles on about school and Halloween.

She twirls in her pink costume. When it arrived in the mail

yesterday afternoon, she pitched a fit about wanting to wear it to school, so I made her a deal that she could wear it after. Which is why she's a fairy queen now. Crown and wings included.

"Gorgeous!" Eloise coos, admiring Mazie's costume. "Are you excited to go trick-or-treating?"

She nods enthusiastically, then asks, "Are you going trick-or-treating?"

Eloise laughs. "I'm gonna hand out candy."

"Come with me!" My daughter points between herself and me. "Come with us! It's fun!"

Eloise's brows shoot up as she slants her gaze up to me, a question in her eyes.

I shrug. "Yeah."

"Really?"

"Not the fun part, but for you coming with us... Yeah."

She rolls her eyes at my fun comment. "You aren't going with your family? Don't Taryn's and Griffin's kids usually go together?"

I shrug. "I guess they used to, but the kids are going on their own now. No parents."

I'm in no rush for Mazie to grow up, but I can't wait until she's old enough to do all this shit on her own. Eloise must be able to interpret my grunt, but she snickers then turns back to my daughter. "I'd love to come with you. Thanks for inviting me."

My kid throws her arms around Eloise's neck, and it's so natural. It's like they've known each other for a lot longer than two months. Feels the same for me too.

She's slipped so easily into my life... Or maybe, it's the other way around. Mazie and I have slipped so easily into life here in West Chester, into Eloise's life.

Eloise stands and fixes her shirt in place, taking away my

great view of her tits, then drops a kiss to my daughter's head before looking to me. "I guess I need to figure out a costume. What are you dressing up as?"

"I don't dress up."

She socks me in the arm. "Come on!" When I shake my head, she pouts. "Why not?"

I arch my brow, asking a silent question. *Do I really give off the vibe of a guy who dresses up in costume?* She giggles, tugging on my T-shirt, and I let myself be pulled to her.

Careful not to touch her, I shove my hands into my pockets, until I notice the smudge of flour on her neck. I swipe my thumb over it, and since I already broke the rule, might as well take advantage, so I pinch her chin. "I'll text you my address."

She licks her lips, the tip of her tongue too tempting to ignore, and I follow the path with my thumb. Her eyes go soft as she releases a long exhale, a silent sigh. She's tortured.

Me too.

I force myself to back up. "Come over around six."

"Sounds good," she says, folding her arms over her chest, covering her pebbled nipples.

A shame.

"See everyone later!" She scoots out through the shop, to the front door, and I pretend I don't understand the looks Luis and Shawn shoot me. As if we're not fooling anyone. *I'm* clearly not fooling anyone. So I don't try.

Instead, I go back to work.

Chapter 20
Roman

A few minutes after six, the doorbell rings, and Mazie tears out of her seat at the table to answer it. I don't have to see her fling the front door open to know she does it with so much force, it rebounds off the doorstop. I can hear the weird clang it makes, and I roll my eyes.

"Jesus Christ, Maze! Chill out," I call from the kitchen, still cleaning up from the gourmet dinner of macaroni and cheese and hot dogs.

"Eloise!"

I poke my head out in time to see my six-year-old daughter literally dragging her into our house.

"You're awfully strong for someone so small," Eloise laughs, careful to shut the door behind her.

"That's 'cause I work out with Daddy." Mazie raises her arms to flex her so-called muscles.

"And I'm not gonna take you trick-or-treating if you're gonna act like this." I cross my arms over my chest, leaning against the doorframe. "Hulking out on the doors and our guests."

"*You* said I'm strong," she argues, but I don't have time to have a conversation about it because she races off toward her room. "I hafta put my costume on!"

I turn my attention to Eloise in a big, fluffy pink Care Bear costume and push off the wall. "How'd you find that in two days?"

She lifts her arms out at her sides, rocking back on her heels. "You think I don't have multiple Halloween costumes in the back of my closet?"

Of course she does.

"And you must be Fantasy Ken," she says, gesturing at me, but I don't get it.

"What?"

She sighs, shaking her head like she's disappointed in me for not understanding. "You have on a white V-neck T-shirt, so I can see your tattoos and your piercings. Plus, you have a dish towel over your shoulder, meaning you've cooked and/or cleaned, and to top it all off, you're wearing gray sweatpants, which makes me feel like you *know* what you're doing. It's gray sweatpants season, and you've got a boa constrictor in them, so..." She huffs an annoyed sound and pops her hands on her hips. "Don't play innocent with me, Roman Alan Stone."

"That's not my middle name."

"Just go put some underwear on!"

For a moment, I'm stunned. She yelled at me. About my dick. And my underwear.

I don't know what to do.

Besides laugh.

Earning what I think is a stern warning with her index finger, but I can't be totally sure because her hands are covered by the Care Bear mitts.

"It's all fun and games until it's time to send me home, but you're gonna have a real hard goddamn time because you've decided to be Fantasy Ken, whose job is to make me fall in love with you."

That sobers me, and I grab the towel from my shoulder, whacking the side of her thigh with it, though I doubt she feels anything through the fur. "Fine. I'll go change if it'll make you happy."

"Well, I'm sure the rest of the straight female population will hate it, but it would make me feel better, since we're keeping this PG."

If that's what she wants.

But I'd be okay fucking a furry.

Didn't see that kink coming.

Then again, never saw Eloise coming either.

I never could have expected that ball of sunshine to lodge so deeply in my chest I don't feel like I can properly breathe unless I'm around her.

"Be right back," I say before heading down to my room. I showered after work and didn't bother putting on "real clothes," but I do now, including slipping on a pair of Hanes before stepping into jeans. Down the hall, I hear Mazie giving Eloise a tour of the house, including the bathroom, Steve's bunny condo, the kitchen, and finally, my room.

I finish pulling my hoodie down as Mazie tosses my door open with a flourish. "And this is Daddy's bedroom."

"Nowhere on the job description of being my daughter does it say to give house tours, especially not to my room."

Mazie angles her head. "What are you talking about?"

"I'm talking about this habit you've picked up of throwing doors open, and about how you can't open my bedroom door whenever you want. I knock on your door. You need to knock on mine."

"Yeah, yeah, yeah," she mumbles because first grade has given her a lot of confidence, and not all of it is good.

"I might hang you up by your pigtails before the night's out," I tell her, and she screws her face up at the threat she knows I'll never follow through on before dashing away, yelling about how she's going to hang me up by my ears.

For her part, Eloise slaps a hand over her mouth, probably to cover her laugh. I glower at her. "Don't you start too. Having one sassy female in the house is more than enough."

She raises her hands in innocence. "I didn't say anything."

I stuff my wallet, keys, and cell phone in my pocket, calling out, "Shoes on, Maze. Let's go."

"I'm already ready!" Eloise and I make our way back down the hall to where Mazie's by the front door, swinging her plastic pumpkin bucket around. "Took you long enough."

"I swear to fucking god," I mumble, motioning her out the door. "One of us isn't gonna make it to her sixteenth birthday."

Eloise snorts a laugh, following my kid out so I can lock up before the three of us head down the block. I pinch Eloise's ass in warning to be good, and she squeals in surprise, earning a funny look from Mazie, who holds out her hand. "Come on, Elle!"

Eloise doesn't hesitate. She takes Mazie's hand, and they walk in step to the first house.

I love my daughter. I love my daughter more than life itself and will do anything for her, but that doesn't mean I don't hate 87% of the shit she wants me to do, like trick-or-treating.

But.

With Eloise dressed up as a Care Bear and Mazie bouncing around as a fairy princess, it's hard not to be swept up in their energy. We hit nearly every house in the neighborhood, Mazie darting from door to door as Eloise's laughter mixes with the sounds of the night.

"You're really a good dad," she comments, watching Mazie run back toward us, her plastic pumpkin swinging wildly as she complains about getting yet another Tootsie Roll.

"Did you say thank you?" I ask, and she nods before sprinting to the next house. "I didn't hear it last time," I call. "You have manners, Maze. Use them."

She throws me a thumbs-up over her shoulder as she waits in line behind Buzz and Woody. I turn back to the Care Bear at my side, feeling a bit awkward about the praise. "She's my kid. I don't really have a choice."

Eloise shrugs. "You could be a shitty dad, but you're not. You're here, making memories with her. That's a choice. You're choosing to be a really great dad."

Her words hit me in a way I wasn't expecting. I've always done what I had to for Mazie, but hearing Eloise say it like that —it makes me feel like maybe I'm doing something right. Without thinking, I place my hand between her shoulder blades, intent on pressing my gratitude into her lips, but before I can, my sweet baby angel runs up between us. "Look at this! Look how big it is!"

Eloise whistles. "King-size? We'll have to remember this house for next year."

I know she said it absently, *we'll have to remember for next year...*

And yet there's a tug, a desire. I want this.

This feeling of rightness.

I don't want it to go away.

I'd like it to be around next year too.

And the year after that.

I want it for a long damn time. Forever.

"Ooh! Do you see that house? I don't want to go there." Mazie shivers as she pulls on Eloise's hand, so we keep walking past the house with the giant fake spider on the front.

Mazie's freaked out about bugs. Apparently, so is Eloise.

Great. Both of 'em sassy and afraid of insects. I wouldn't be able to catch a break with these two.

But who the fuck am I kidding? Like I'm not taking care of them both. Bugs or not.

When we return home, Mazie bulldozes over Eloise again, begging her to stay to watch a movie, and Eloise puts up the fight of a feather, agreeing almost immediately.

Neither one of them consulting me.

Because they're already teaming up, and I apparently no longer rule the house. If I ever did.

Kicking off my shoes, I watch as Mazie tosses her fairy wings to the floor before jumping onto the couch. She waves at Eloise to follow her. "Come on! Come on!"

But Eloise hesitates for a moment, meeting my gaze. "I'm actually really hot in this. Would you mind..." She lifts her paws, waving them back and forth. "I can't unzip with these."

She doesn't wait for my answer and turns her back to me. I unzip it, feeling exactly how hot she must have been when the material splits down her back, giving her room to step out of it with a burst of humidity. With Mazie busy mashing buttons on the television remote, I take the opportunity to brush my knuckles across the nape of Eloise's neck. Her skin's warm and slightly clammy, and I rake my hand down her spine when she bends to step out of the giant onesie.

Once she stands up, she faces me again, hands in her hair, tying it up in a knot on the top of her head, offering me time to blatantly check her out in her thin T-shirt and tight workout shorts. I imagine bringing her to the gym with me, her ass as she squats, her tits jiggling as she runs on the treadmill.

She said she used to be an athlete, and she has an air about her that makes me think she'd give me a run for my money. She'd no doubt want to have some kind of competition.

I'd let her kick my ass, so I could give her the reward and lay her down on the floor and lick up her sweet pussy until—

"*Spookely*! Fuck yeah."

"No." I lunge at Mazie and steal the remote from her. "Absolutely not. And watch your mouth."

"Daddy!"

"No." Ignoring Eloise's giggles behind me, I point the remote at the TV to stop the goddamn show about the square pumpkin and find something else. Something better. I settle on *The Addams Family* and place the remote on the shelf that Mazie can't reach, and she whines for a minute. Until I toss her a candy from her stockpile. Then she doesn't care about what's on the screen anymore, only how fast she can rip into her haul.

"Have a seat," I tell Eloise, then head into the kitchen to pour both of us water and pop a bowl of popcorn. It can't be said I'm not a semi-decent host.

"Ooh, thank you," Eloise says, accepting the popcorn from me, and I settle on the other side of Mazie, so she's between us. I stay quiet, enjoying the chatter between my two girls, talking about their favorite candy, sorting it into the good and bad piles. Obviously, they give the "bad" candy to me.

And it hits me while I'm on the third Tootsie Roll how domesticated this whole scene is. How peaceful and nice it is. How this is what I've always wanted for Mazie.

And it's a little too close to reality. A little too fucking scary to realize all it would take would be a few words.

I'm not sure I'm ready.

Distracted by my thoughts, I don't register how much time passes until Eloise gently taps my arm, motioning to a sleeping Mazie, her head in Eloise's lap.

My chest aches, and I can't do anything but smooth my hand over my daughter's hair. She doesn't shift or flutter her eyes, conked out. Completely comfortable with Eloise.

"I'll be right back," I whisper and carefully gather Mazie in my arms. I carry her to her room and tuck her into bed. Still, she doesn't stir. I should feel guilty about not changing her into pajamas or all the sugar she's had—I'll probably pay for it later when she has four cavities—but I know what a dragon she can be when woken up. I press a kiss to her forehead then slip out, quietly closing the door on the way.

I find Eloise in the living room, slipping her shoes back on. She smiles when she sees me. "That was fun. Thanks for letting me tag along."

I don't want her to leave yet and move to stand in front of her, effectively blocking her way because I'm a greedy son of a bitch. I want all her attention. All her time. "You're not in a rush to head home, are you? You can stick around if you want."

She considers it for a moment, eyes slanting to the door, before meeting mine again and toeing her shoes back off. "Yeah, all right."

She hops onto the couch, and I internally fist-pump like the fucking chump I am.

She's staying. In my home. And at least for a little while, she's all mine once again.

I sit right beside her, draping my arm along the back of the couch, but instead of curling into my side like I expect, she sits on her knees facing me. "So, I think this is when you finally tell me."

"Tell you what?"

She tips her head to the side. "About Mazie's mom."

Chapter 21
Eloise

Roman's eyes widened like a bunny being hunted, and I supposed *this* is what my mountain of a man's afraid of. He's let me in, has told me about his addiction and family, but bringing up Mazie's mom?

Pure terror.

"Why?" he asks, rubbing at the back of his neck.

"*Why?*" I cough a dubious laugh. Isn't it obvious?

Roman's an amazing father, and the more time I spend with Mazie, the more I'm coming to care about her. I can't go on like this—*we* can't go on like this—without having the truth between us.

I have feelings for Roman. Big feelings. The kind that make me daydream and keep me up at night. And I think he has feelings for me too, but there's no way I can keep putting myself out there with him if he's not going to allow me into his life completely. I've been burned enough in the past, and I deserve someone who puts as much energy into a relationship as I do.

To say nothing of how nosy I am. Clearly, there's something

going on that is out of the ordinary, and I want to know. *Need* to know.

"Because..." I wave a hand between Roman and me. "Don't you want to tell me? I mean, I basically word-vomit every thought I have in my head to you, and it's a bad habit I have, but I also do it because I want you to know everything about me. And I..." I shrug, plopping my hands in my lap. "I want to know everything about you. That is...if you feel the same way about me. I had a lot of fun tonight with you and Mazie, and I'd like to keep hanging out with you because I like Mazie. But I *really* like you. And I feel I need to draw boxes on a note or something embarrassing like that, like, 'Do you like me? Check yes or no.' 'Cause I'm checking yes, and I'm hoping by you telling me about Mazie's mom that means you'll check yes too."

The room falls silent after my chaotic confession, the echo of my words hanging in the air like I screamed them. I might as well have for how he's staring at me.

I start backpedaling, scooting to the other end of the couch. "If you don't feel the same way—"

"I want to tell you," he says, his dark eyes searching mine. I can see the gears turning behind them, weighing his options, deciding how much of his guard to let down. "I want to tell you everything about me because..." He dips his chin, takes a breath that raises his shoulders and chest before licking his lips and meeting my gaze again. "I'm checking the yes box."

I smile. A big, huge, idiotic smile.

Then I immediately lose it because he says, "But this isn't easy to tell, and I don't..." He trails off, scrubbing at his beard for a while, then leans back against the cushions, his focus on the wall across from us. "You were the last thing I expected when we moved here. I wanted to come here for a fresh start, and ever since I've met you, I feel like I didn't just get a fresh start, I got kicked into another universe."

I wince. "Is that good?"

He angles his face to me, lips quirking to the side. "Yeah, sunshine. It's really good. Real fucking scary too."

I crawl back to his side, sitting next to him, hip to hip, my thigh against his, and lean my head on his shoulder. "I get that, and if you don't want to tell me right now, you don't have to. I'm not going anywhere."

Two minutes pass, Roman's steady breathing the only soundtrack as the movie has finished, the television screen displaying the streaming menu, and I watch the digits in the corner change. But then I feel his lips against my head as he inhales audibly, like he's smelling my shampoo.

Then he tells me, "Her name is Amy. She was...broken. Like me. So, being with her was easy. I didn't have to face any hard things since we were running away from them. We ran away together."

He shifts, forcing me to pick my head up from his shoulder, and he takes my hand in his, completely encompassing it. I stay quiet, but I do place my other hand on top of his, silently encouraging him.

"We burned hot and fast, moved in together almost immediately and spent every night getting drunk and high on whatever drug we could find. We both liked pills, but she could be more adventurous than me, and for as big as I am, her tolerance was much higher than mine." He lifts his eyes to mine, unflinching in his truth. "Then she got pregnant, and we were both really excited. You pretty much know the rest of my story, except the part about Amy."

"Doesn't go in the same direction as yours?" I guess, and he shakes his head.

"I had times of intermittent sobriety, but I needed this time to stick, and since we were doing it together, I thought we could keep each other on track, but..." He exhales raggedly and drags his hand over his hair and face. "I don't know what it was like for her after she had Mazie. I don't know what women have to go through, but I know what I saw, and I didn't like it. Whatever she may have been feeling or dealing with, it wasn't an excuse to start using again. I know that's hypocritical of me to say. We're both addicts, and I have no room to judge her, but we had a *baby*. If she couldn't stay sober for her, then she wouldn't ever be sober."

I hide my frown, feeling sympathy for the woman. Though I've never been pregnant, I know postpartum is hard. I sat with Sloane after she had both of her babies. It's not easy, physically or mentally, and while I don't think it's my place to tell Roman what to think or feel about his situation, I also think it's easy to sit in judgment of others' mental health struggles. It's easy for us to know what's best for other people when we haven't been in their shoes.

Sure, she made terrible choices, but she's human, like the rest of us. Flawed and struggling.

"I tried to make it work for Mazie's sake. But in the end, I had to put my daughter first. Amy's usage got worse and worse, and she was eventually arrested."

I suck in a breath through my teeth, but he plows on.

"It was... It was horrible. We were there—me and Mazie. She saw her mom be arrested, and I don't..." He blows out a big breath. "I'm not sure if that's something she'll ever get over, but Amy is going to be in prison for a few years. It's been almost thirteen months that she's been there, and Mazie needed a change. I don't want her childhood to be *that*. I want her to have good memories and feel safe. There is minimal contact between Amy and me because I need to protect my daughter. Amy's not the mother Mazie needs right now. So..."

He clears his throat, but his voice still cracks with the

weight of years-old heartache, and I wonder how many times he's told this story. Or to whom.

I bet not many. Probably only his siblings.

Though my mind is quickly brought to a screeching halt when he tells me, "I'm now sure how to do this—you and me—so Mazie doesn't get hurt. I feel out of my depth."

This man. He could not make me care for him any less, if that's what he's afraid of. With his gaze down, obviously expecting me to be upset over him wanting to protect his child.

That could never happen. I curl my hand around his bearded jaw so he'll meet my eyes, and I offer him my best reassuring smile. "It's okay. We'll figure it out together."

He blows out a relieved breath that makes me wish I were big enough to protect him. But then again, my heart is. If anything, I can cloak him with my love. Make sure he and his daughter will always be protected.

I lift Roman's hand to my mouth, kissing Mazie's name, tattooed across the knuckles of his right hand.

He watches me for a long time as if he doesn't know what to do with me, and for a moment, I think I did the wrong thing. Maybe he thinks I'm babying him or treating him too delicately. What huge guy wants to have his knuckles kissed?

Mine does apparently because he lowers his forehead to mine, wrapping his free hand around my neck, breathing deeply. My heart aches for the pain he's endured, for the little girl who's been caught in the crossfire of her parents' mistakes, and when he finally leans back from me, his eyes are red, mouth tight. This conversation has taken a toll on him.

I want to say something profound, something that will ease his soul, but words seem cheap in the face of his honesty. So I simply press my lips to his, a soft, lingering kiss that's meant to comfort more than arouse.

But Roman is quick to find my hips, pulling me closer, obviously done with the sweet and honest portion of the night. I roll with it, straddling his lap.

"Change of subject," I say, whipping off my T-shirt, and his eyes lose the sadness in them, replaced by raw lust. He rids me of my bra and takes my breasts in his hands, nothing gentle or tender about it when he pushes them together, licking and biting at the valley between them before sucking on my nipples in turn.

I grind on him, feeling his erection grow beneath me, and my pussy has no muscle memory. Just straight up in *give me that monster cock* mode, and at the moment, I don't really care that I was sore the morning after either.

I want him in me. *Now.*

But instead of helping me when I dive for the button on his jeans, he pushes my hands away, murmuring something that sounds a lot like "Not yet."

Not yet?

Not yet?

Yes, yet.

Standing, I strip completely naked in front of him, flinging my bike shorts off to the side, and Roman's laid low for a moment, surprised. He trails his gaze over me, hanging out below my waist for a while before journeying back up, and my nipples are so tight they hurt. Never mind the tingling between my legs.

"Eloise," he growls like a reprimand, but there's no real bite to it, especially because he pulls off his shirt then shucks down his jeans and underwear, revealing the maker of dreams and destroyer of pussies.

"Get over here," he demands, spreading his thighs, and when I happily comply, he grabs hold of my hips with a bruising grip, pushing me down to grind against his thick length.

"What are you...?"

"Gotta get you warmed up." He kisses me before I can protest, urging me to roll my hips, working my clit over his hard cock, and it doesn't take long before I'm lost, whining and undulating over him. "There she is," he rasps. "Almost there."

I don't remember the last time I did this—if ever—but it's erotic and deliciously dirty. Especially with all the lights on and nothing to take away from his quiet grunts and the way our skin sounds, rubbing together, wet and purely obscene. Makes me want more. Makes me want it all.

Roman lowers his mouth to my nipples, sucking hard on one while twisting the other, and I barely start to orgasm before his hand is there, thrusting fingers inside me. It takes my breath away, and I whimper, rocking back and forth, wave after wave of pleasure hitting me as he nods over and over, his mouth so close to mine, when he licks his lips, he licks mine too. His thick fingers don't let me rest, forcing me up another crest, and mere minutes later, I come again, spasming and shuddering, my head lolling back to my shoulders.

"You wet enough?" he asks, and it takes me a few seconds to even understand he's talking to me.

"What?"

He growls impatiently, physically spinning me around so I'm seated on his lap, my back against his chest, his cock trapped between my butt cheeks and my knees on either side of his.

Before I even fully settle, he fists my hair. "Gimme this hair." Tugs my head to the side. "Gimme this neck."

He lands a hot, openmouthed kiss there while gently curling his hand around my throat. I moan. "Oh god."

Nipping at my earlobe, he trails his fingers down to tweak at each of my nipples before palming my belly, his hips pushing up enough to lift us a few inches so we sink lower on the couch.

And then he circles my clit, spreading my wetness around, making sure I'm ready to handle him.

"Please," I beg, but he doesn't give me what I want yet. Not until *he* thinks I'm good and ready. Even as I beg and plead and yank on the back of his head.

He merely bites the slope of my neck and grates out, "Don't rush me, girl, or I'll fucking tear you in two, and not in the way I mean to."

"Yes, please." I slant my head to kiss his bearded jaw, search for his mouth. "I want you inside me. Please, *daddy*."

He growls and smacks the side of my thigh. "Fine. You want it so bad, take it." He releases his hold on me and throws his arms out to the sides. "Fucking take it, Eloise. Show your daddy how good you can ride his cock."

Challenge accepted.

I place my feet on the floor between his and lean forward so I can reach behind me and position the tip of his erection at my entrance. Before I *fucking taking it*, I meet Roman's gaze, and he arches a brow. Smug bastard.

Then I bend my knees and sink down, taking the first inch or so, and *ohh god*.

I moan, tossing my head back, and Roman shifts, wrapping one arm around my middle, and claps his hand over my mouth.

"Shh, sunshine," he whispers in my ear. "We don't want to wake Mazie."

I nod, but he doesn't let go right away.

"You sure you can be quiet?"

I nod, frantic now, my body naturally accepting more of him simply from being this close. There is nowhere else for me to go. Nothing else for me to do but let gravity do its thing and *take it.*

A few seconds pass before he finally releases me, relaxing back against the cushion, and I place my hands on his thighs to support myself as I sink even farther down, biting into my lip to smother my sounds.

His big palms land on my ass cheeks, holding me up, helping me move up and down his shaft as much as I can. Each stroke radiates through me like an echo of a bell, and I have a hard time *taking it*.

I can't keep up.

It's impossible for me to keep going.

Instead, Roman tightens his grip on my butt, fingertips digging into my hips as he basically lifts me up and down, thrusting without thrusting inside me.

I hang my head, squeeze my eyes shut, and merely hold on...let go. Say hello to the angels.

Because I'm done.

And I fly straight to heaven.

Behind me, I hear him mumble a string of curses, his thigh muscles coiling under my palms as he follows me up. Or down.

Either way, he tows me against him, careful to slip out of me before cradling me against his chest, both of us breathing hard. He smooths his hands all over my hair and back, and it would be too easy to stay right there, wrapped up in his warm embrace. So instead of falling asleep on him, I disentangle myself and stand on shaky legs, scooping up my discarded clothes off the floor.

"I should get going," I say softly, and he opens his mouth like he might reply but stays quiet, watching me with a heavy-lidded gaze instead. I duck into the bathroom to clean up and put on my clothes, and when I emerge again, I find him by the front door in his jeans with the zipper open.

And he truly must be *trying* to kill me.

He walks me out to my car, his sharp gaze sweeping over it critically. I nudge him playfully. "Don't even think about buying me a new car just because you got me that bike. This one runs fine."

"At least fix it up," he mumbles, and when I start to argue, he silences me with a scowl. My stubborn protector of a refrigerator.

I unlock my car, then pause to smile up at him. "Thank you for tonight. For...everything."

His hard expression softens, and he pinches my chin to drop a kiss on my lips. "Drive safe, sunshine."

Reluctantly, I offer him wave before pulling away into the night. Body pleasantly wrung out, heart achingly full.

Do you like me? Check yes or no.

Try *do you love me? Check yes or no.*

Chapter 22
Roman

Less than twenty-four hours after Eloise left my house, and I'm already back in her presence, pretending as if seeing her hold Mazie's hand doesn't have me coming up with all these ridiculous ideas that involve rings and changing last names.

It was Mazie's idea to go to the park today, but it was my idea to see if Eloise wanted to come. Since it's right by her apartment building, she could walk there. When I offered the suggestion to my daughter, she jumped on it and demanded my cell phone so she could personally invite Eloise. I found her contact then handed it over, happy I didn't have to admit how much of a simp I am.

Not like now.

Standing off to the side with Eloise's pink purse over my shoulder as she helps Mazie across the monkey bars. They go up and down the slide a few times before moving on to the swings, but Mazie doesn't stay there long once she spots a kid from her class, and the two run off to the slides together.

Wordlessly, Eloise and I decide to take a seat on one of the benches, watching Mazie run around the park, talking with a third child now. I'm so proud of her.

"Last year, if you'd told me Mazie would walk up to other kids to play with them, I wouldn't have believed you."

Eloise's light brown eyebrows rise. "Oh yeah?"

I glance over, noticing the tip of her nose is red, along with her cheeks. Even though she's got a cream-colored beanie on her head, she must be cold, and I drape my arm over her shoulders. "She used to be afraid of her shadow."

Eloise huffs out a dubious sound. "Hard to believe. She's so amazing."

I nod, finding a bit too much comfort in the words of the woman who's not Mazie's mom, but who so easily slips into a maternal role that it's hard not to imagine it.

"I was worried," I confess as her green eyes drift back and forth between my own, her hand finding mine over her shoulder, linking our fingers together. I don't understand how she always knows exactly what to do to make me feel less anxious with her touch alone, but it's enough for me to beg her never to stop.

Never to leave.

Yet it's not like we're even *together*.

We had one weekend pretending.

Then an afternoon.

And last night.

And now...whatever this is. Sitting here, sharing a bench, watching Mazie run around with friends.

I keep my eyes on Mazie climbing the jungle gym. "I only ever wanted to give her a stable family, a stable life."

"You are. Look at her out there. Look how happy she is. Not everyone would have the courage to do the hard things for their kids, but you did. You do." Eloise places her hand on my jaw, her palm cool when she turns my head to face her. "Tell me one thing you're good at."

"You gonna show me what you're good at in return?"

"Maybe."

I relax my legs, widening my stance. Being a big guy, I try to be careful of the space I take up, but I forget all about that with Eloise. She doesn't mind that I crowd her. In fact, I think she likes it.

"Something I'm good at," I repeat, and she settles more into my side, her right hand on the top of my thigh. "Fixing up cars."

"Obviously. Something else."

"Making you come."

"Shh!" She backhands my stomach. "Not on the playground, Roman."

I lean over, my mouth against the shell of her ear when I say, "Making you scream."

She flushes pink, and I give her the answer I know she wants to hear. "And I'm a good dad."

"Fuck right, you are."

I tug on a lock of her hair. "Watch your mouth in front of the kids, sunshine."

She snorts, nodding sarcastically. "Okay."

"So much attitude," I mumble. "I'm not sure if I want that rubbing off on my daughter."

She gasps, pretending to be shocked before socking me in the shoulder. "Mazie loves me."

"You're right," I say, all the humor gone from my voice. "She does."

I think I do too.

But that is fucking bananas, and no way am I going to admit that out loud. Instead, I clear my throat and move on. "What about your dad?"

"What do you mean?" she asks, leaning against my side

once again, waving at Mazie when she calls our names at the top of the slide. I should probably be more cautious of letting her see us being so physical together, but I think Mazie likes it.

She certainly doesn't seem confused or upset by it.

Because after she slides down, she runs over to us, a leaf in her hand. "Look at this! Here." She hands it to Eloise. "Hold this for me."

"How 'bout you use some manners?" I interject, and she tries again.

"Hold it for me, *please*."

Eloise laughs at her overenunciation. "Yes, of course I will."

"Watch me," Mazie tells her. "I'm gonna go down the slide again. Watch me, okay?"

And she does. Eloise never takes her attention off my daughter as she climbs the ladder then pivots around to make sure Eloise is indeed looking. The woman straight out of my dreams next to me points to her eyes then at my daughter. "I'm watching!"

Mazie shrieks and goes down the slide with her arms up. "Did you see?" she yells. "I went so fast!"

Eloise claps. "Awesome job, babe!"

Mazie smiles brightly and zips off to run across the planks to the tower in the corner, and Eloise turns to me as if she didn't grind the last bit of fight I had against my growing feelings for her to dust. She tips her head to the side, hitting me with a cute, distracted scowl. "What were we talking about?"

"Your dad."

"Right." She snaps her fingers. "Yeah, my dad... He's supportive."

"That sounded like a question."

"No, he is," she says but then backtracks. "Kinda." When I stare at her blankly, she circles her hands in the air. "It's hard to describe because he's the kind of dad who'd give me a pony if I wanted, but then he won't say anything to my mom about me or jump in to defend me. So what's the point of the pony, you know?"

I've never had the kind of money to be able to buy somebody a pony, but I understand the sentiment.

"He thinks he can throw money at a problem," she goes on, although that immediately sets me on edge.

"You're not a problem to solve."

She scrunches up her face. "Maybe a little bit."

"Not even a fucking crumb of a bit, Eloise. Do we need to play our game for real? 'Cause I'll take you home right now, woman. Don't—"

She quiets me with her index finger against my lips. "This isn't a confidence thing. This is a reality that I have to live with. I do need to find ways to live my daily life that are not typical for other people. I have problems I need to solve, and my dad is unlike my mom in that he knows it. He believes me when I say I need help, and he's more than happy to write me a check. He's more than happy to pay off my student loans then lend me money to open my bakery. He's more than happy to buy me an electric toothbrush or smartwatch or robot vacuum. Anything to make my life easier, except what I *really* need."

"Somebody to tell your mom to fuck off," I say, and she nods.

"More or less."

I cup the back of her head. "I'm happy to do it."

"I know you are." She laughs a bit sadly, and I hate it. "And I appreciate it, but it feels different coming from someone who loves me, you know?"

I swallow the words down. Hard. "I get it. I just don't like that you don't feel supported."

She shrugs. "I have my friends. Sloane. My chosen family."

My heart's in my throat, and I can barely force the words out. "You have me too."

Her eyes sparkle with a little surprise but even more gratitude. "Yeah?"

I nod. "Definitely."

Pressing my forehead to hers, I breathe in her cinnamon-and-sugar scent that lingers on her even when she's not in her bakery, even when we're sitting outside in the middle of fall with dried leaves all around us. Still. She's the sweetest, brightest thing in the world.

"Do you and Mazie want to come to my place?" she asks, lifting her head, a small smile gracing her hopeful face. "It's getting colder, and the sun will start to set soon. I don't have much to eat, but I do have tomato soup and I make an excellent grilled cheese."

Without breaking my gaze, I call out, "Hey, Maze!"

"Yeah?"

"You want to go to Eloise's house for dinner?"

"Fuck yeah!"

Eloise bursts out in a giggle as I stand, rolling my eyes at the scandalized gasps of the other adults around the playground. Waving my troublemaking daughter over, I take her hand. "You really gotta knock that shit off."

"What shit?"

"The fucking cursing, Maze. People are gonna think I'm raising an animal."

She sticks her finger in the air with an idea. "What animal? A butterfly? Or chipmunk? Or penguin?"

"Rat," I say, meeting Eloise by the edge of the park, her purse over her shoulder as she digs through it for her keys.

"A rat?" Mazie makes a face. "Rats aren't cute. I wanna be a bunny."

"Be whatever the fuck you want, just stop cursing." I open

the door to Eloise's building for her and Mazie. Eloise's apartment is on the second floor, but instead of taking the elevator, we hike up the staircase. Mazie loves the fall wreath hanging on Eloise's door, and she flies inside when Eloise unlocks it.

Since I didn't get much of a look last time I was here, too obsessed with giving her an orgasm, I study the place. It's not huge, but it's nice. Her pink cruiser rests against the far wall, and Mazie goes right over to it, patting the basket on the front before asking Eloise, "Can I see your bathroom?"

Eloise laughs and points to the door in the hall. "Sure. It's right down there."

Mazie makes a beeline, and I shrug when Eloise turns her questioning gaze on me. "I don't know. She likes toilets and soap."

I take off my boots, afraid to somehow mess up her obvious aesthetic by keeping them on. The living room is cozy, with plush pink blankets and pillows, a fluffy white rug, and a bookshelf filled with books and knickknacks.

There are framed pictures on the walls, including one of a young Eloise and Sloane, probably in high school. There's also one of her holding a huge cake that looks like it could feed a small army. When Mazie's finished inspecting whatever-the-hell in the bathroom, she meets me in front of the picture. She points to it and asks Eloise, "Did you make that?"

"I did," Eloise says.

Mazie's jaw drops. "It's huge! Can I have some?"

"That one's all gone, but I can make you another one sometime."

My kid's eyes light up. "Really?"

"Really," Eloise confirms, and Mazie squeals, running over to hug her, accidentally knocking into a small table so the flowerpot on top wobbles. The pot's got a pair of boobs painted on it, and Mazie snickers.

"Those are funny."

"They are." Eloise nods, surreptitiously hiding another pot, one that I'm pretty sure has miniature dicks all over it. I shake my head at her in mock disappointment. She silently laughs in return.

"So," she says, waving Mazie and me to follow her. "Come have a seat at Café Eloise." She offers us water or orange juice to drink with an apology. She explains that she has meal kits delivered, but nothing much in the fridge beyond that. "Groceries and meal planning are something I'm terrible at," she tells me as if that will somehow be a turnoff.

Not possible.

As I sip on my water and Mazie drinks her OJ through a squiggly-shaped straw, which Eloise has a dozen of because of Sloane's kids, Micah and Olivia, she prepares our dinner.

She moves with a natural grace, even in her small kitchen, and I'm captivated. The way she wiggles her hips, dancing to the music playing as she butters the bread, entertaining Mazie with flourishes of her hand, waving her spatula in the air. Soon, the three of us are seated with bowls of soup and perfectly browned grilled cheese.

With my girls on either side of me, exchanging giggles and stories, it's the best damn meal I've had in a very long time.

Chapter 23
Eloise

I'm more of a daydreamer than usual, my head in the clouds, thinking of Roman.

After I spent the evening with them Saturday night, they came to visit me yesterday, waiting out the Sunday breakfast rush so the three of us could hang out at a table for a bit, sharing a warm cinnamon roll. And I couldn't help but notice how we were becoming more like a couple—like a family—with every one of these near-daily...dates?

It's absurd.

The idea of hanging my hat on the eighteen-foot-tall bull of a man and his delightfully foulmouthed daughter is absurd. There's no way I could fall in love with someone—and their child—so quickly, but the funny feeling in my stomach and the lightness in my chest convince me it is possible.

Normally, I'm a terrible decision-maker. I'm paralyzed by choices, to the point that I avoid them at all costs, but these emotions are real.

There was no choice.

There *is* no choice.

Which is why I think I love Roman.

"All right over there, Elle?" Leonard asks, and I shake myself from my reverie.

"Hm?"

"Are you feeling okay?"

"Oh yeah. I'm fine." I toss a smile his way, though his brows stay furrowed. "Just thinking..."

He hums barely louder than the quiet whir of the appliances, his eyes studying me closely.

"I'm fine," I reiterate, forcing myself back to work, but I can feel his stare on me and lift my attention from the pie crust. "Yes, Lenny?"

"What is it? What's wrong?"

"I'm not paying you to be my therapist," I playfully snap, and he raises his hands, looking side to side.

"Don't see anybody else here, so you might as well tell me what's bugging you. Or you'll never get anything done today."

"It's really rude how you know me so well."

He scoffs an amused sound, deep from his chest, waiting for me to spill it. So I do.

"How did you know you were in love with Ann?"

His bushy brows rise, and his features give way to a knowing smirk. "This about that big guy who's been hanging around?"

"Maybe." I shrug, fooling exactly no one. "What was it like for you? How did you know she was it? Was it a gradual kinda thing or, like..." I explode my hands. "Boom?"

"Boom." He repeats with a soft chuckle that rattles around his chest. Another grump who needs some practice laughing. He places his dough into a bowl and covers it before washing his hands and turning to me. "The moment I laid eyes on her, it was like someone had punched me in the gut. I knew, without a doubt, that she was the one for me."

"Really?" Fully invested in his story, I lean against the counter, watching as Leonard's gaze goes somewhere far away from here, to another time and place, absently wiping his hands off on a towel.

"Really," he confirms. "We were in high school—she went to a different one than me. Her father owned a small grocery store, and I'd just gotten a job there. I had to wear this orange apron and name tag and could not have felt more like a schmuck when she walked in. Breezed right past in this short skirt and long hair like some shampoo commercial. I couldn't stop staring, stopped stocking so I could watch her."

Leonard pauses, a fond smile pulling his mouth up. "Of course, she didn't see me or know who I was, but any time she came in to visit her father, it was like being struck by lightning. And she had no idea." He folds his arms over his chest and meets my gaze, coming back to the present. "Until this one day, she was in the parking lot, arguing with her boyfriend at the time. I'd heard grumbling from her father that he didn't like the guy much, and naturally, I didn't either since he was with the love of my life. But that day, she yelled at him, 'How about I kiss someone else even though it means nothing and see how you like it?' That jackass said, 'Go ahead and try it.'"

I clap giddily, guessing at what happened next. "And she did! With you!"

He nods, a triumphant smile on his face. "It was my lucky day to be walking past, because she grabbed me by the collar and laid one on me."

"I can't believe it! What happened? What did the boyfriend say? What did you say?"

"The boyfriend was pissed and took off. I was...stunned. I couldn't do anything, especially because she wiped her thumb over my lips and apologized for—" he crooks his fingers in quotation marks "—proving a point with me. I said she could prove a point with me anytime."

"So smooth, Lenny!"

"Not that smooth because it took a while before she broke up with him for good, but we eventually got together when her father asked me to give her a ride home. I knew I was going to marry that girl, and I would've waited forever for her. Thankfully, she didn't make me wait that long." He sighs, his eyes going red-rimmed. "We married a few years later, young, dumb kids in love, and every day, I thanked her for proving a point with me."

It's too much, and I press my hands to my chest, flying high from the romance and his love for his wife, sad because she is gone and they are separated now. Unable to take it, I fling my arms around his neck. "That story is so lovely. Thank you for sharing it with me."

He eventually pats my back then gives way to a hug after a few moments. "Thanks for asking me about her. About us."

I bat at my tears before they can spill from my eyes then back away, slugging him in the arm to rid ourselves of the melancholy. "You big softy."

He clucks his tongue, dragging his knuckle over his eyes then props his hands on his hips, back to his usual gruffness. "So, what's the story with your giant?"

"He *is* a giant, right? I don't understand how nature makes people that big."

Leonard washes his hands so he can get back to work. I do *not* get back to work. "I think I might love him, but I'm not sure. I've never been in love before. I mean, I thought I was, but it never felt anything like this, and I don't know if what I'm feeling is love because who falls in love after hanging out literally five times."

"Hanging out," he says, glancing over his shoulder at me. "That's what you kids call having sex, right?"

I whack his shoulder. "You scandalize me!"

He rolls his eyes at me before plucking eggs from the fridge. "From the way you've been walking around here lately, I figured you were *hanging out* a lot more than five times."

"Leonard!"

He shrugs. "There's nothing wrong with it. Ann and I were *hanging out* a lot too. As long as you're being safe."

I cover my face with my hands. "Oh my god. This is worse than the time my parents had this talk with me."

"You can never have it too many times with your kids," he says, and I'm hit with a pang of gratitude. Leonard didn't even realize what he'd said. A slip of the tongue. Referring to me as one of his kids.

But I find myself hugging him again, this time from behind, my head on his shoulder with my arms around his chest. "I love you, Lenny."

"Don't get all weepy on me. Too early for that."

"But you said—"

He nudges my arms off him so he can meet my watery gaze. "I know what I said because I think of you like one of my own, and I'm glad you're happy. If this man makes you happy, don't second-guess it. Hold on to it and don't let go. Love is too fleeting in this life to ever wonder if it's right." He points to his chest and then to mine. "You know in here what it is."

"Thanks, Len."

He elbows me. "Come on, kiddo. We got a lot to catch up on. You can daydream about your boyfriend later. Now, we bake."

"Now, we bake," I agree with a laugh.

* * *

I received a text message from Roman that June was sick and Riley was working, so he didn't have anyone to pick Mazie up from her after-school care and asked if I could. Happy that he asked me, I immediately agreed and made plans for me to go to their place to have dinner and *hang out*.

It's not until after I've had a snuggle with Steve and cut up an apple for him and Mazie to share that I accidentally find a letter. It's while I'm picking through his kitchen, because I'm obsessed with finding out whatever I can about the man I apparently love, and I spy the envelope tucked in a napkin holder with a bunch of other paperwork, like bills, receipts, and coupons for a sandwich shop downtown.

Too curious for my own good, I open it, careful not to rip the envelope any more than it already is, and unfold the paper.

My heart is a drumline in my chest as I skim it, finding who I already have guessed it's from: Amy. I'm not sure when she sent this or if Roman responded to it, but the words are a mix of heartache and hope, a desperate attempt to reach out to the family she's been separated from. She talks about missing Mazie and how she wishes Roman would stop being so stubborn. She also calls him an asshole, which I don't find helpful, but the more the lines of her handwriting slant, the more emotional she becomes. A plea for forgiveness, a written *scream* to be able to see her child.

It guts me, and my hands tremble slightly as I fold it back up and place it in the envelope like I never touched it, but I can't forget it.

The stark reminder of the complexity of their lives, the pain that lingers in the background. It's not my place to pry, but the words in that letter have touched something in me, a newfound tenderness for the woman whose choices have led to so much heartache.

Of course I can understand Roman's anger and pain, but

it's impossible for me not to feel bad for Amy as well. She made bad choices, and now she's paying for them, but for how long does she need to?

I can't think about the question too long because the front door opens, and Roman steps inside, bringing with him the crisp scent of autumn air. I poke my head out of the kitchen, and his eyes find mine immediately. There's a warmth in his gaze that tells me I'm exactly where he wants me to be.

I meet him by the door, sneaking a kiss. He pinches my chin in the now familiar gesture. "Hi, sunshine."

"Hi."

"Thanks for picking her up."

"Whenever you need me to, I'm here," I say, and he answers with another kiss then kicks off his shoes and hangs up his coat on the hook next to the front door.

"Hey, Maze." Roman holds his arms out, and she runs into him so he can pick her up, swinging her around until she shrieks in glee. He kisses her head and cheek before setting her back down. "Hungry for dinner?"

"Yes!"

He holds out his palm for a high five. "No cursing that time, nice."

She slaps it, yelling, "Fuck yeah!"

I hide my laugh, and Roman heaves a sigh, heading toward the kitchen, mumbling his own curses.

When I try to help Roman with the food, he sends me away to keep Steve and Mazie company in the living room, so I spend the next hour watching *Beauty and the Beast* while my mouth waters because of the delicious scents wafting from the kitchen.

"This smells so good," I tell him when he finally calls us to the table, set with our plates, glasses of water, and a big pot of chicken and rice in the middle. He gestures for us to sit down then scoops me out a generous serving. "I'm seriously impressed."

"Don't be." He fills Mazie's pink plate and then adds two scoops to his own. "Mostly everything I make has five ingredients or less."

"Well, I hate cooking, so it looks like you'll be making all our meals," I blurt before I think better of it and freeze with my fork halfway to my mouth.

Roman merely lifts his huge shoulder, his eyes shining, lips quirked to the side, not at all offended by my proclamation. "Guess so."

During dinner, Mazie chatters on about her day at school, her friends, and how she wants a leash for Steve so she can take him for a walk, but Roman immediately vetoes that idea. I stay out of the argument, hiding my amusement by stuffing more of Roman's delicious dinner into my mouth.

Afterward, he announces it's bedtime. She looks up at me with those big brown eyes, so much like her father's. "Will you read to me tonight, Eloise?"

"Yes, of course," I reply, meeting Roman's eyes over her head, seeing nothing but acceptance and love in his gaze. There is no second-guessing. I smile at his daughter. "I'd love to."

I leave Roman to clean up the kitchen while Mazie changes into her PJs, brushes her teeth, and then we settle into her bed, the book about a cat and a unicorn throwing a party spread out between us. It's silly and cute, and she knows almost all the words, mouthing them with me as I read. And when I finish, she tucks the comforter more fully around herself, asking quietly, "Stay with me a little while?"

"Always," I answer and kiss her head, but it's barely five minutes before she's asleep, her breaths even and deep.

When I return to the living room, Roman's waiting for me on the couch, but instead of pulling me down with him like I expect, he stands and wraps his arms around my waist. "Thanks for doing that. It means a lot to her. To both of us."

"Thanks for letting me. I think..." Stopping myself from admitting something I'm not sure I'm ready to say out loud—that I love him and his daughter—I say, "I think if I had a kid, I'd want her to be like Mazie. You've raised a great girl."

"And you're great with her." He brushes a stray lock of hair behind my ear, and I should tell him I read the letter, that it broke my heart all over again, knowing what he and Mazie have been through, but I don't want to betray the trust he's placed in me. Hopefully, we'll have more conversations about Amy, although now is not the time.

Because his lips are on mine, melding our mouths together. It's intense yet soft, emotions behind every lick of his tongue as good as speaking words. I feel love and safety, comfort and passion. It's a slow burn, his hands lazily roaming all over me, keeping the embers sizzling in my belly, but anytime I try to speed him up, he stops and offers me a shake of his head.

Almost like he's trying to tell me something too.

In the way he takes my hand and leads me to his bedroom and gently pushes me to the bed. His eyes track over me with reverence as he removes my clothing. There's no rush, no urgency.

But there is a depth of unspoken feelings, a silent declaration in the tender glide of his hands over me like I'm precious and what we have between us is something to be treasured.

Roman worships me with his fingers and mouth, exploring every curve and dip, pressing soft words into my skin.

My beautiful girl.

Sunshine.

You're perfect.

You're a dream.

"God, Eloise," he rasps against my innermost flesh. "You

are so fucking sweet." He licks up my center, moaning like it's the best thing he's ever tasted. "I want to do this forever."

I breathe out a laugh. "Please do."

In return, he pushes my legs wider, fingertips pressing deep into them with a bruising grip. Then he deliberately scrapes his beard along my hips and thighs, grunting. An animal marking his territory.

I don't mind.

I like the idea of being marked by him.

But when he slips his thick fingers inside me, I can't think about anything other than the fire he stokes in my belly, the heat crawling up my spine, setting my skin aflame. I curl my fingers into his hair, keeping him in place as I reflexively fight his hold against my legs, and he releases a sound that I feel more than hear, rumbling against my clit, and it nearly sends me into a different stratosphere.

I am a panting, sweaty mess, begging to come, and when he finally crooks his fingers against my swollen inner wall, he slaps a pillow over my face to drown out my shout. Though, he doesn't let me rest, dragging me to the edge of the bed, keeping one hand shackled around my ankle while he digs through a side table for a bottle of lube. I happily note that it is brand-new because he has to unwrap it, and the jealous shrew that popped out of its hole can slink away because Roman is mine. No one else's.

He pops the top and squeezes a good amount on his index and middle fingers, smoothing it over the length of my pussy and inside. I'm already swollen and wet, but he mutters things about how I'm not ready for him yet. He bends to suck on one of my nipples, torturing me with his teeth and tongue until I'm squirming all over the bed, and he has to drag me back to him, flipping me over so I'm on my stomach and my feet are on the floor. He moves a pillow under my hips, so my ass is even higher, back arched slightly.

"Fuck yeah, sunshine. Look at this," he growls a moment before his mouth is there, biting my cheek. Then he slaps it, gripping it roughly to pull them apart, revealing *everything* to him. He sinks his face down, the wiry yet soft hair of his beard a stark contrast to the wet touch of his tongue as he licks and kisses me all over before focusing on that hole. I gasp into the sheets, jerking forward, earning another smack.

"Oh god, Roman. Oh my god."

I feel him nod, groaning like he enjoys this as much as licking my pussy. I think I do too.

After another minute, he stands up behind me, and I glance over my shoulder to see him adding more lube to his fingers, dragging it from my front entrance to my back, the tip of his finger invading. "Okay?" he asks, and I nod, pushing my hips up even more, offering all of myself to him. To do with what he wants. "One day, I'll fuck you here. But we have a lot of work to do before then, don't we, Eloise?"

He bends, the thick and heavy length of him settling in the crease of my ass as he nips my earlobe. "What do you think, sunshine? You ready to work?"

"I think you're trying to kill me," I mumble into the sheets, his amusement rumbling in his chest on my back.

"Nah. I like you alive and chatty. So, talk to me. You ready for me to fuck you hard?"

"Yes, daddy," I say against his mouth, a brush of his lips against mine before he calls me his good little girl and straightens once more, pulling my hands behind, settling them at my lower back, holding them together in one of his hands, keeping me exactly where he wants me. Then he's there, pushing his huge cock inside me, giving me a mere few seconds to get used to the feeling before he easily slides out with all of the lube and thrusts back in. True to his word, he fucks me hard, pumping in and out in an unrelenting rhythm, and I can't do anything but lie there, grunting and panting, my body held in place by his.

He is so deep, hitting so far inside me, that it prevents me from taking a full breath, and still, I rise on my tiptoes, needing more. Behind me, Roman grunts a "good girl" that is barely audible, like his teeth are clenched. But a moment later, he slows enough to squeeze out more lube. I'm pure sensation, so worked up and overheated that the cool gel is a shock, and I jolt. "It's okay," he tells me in a low, grating voice that is like sandpaper over my skin. "You're doing so fucking good. Such a good girl, taking me so well."

He smears the lube all over, teasing my clit with a few circles then up to where we're connected, rubbing it all over my pussy and his cock, and up even farther. He pushes his finger inside, deeper than before, ordering, "Relax, sunshine, relax. That's it. Fuck, you're perfect."

And I've never felt fuller as he begins to move again, but this time, it's nowhere near as rough. It's gentler, lazier, a slow glide in and out, his finger mimicking the movement, and I am lost somewhere in space, moaning into the bed, strands of my hair stuck to my lips, my breasts and belly pinned beneath me even as my legs quake.

I am close. So close, all it takes is one synchronized roll of his hips and thrust of his finger, and I am gone. Bright lights spark behind my eyelids and rushing fills my ears, and I feel like I'm being pulled out to sea, unable to see or hear or breathe, wave after wave hitting me, dragging me back under each time I'm about to reach the surface.

The only thing that brings me back is Roman curled over me, his face near mine, his breath hot on the side of my face, his hands massaging my arms and hips and legs. That's when I realize I'm free to move, yet I can't.

Might as well throw me back into the ocean, so I can float.

"You okay?" he asks, and I manage a nod. "You did so good," he tells me, and I nod again. "I'm going to clean you up. Don't move."

I couldn't even if I wanted to, and Roman draws himself up, pulling out of me with a quiet hiss, and drops a smattering of kisses on my neck before leaving me still splayed out on his bed. My body temperature quickly plummets, and goose bumps break out all over my skin. I slowly wiggle my fingers and toes then bend my knees and elbows, working life into my limbs so I can roll to my back. In time for Roman to reappear with a glass of water and a warm washcloth. He carefully swipes the cloth over my face, tucking my hair behind my ears, leaving a kiss on my forehead, then he tenderly wipes it over my most sensitive flesh and places an openmouthed kiss on my throat.

He tosses the cloth in his laundry basket then hands me the water, watching as I drink down the entire thing. Only then does he settle back on the bed, stark naked and entirely too self-satisfied when I mumble, "I think you broke me."

"Fucked you so good you won't be going anywhere anytime soon."

He shuts off the light and wraps his arm around my waist, settling us against the pillows, and I relax into him. "That was your evil plan all along, wasn't it?"

He kisses my shoulder. "Anything to make you stay."

I yawn and close my eyes. "I'm not going anywhere."

Chapter 24
Eloise

It's after nine o'clock in the morning in the middle of the week, and I'm elbow-deep in dirty dishwater in the kitchen at Sweet Cheeks when my phone buzzes with an incoming call. Very few people actually call me because those who know me know I don't answer my phone. So, when I peek at the screen and see my best friend's name, I frown. She, of all people, wouldn't be calling me, and a rock forms in the pit of my stomach, my brain spiraling with every kind of possible reason she might dial my number, and none of them are good.

I wipe off my hands and answer. "What's wrong?"

"Ellie," she says, voice breaking, and so does my heart.

"What? What's wrong?"

"Can you come over? To my house?" She sniffs a few times, and I'm already on the move, ripping off my apron.

"Yeah, of course. I'm on my way." I pocket my phone and tell Leonard I've got an emergency. He wishes me luck but doesn't question it as I head out to the front, flying past Morgan, instructing them to hold down the fort until further notice. They salute me, and I run out to the sidewalk, forgetting that I don't have my coat on until I run headfirst into Roman.

"Jesus fuck," he grates at the same time I rub at my head, having hit it on the middle of his sternum in my rush to get to Sloane. "Are you all right?"

I rub my forehead and blink rapidly. "Sloane called. Something's wrong. I've got to get over to her house right away."

His brow furrows with concern. "Is she okay? What happened?"

"I don't know, she didn't say. Just that she needs me." I'm already moving to step around him, urgency propelling me forward.

He puts a hand on my arm, stilling me. "Hey, take a second. Breathe." His dark eyes search mine. "Do you want me to come with you?"

I'm touched by his offer, but I shake my head. "No, it's okay."

"Where's your coat?"

"I...oh."

He curls his hands around my biceps. "Sunshine, take a minute. You won't be able to help her if you're not in the right frame of mind."

I nod at his direction and inhale deeply through my nose, blow it out of my mouth. "It's only that Sloane always has it together, you know? She's the problem-solver. She's not..."

He kisses my temple. "I get it. It's okay. You're worried for her, and I'm sure you'll be able to help, but you need your coat. It's forty degrees out. Where did you park?"

I wince. "I rode my bike today."

"Eloise." He sighs. "It's November. What the fuck are you doing on a bike in November?"

"I felt like a bike ride this morning." I shrug. "And it didn't feel so cold."

"When the sun was barely up? Jesus." He scrubs his hand over his face. "I gave you that goddamn thing, and I'll take it away if you're gonna be reckless with it."

For a moment, I put aside my worry and lean into him. "You can't take Betsy away from me."

"Who the hell is Betsy?"

"The bike."

He snorts an amused sound. "You're a trip."

Regaining my purpose, I back away from him. "And I have to go."

"Go back inside and get your coat. I'll drive you," he insists in a tone that brooks no argument, so I do as he says and meet him back outside, where he walks me to his car, telling me he'll pick me up later after I give him directions to Sloane's house, about a ten-minute drive from downtown.

"Text me," he says when he parks outside of the brick-and-stucco house.

"I will."

He grasps my chin and presses a hard, bruising kiss to my lips. "Be safe. Let me know if you need anything."

My lips tingle as I pull away. "I will. I've got to run."

With a last squeeze of his hand, I'm jogging to the front door, where I let myself in with the key code, and since no one is screaming and there are no kids here, I take that as a semi-good sign.

"Sloane?" I call out, moving through the entryway toward the stairs. "It's me! I'm here!" I take the carpeted steps two at a time and turn right to her bedroom, pushing open the door to find her crumpled on the floor at the foot of her bed, face buried in her hands.

"Sloane?"

She tips her head up, and as soon as she spots me, she breaks.

Completely.

I sink down beside her and latch my arms around her slim body as she sobs. Sloane is not a crier. For all the bullshit *her* mother feeds her, she's not super emotional. At least, not that she lets out.

I am the emotional one. I am the wreck.

But I am happy to return the favor, to be the one who dries her tears for once.

Holding her close, I press my cheek to her forehead and stroke her hair as she cries into my shoulder. I don't know what to say, so I go with the old standbys. "I love you. It'll be okay. We'll figure it out. I've got you."

Eventually, she quiets and sits up to pull in ragged breaths, and I use the hem of my T-shirt to wipe her face free of snot and tears, not bothering to waste time searching for tissues. She combs her fingers through her long black hair then rubs at her blotchy eyes before apologizing.

"Sorry for—"

"Nope." I hold up my hand. "We're certainly not doing that. Try again."

She takes a breath that makes her shoulders rise as she closes her eyes. "Trevor's cheating on me. He's been cheating on me."

My jaw drops, and that really wasn't on my list of possibilities when I tried to think of what could be wrong.

She meets my gaze, and my best friend is one fucking unbelievable woman because she delivers the rest of the story to me without flinching. "He told me last night after the kids went to bed. There's another woman, and he wants to be with her. He wants a divorce."

"Motherfucker," I seethe. "What the hell? Where is this coming from?"

She shakes her head, chewing on her bottom lip. It's

swollen and chapped. "Apparently, he felt bad for lying to me. That's why he told me. He didn't want to keep lying to me when he loves her."

I choke on a laugh. "*What?*"

Still gnawing on her lip, she stares at me with bloodshot eyes and nods.

"You're ruining your best feature," I say, tapping at her mouth, trying and failing at levity when she cracks, chin wavering as she bows her head and begins to cry again.

"Oh babe, I'm so sorry."

"I just never thought..." She sniffs a few times, and I decide it's time for me to find the tissues. I locate a box then fill up a small cup of water from the faucet in the attached bathroom. She accepts both and dutifully drinks the water.

After a few minutes, she tells me, "He doesn't want to try counseling. Doesn't want to work on things. He just wants her. I was stunned when he told me."

I nod like a bobblehead because...yeah. This is fucking stunning. I always thought the guy was kind of a douche, but I never thought he'd cheat on Sloane.

"And he told you last night?" When she nods, I ask, "Why didn't you call me then?"

"Because I knew once I started crying, I wouldn't stop, and I still had to wake up this morning and get the kids on the bus. I didn't want them..."

I wrap my arm around her shoulders. "You're the best mom I know. Literally. You should be on the cover of magazines and on podcasts and stuff. I don't know how you do it. You do everything for your family. You're an amazing mom, and wife, and you don't deserve this. I hope you know that. I hope in the dark recesses of your mind, you're not letting all the BS make you think this is your fault, because it's not."

She blows her nose, and I know she hears me, but I don't think she *hears* me.

"The funny thing is, when he told me, my first reaction wasn't even about me or my marriage, it was about the kids. What about the kids? What are we going to do about the kids?"

And that's exactly what I was talking about.

Sloane lives for her children.

"The kids will be fine," I say, hoping I'm right. "They're resilient. And with you as their mom?" I wave my hand in the air, swatting away the bad vibes. "There is no way those kids don't turn out to be perfect, loving individuals."

She nods a few times, tears sliding down her cheeks. Then she rasps, "They're all I care about."

"I know, I know, I know." I pull her in for another hug as a new wave of sobs overtakes her, and we sit on the floor for a long time. Until she seems to have dried out.

Then I hold her hand to help her stand and stay with her in the bathroom as she showers because this isn't the first, and I doubt the last, time one of us will need help like this. I hand her a towel and get her dressed in comfy clothes then French braid her hair before we head to the kitchen.

I make us hot chocolate with a tiny splash of vodka because Sloane—of course—has to pick up the kids from the bus stop today. I admire my best friend for a lot of reasons, her big heart, her bravery, her artistry, but also for how she so willingly puts everyone ahead of herself.

It's also the one thing that can and will be her downfall.

It's while I'm making us lunch that I think of the letter I found from Amy. The writings of another mother, wanting to be a part of their child's life. I don't know her apart from what Roman has told me about her, but being here with Sloane, knowing how much she loves her children, makes me think

Amy must feel something similar. She wouldn't write a letter to Roman without wanting to atone.

And I feel the call to help.

I can't stand seeing my best friend hurt, and if Amy is suffering with even a quarter of the same pain, I want to help her too.

I could possibly do something. Maybe act as an intermediary between Amy and Roman. It couldn't hurt to reach out.

But first, I need to get Sloane on her feet and make sure her two munchkins come through this whole nightmare unscathed.

And possibly invent a murder plan for Trevor.

Poison in a cinnamon roll sounds easy enough.

Chapter 25
Roman

"No way! That doesn't count."

"Fuck off," I mutter, muscles twitching, struggling to hold myself up anymore. Wondering how the hell I got here.

I met Ian, Griffin, and Taryn for coffee at Cuppa Jo, and after they took turns giving me shit about *finally* showing up, we chatted idly about nothing in particular until Dante arrived.

It was my first time meeting Taryn's boyfriend, and I liked him right off the bat for how completely and clearly he loves my sister. He struck me as a bit of a goofball, but he said he had some time between project meetings and thought he'd pop down for coffee, hanging out even after Taryn slipped away to return to work.

And somehow I found myself at Stone Ink with my brothers, Taryn's boyfriend, and Ian's kids in a push-up contest. It was Jaybird's dumbass suggestion after he made some comment to Griffin about how he was looking a little weak lately, and then the two were on the floor. All of us agreed to this competition. Loser with the least number of push-ups gets a new tattoo picked out by the winner with the highest number.

Which, in this particular group of men, could mean anything. Especially because we are all gym rats.

"Nah, come on," Jay argues, kneeling down on the floor at my eye level, showing me how I wasn't parallel to the floor. "Your elbows aren't ninety."

I blow out a breath, lowering a smidge before pushing back up.

Jay holds his finger up. "Judges?"

"It counts," Jasper says, but Cash disagrees with a shake of his head.

Dante, the fucking traitor, is the one who declares, "Doesn't count."

I can't take it anymore and give up, flattening myself to the floor and rolling to my back, breathing hard. "That's bullshit. I did chest and tris this morning. You caught me on a bad day."

Ian sticks out his hand to help me up from the floor as Griffin clucks his tongue. "Bad day?"

"Fuck off."

The guy has five years on me, and he's a machine. Dante scrubs his hands together. "So, what's it gonna be, Cap?"

Griffin tosses him a scowl. "Don't call me that."

Dante merely grins. "Ah, come on. You love me."

Griffin shakes his head, earning snickers from all the young bucks.

Cash gestures to his chair so I can accept my punishment while the others quietly discuss options. I hear the words "alien" and "Mickey Mouse" and "pussy." And after hearing some of their stories, I don't doubt they'd put an alien-looking Mickey Mouse with a pussy on me somewhere.

Deciding to text Eloise to check in while they decide my fate, I pull my phone from my pocket.

> How do you make a baker smile?

She messages back almost immediately.

SUNSHINE

How?

> Butter them up.

SUNSHINE

That's so stupid. I love it.

SUNSHINE

Speaking of, don't ever use butter as lube.

> I hope this isn't coming from experience.

SUNSHINE

No! Just spreading the word.

SUNSHINE

Get it? Spread.

SUNSHINE

But seriously.

SUNSHINE

I fell down a rabbit hole about household products and lubricants.

> ?

SUNSHINE

Well, you can use coconut oil as lube and I thought what else can you use that might be in the kitchen? Because I keep coconut oil in the kitchen at all times, so I wanted to know my options. If any. You know?

> No. I've never had that thought.

> Ever.

For The Weekend

SUNSHINE

So do you want to hear what else?

Yes.

SUNSHINE

Crisco, which is not surprising but also ew, right? Then the other natural oils like olive and sesame, avocado, etc. Makes sense. BUT THE MOST SURPRISING IS

SUNSHINE

Drum roll...

When she doesn't text me after a minute, I text her.

Are you going to tell me?

SUNSHINE

I was waiting for the drum roll.

I refuse to laugh, even to myself. Yet, still, I indulge her.

SUNSHINE

Thank you.

SUNSHINE

YOGURT

What?

SUNSHINE

You can use yogurt as lube as long as there is no sugar in it.

That sounds disgusting.

SUNSHINE

Right? But also

SUNSHINE

I am a little curious.

That's too bad because I'm not.

SUNSHINE

Ok. I can still try it.

I almost fumble my phone in my haste to message her back.

the fuck you can

Eloise.

You're not trying anything with anybody.

SUNSHINE

I didn't say I'd try it with other people.

You better not be.

SUNSHINE

What are you trying to say, Roman?

I don't think. I just type.

I'm trying to say you're mine, and you don't try anything with anybody else.

SUNSHINE

🖤

SUNSHINE

You're mine too.

Good.

How's Sloane?

SUNSHINE

Ok.

SUNSHINE

He's been staying with his girlfriend, so it hasn't been much different for the kids since he's away for work a lot anyway. But I can see it wearing on her. I'm just trying to do what I can for her.

You are. You're a good friend.

SUNSHINE

Text me later? I was thinking about trying to convince Sloane to take the kids out to eat for dinner. Maybe you and Mazie can come?

Yeah. We can do that.

SUNSHINE

By the time I slide my cell phone into my back pocket, my so-called family is all staring at me, a mix of curiosity and goofy grins across their faces.

Jaybird starts in on his bullshit. "Who was that?"

"Eloise, obviously," Ian says, and he used to be my favorite brother, but Griffin is now.

"You two a thing?" Dante asks, head tipped to the side, and I shrug even though I basically just laid my claim on her during that text exchange.

Ian takes a seat on his rolling chair. "Never a question."

"Like you have room to talk," I say, and Ian bows his head, not bothering to argue or hide his growing smile. He's the definition of pussy-whipped by the cute bookstore owner next door.

Not unlike how I'd follow the baker next door on my hands and fucking knees if she asked.

"Stepmommy's got him by the balls," Jay teases, and Jasper actually chimes in.

"Literally."

That gets Ian's attention, and he faces his eldest son. "What?"

"You scarred June for life. She found...something in the bathroom and came screaming to me about it last night."

Ian freezes as Jay leans in. "*What?*"

Griffin and I trade glances. I fear whatever it is that's about to come out might scar us all.

Jasper rubs at his forehead and blows out a pained breath. "She..." He meets his father's gaze head on. "She found your cock ring."

Jay slaps his hand to his chest as Dante splutters a laugh. Griffin coughs a few times while Cash turns away from us all, becoming very busy with his tattooing instruments. I drop my head, tunneling my fingers into my hair, not sure whether to laugh or cry or run for the hills.

Ian clears his throat and waits until the rest of us are all looking at him before he crosses his arms and gives us his best paternal eyebrow arch. "We're gonna need to have a conversation—"

"You gave us the sex talk in fourth grade," Jay interrupts.

"And in sixth," Cash says, presumably because he received every talk right along with Jay and Jasper.

"And you gave me a book on female pleasure in high school," I add, which cracks his boys up.

Griffin mutters a "dear Jesus" as Dante props his hands on his hips, saying, "Man, I wish I grew up in this family."

Ian ignores it all, focusing on Jasper, Jaybird, and Cash. "We're gonna need to have a conversation about living arrangements soon."

"Because with Junie still living in your apartment, you can't fuck your girlfriend wherever you want?" Jay guesses, and Ian isn't at all embarrassed.

"Yep."

Jay smacks at his ear like he's trying to rid that information from his head, while Cash appears deliberately uninterested, readying his tattoo gun for me while Jasper and Ian talk about where Juniper might move and when, though I really doubt it would ever really happen. They're all so protective of her. Hell, so am I.

But being here, in this community, spending time with my family, is changing me. Making me care about inane things I never would have before. Like push-up contests, cock rings, and the living arrangements for my twenty-one-year-old niece.

"So," Cash says, standing next to me with his rubber gloves on. "Where you want it?"

I check out what space is left on my arms, not really wanting to drop trou, even though I have more free skin on my legs. Instead, I hike up the sleeve of my T-shirt and point to the bit of open space on my triceps, next to my mom's tattoo.

Cash has a seat and gets to work on my loser tattoo as Griffin clears his throat. "As a reminder, Thanksgiving is at our house at five. Everyone needs to text me what they're bringing." He fixes his gaze on me. "I assume you'll bring Eloise."

I don't answer, the sting of the needle in my arm and the overwhelming feeling of being part of this family fogging up my mind. It's been years since I've seen them, and they so easily accepted me back into the fold. I'm not sure I deserve it, but there is nothing I appreciate more.

I think Griffin can see everything I'm not able to articulate because he nods once. "She's part of the family, right?"

Ian agrees then says, "Sloane will probably come too. With everything going on..."

The trailed off thought sends all seven of us into a moment of silence.

And then we all talk at once.

"Fucking scumbag."

"I always thought he was a fucking weasel."

"If he didn't have money and connections, I'd go fuck him up."

"He's got a punchable face."

"Such a punchable face!"

"He's not worth it, though. Karma will take care of him eventually."

"And if it doesn't? My right hand likes karma."

"Sloane doesn't deserve that shit."

"I'm surprised Eloise hasn't murdered that fuckwit yet."

They all turn to me, and I shrug. My girl struggles with standing up to her own family, but I think if given the chance...

"I'd imagine she'd go for his eyes first."

They all agree and eventually move on to a different topic: food.

After another few minutes, Cash announces he's all finished and wipes down my new ink. I turn, holding up my sleeve to view it in the mirror, and I can't help the idiotic grin that crawls across my face at the tribute to Eloise.

"It's perfect," I say eventually and dap him up before clapping hands with the rest of the younger guys and hugging my brothers.

"Thought you'd like it," Griffin says, and I nod.

Ian slings his arm around my shoulders, telling me seriously, "Don't break her heart. She's one of our favorites around here."

"Mine too."

Chapter 26
Roman

Between my schedule and everything going on with Sloane, Eloise and I haven't been able to connect for time together until now. So when she texted, asking if I wanted to go out, I immediately asked Riley and June to babysit Mazie and made a reservation at Tabby Cat.

Eloise and I had seen each other over the last few days and exchanged plenty of text messages, but the thought of finally being alone with her makes my skin buzz with anticipation. I missed her.

I fucking missed her.

When she opens the door of her apartment, I'm not prepared. She's wearing her hair piled on the top of her head with loose strands by her temples and the smile I've come to think of as my own. The one that crinkles her eyes but is a bit shyer, her teeth digging into her bottom lip like she's afraid to unleash her full wattage. I love it.

I fucking love her.

Her chunky sweater with huge sleeves reminds me of a blanket, and there's nothing I want more than to wrap myself up in it with her. Instead, I use it to pull her to me. "Hey, sunshine."

"Hi, Rome," she says, voice all smoke and gravel and choking me.

Or maybe that's my heart in my throat.

I'm not sure. I can't tell.

But I am sure that the day I first saw her, laughing in Wawa at Mazie, I was attracted to her. Then when I spotted her out back of her bakery, covered in flour and laughing at herself, I fell in love. I loved her then without knowing.

I love her even more now.

It overwhelms me. Like I can't breathe without her. She's everywhere. The air in my lungs, the never-ending loop in my head, the steady beat in my heart.

I love her smile and energy, her compassion and humor. I love the way she makes me feel and how she takes care of Mazie. I love the way she tells me everything that crosses her mind and texts like she's having a conversation in person. I love her insecurities and all of her confidence. I love every piece of her. Every bit of sunshine and every shadow.

And I can't do anything besides crowd her against the door. My mouth finds hers in a kiss that's equal parts hunger and reverence. It's been a week since I've tasted her, though it may as well have been a year.

She tangles her fingers in my hair, and I lift her up, wrapping her legs around my waist. We're a jumble of limbs and need. It's frantic and desperate, a clash of desire that neither of us can contain.

"Missed you," she breathes against my lips, and I growl in agreement, roaming my hands over her body, reacquainting myself with every dip and curve.

"Need you," I admit, and it's more than physical. It's a craving that goes deeper than skin, an ache only she can soothe.

I carry her past the kitchen, but my eye catches on a bottle, and I can't help the amused sound that escapes the back of my throat.

Eloise lifts her head, eyes dazed, lips swollen. "Hm?"

"The olive oil," I say with a jut of my chin toward it. She follows my line of sight and inhales sharply, a wild grin taking over her face.

The smile when she's really excited about something. "You wanna?"

I set her on the counter to pull her sweater over her head and lean down to draw my tongue over the soft flesh barely contained by her bra. "Wanna what?"

"Try olive oil?"

I step back and tug my own shirt over my head, still not comprehending the suggestion until she unscrews the cap and pours a drop on her index and middle fingers before rubbing her thumb over it and smearing it over her collarbone. She drags her fingers down the dark valley between her tits, and I swallow thickly, imagining oiling her up all over.

I nod, take the bottle from her hand, and throw my woman over my shoulder. She shrieks in laughter, smacking my ass a few times. As soon as I toss her on the bed, I kick off my boots and strip off my jeans and underwear. "Naked," I tell Eloise. "Get naked now unless you want your clothes ripped in half."

She doesn't hesitate, yanking off her black leggings and flinging her thong at me. Before she can remove her bra, I pounce on her, unclasping it myself. I should be moving slower, taking my time, worshipping her properly, but I'm too keyed up from being away from her for so long. I need to inhale her. Drink her in. Swallow her down.

Eloise is my new addiction, and that is the one thought that has me taking a pause.

A breath.

So I don't completely lose myself and ruin my fresh start before it's barely started.

Kneeling between her open legs, I reach for the bottle of olive oil and spill some into my palm, rubbing my hands together before spreading it over her thighs and stomach. Eloise is already soft and pliant, but with the way she trembles under my touch, I can tell she wants more.

I dribble a line across her chest from nipple to nipple and rub it in, flicking my thumbs over the stiff pink points, admiring the sheen on her skin, the visible tracks of my fingers across her breasts and belly. When I drag my hand between her legs, she shudders, and I watch as she flushes pink all over as I press my fingers into her already wet pussy, stretching it, working her sensitive flesh until she's coming on my hand.

She mewls and closes her eyes, shifting under me, and I place my right hand around her throat in a hold that isn't at all tight, but does always seem to settle her. She likes my palm around her, my fingertips against her beating pulse. She knows I'd never hurt her, and when our eyes meet, she curls her fingers around my forearm, keeping me in place. Then she hits me right in the solar plexus when she says, "You make me feel safe. Like nothing can touch me. Nothing can hurt me."

I hope so. Because I protect what's mine, and as long as she'll have me, I will always keep her safe.

Bending, I lick into her mouth as if I could draw her words into my mouth, and I roll us so we're on our sides, her back to my front and wrap my left arm around her neck to keep her close, smoothing my right hand down the length of her. I pull her top leg up and back over my thigh, meeting her lips when she turns her face to mine for a kiss, and I toy with her clit for a few moments until she's rolling her hips too much.

Too much for me to handle without being inside her.

With so much oil between us, it takes almost no effort to

slowly thrust inside her, and she cries out. I stop, waiting until I know she's all right, until she reaches for me, wanting another kiss, until she begins to rock back and forth.

Then I let her go, let her use me how she needs, taking my cock inside her with every shift forward and back. I palm her hips, her ass, her breasts, kiss her shoulder and lick along the shell of her ear. I strum her clit, bringing her to the brink again, her inner walls pulsing around my shaft, taking me farther inside her. Seated to the hilt, I'm sure she'll be sore tomorrow, but when I check in with her, she wants me to keep going, so I do. I roll her to her back and hold myself above her, sliding inside her easily, taking over when she's too wild with pleasure.

I'm not sure how long we're at it, wrapped up in each other, slick with sweat and oil, but time has ceased to exist. There's only Eloise, her body moving in perfect harmony with mine, her sighs of pleasure echoing my own.

The olive oil has turned our sex into something almost primal. The evidence is everywhere—on our skin, in our hair, smeared across the sheets. It's a mess, but the best kind, and with Eloise beneath me, her eyes locked on mine, sweat dotting her brow and upper lip, she's never looked more untamed or beautiful. I can feel her tightening around me, her body coiling like a spring as she nears her peak. The same one I'm climbing. I grit my teeth, willing myself to hold on a little longer.

"Roman," she gasps, her voice a plea. "I need... I need..."

I cut her off with a kiss, swallowing her words as I thrust into her one last time. Her fingers dig into my back, her nails scoring my skin, and I welcome the sweet sting of pain. It's a reminder that this is real, that this incredible woman is mine and I am hers.

Then with a final whimper, my girl shatters around me. Her body convulses, clamping down on my cock as her orgasm sweeps through her. It's too much, and with a hoarse shout of my own, I follow her into the abyss.

For a moment, there's nothing but the pounding of our hearts and the tattered sound of our breathing. We're both covered in a fine sheen of sweat and oil, our bodies slick and spent. But it's a good feeling, satisfying, and I pull her into my arms as I roll off her.

We lie in silence, our bodies entwined, our breaths slowly returning to normal. I feel the steady thump of Eloise's heart against my chest, and I know we're right where we're supposed to be. I tell her the one thing I know to be true in life. "You make me happy."

She smiles against my shoulder a moment before she drops a kiss there. "I think we missed our dinner reservation."

"I'll order us delivery."

"Sushi?"

"Whatever you want."

She eventually sits up, grinning. "You really know how to woo a girl. Fuck her until she walks crooked then order her whatever she wants. I think I'll keep you."

My eyelids are heavy, but I force them to stay open as I pinch her chin between my fingers. "I'm keeping you too."

She twists her face and kisses my palm before slipping off the mattress. "We'll have to do laundry."

"Whatever you say."

"And take a shower. Get all this greasy stuff off us."

"If you insist."

She nods, mischief glittering in her green eyes. "I insist."

The problem is, once we're both in the shower, it's not at all like we expected, and I can barely fit in behind her.

Under the spray of the water, Eloise pouts. "Movies make two-person showers seem a lot sexier."

I nod, attempting not to elbow her as I soap up.

"Doesn't help that you're the size of Godzilla," she teases as I carefully step around her to rinse off.

"You never had a problem with it until now."

"That's because we never showered together until now. We're going to have to win the lottery to buy a shower big enough to fit the both of us."

I plant a kiss on her temple. "Finish up. I'll order dinner. What'd you want?"

"Get it from Mio's parents. They have the best seaweed salad. I like pretty much any roll from them, except for the specials. They're too big. I can't fit them in my mouth."

I can't help it. I laugh, and she points at my face. "Adding it to my tally!"

"Tally?"

"The I made Roman Edgar Stone laugh tally."

I roll my eyes at her ridiculous guessing game of my middle name and step out of the shower. "My middle name is Yousef."

"Yousef?" she repeats, clearly surprised.

"My mother's father was from Iran. She gave all us boys the same middle name in honor of him."

Eloise presses her hand to her throat. "That's really sweet. I had no idea—"

"Hurry up," I tell her. "I'm hungry, and we can talk about that more while I'm eating."

She salutes me and pulls the shower curtain closed, starting in on an off-key version of the Stones' "Beast of Burden," and I laugh silently to myself. Eloise Thorne is my absolute favorite.

After dressing in my jeans and T-shirt, I head out to the living room to place our food order. Grabbing a seat at her kitchen table, I notice the pile of mail scattered on her kitchen counter. I wouldn't normally pay it any mind, but a specific envelope catches my attention. It's from Champlain Valley Rehabilitation Facility for Women. Amy's prison.

My heart rate spikes, and everything slows as I move to get a better look. I glance down the hall to where Eloise is still in the bathroom, being adorably bad at singing, and yet somehow my world is crumbling out here.

Because I know whatever is in that envelope will wreck this.

I pick it up, seeing Eloise's full name and address scrawled in handwriting I know all too well. Turning it over in my hands, I find the envelope unopened, and before I can think better of it, I tear it open to pull out the thin sheet of paper.

The words blur together at first, my mind struggling to process what I'm reading. But then, it all comes into focus. Amy's writing to thank Eloise for reaching out then goes on to say how she's changed, how she deserves a second chance, and how all she wants is to see Mazie.

I know he's stubborn, but I think he's being cruel now just to punish me. I'm not sure how good of friends you are, but you should know he's not very loyal. Look at what he's doing to me. I appreciate you reaching out, and I hope you can help, but I won't hold my breath. Because look where he is, and look where I am.

I love my daughter, and he doesn't care.

My vision goes red, and I have trouble reading the last few sentences.

I slam the letter down on the counter and lean onto my elbows, gripping my hair by the roots, pissed that Amy would attack me. Would dare to say I don't care, when all I do is care.

But more than that...Eloise.

She knew about this.

She contacted Amy and didn't tell me.

The woman I loved went behind my back when I trusted her. I told her everything, more than I've ever told anyone else. And she twisted it for her own means.

Why? I can't begin to fucking imagine, but the pain in my chest isn't the good kind anymore.

It's betrayal.

I shove the letter back into the envelope, my hands shaking with anger as I hear the shower shut off.

She was in there for fucking ever, and now... Now I don't even want to see her.

Needing to get out of here, to clear my head, I storm out her door, not bothering to tell Eloise where I'm going or what happened. If she can't be bothered to inform me she's communicating with my ex and the mother of my child, I certainly don't owe her any goddamn explanations.

Because one thing is for sure—I'm not ready to let Amy back into Mazie's life. No matter how much she begs and pleads, she obviously hasn't changed. Still hanging the blame for her choices on anyone else besides herself. And if Eloise thinks otherwise, if she believes she can hide something like this from me...

Moving to West Chester was supposed to be my new start.

Eloise was my breath of fresh air.

Except it's all poisoned. I don't want to breathe it in anymore. I can't let it near Mazie. I can't let it ruin what I'm trying to rebuild.

And if Eloise is going to force my hand, I'll do what I have to. Even if it means breaking my own heart.

Chapter 27
Eloise

Last night had been amazing.

Until it wasn't.

It started with Roman showing up at my door and staring at me like I created the moon and stars. He kissed me like he never wanted to stop and made love to me like...like he loved me.

But then he left. Without a word. Or text. Or note. Nothing.

By the time I finished cleaning myself up and tossing on some sweats, he was gone. Like he was never there.

Save for the open and slightly crinkled letter on my kitchen counter. The one from Amy, a reply to my letter.

And I knew I'd fucked up.

My attempts to reach out to him, to explain, were met with silence. Texts went unanswered, calls right to voice mail. For how he opened up to me, he certainly shut down even easier.

I knew he was pissed. There would be no other reason for him to ignore me, but I deserved to be heard out. We needed to have a conversation about this.

I loved him, and even though he might assume I contacted Amy for other reasons, it was only to help. I would only ever want to help him and Mazie.

But with every hour that passes, my own anger rises.

I thought he would be more mature than this, giving me the cold shoulder. No, we'd never officially declared anything about each other, but we were together. I didn't need to label him as anything other than mine. I hurt him, but his ignoring me hurt too, and nothing could be solved in this endless cycle.

Trying to take my mind off it, I ended up at Sweet Cheeks at five in the morning and worked straight through for hours with music in my headphones and flour on my hands. It's not until after noon that I finally take a break. As I'm lugging trash out to the bin in the back, a familiar black monster of an SUV pulls into the lot. Then the familiar figure steps out, his dark eyes finding mine immediately.

"Why are you outside without a coat on?" he asks, his breath forming clouds in front of his mouth.

"Because I was running the trash out, but then I saw you and... What happened?"

"You want to talk? *Now?*"

I shrug. Now is as good a time as any. "Why not?"

He mumbles a curse and yanks off his coat to put around my shoulders. The fleece is warm, and it smells like him. I slide my arms into it, pulling it tight around me, and inhale deeply until my eyes sting. Roman's hard, angry features cause my throat to clog.

But he doesn't speak. Merely folds his big arms across his even bigger chest. The place I'd lain my head yesterday, listened to his heartbeat. Now, he might as well be a stranger. Less than that.

An enemy.

I swallow down the lump in my throat and cling to indignation. He has to hear me out. It's not fair he ignored me all night. It's not okay that he's purposefully trying to hurt me.

"Why did you leave?" I ask. "Why didn't you answer any of my calls or texts?"

He scrubs his hand over his face and hair, his posture losing some of its rigidity. Like maybe he can't hold on to his resentment or whatever it is he's feeling about me right now. It takes him a while, but finally he answers, "I didn't want to say anything I'd regret."

"But I'd rather have you be mad at me and talk about it than completely shut down and shut me out. That hurts. I—"

"It hurts?" He scoffs. "How about finding out the person you trust most in the world has been communicating with the person who destroyed that world? How about that fucking hurt, Eloise?"

I flinch at his tone. "I didn't mean to hurt you."

"But you did. You went behind my back and contacted her. After everything I told you about her, about everything that went down, you still thought it would be a good idea to talk to her. Without talking to me." He slaps at his chest like a wounded animal.

I wounded him, and I take a step toward him. He takes one back. "Why did you even do that? How did you know how to reach her?"

He asks his questions like I'm a threat.

I guess that's how he's interpreting it.

"The other week...I saw a letter she sent you. It was in your kitchen, and I felt... I was heartbroken reading it. For you and Mazie, and for Amy, and after everything that's been happening with Sloane, seeing the breakdown of her family, I guess..." I blink away my tears, trying not to back down in the face of his contempt. "I was trying to help. I thought maybe if she changed—"

"Changed?" he interrupts, his laugh bitter and cold. "You think she's changed because she wrote you a letter? You don't know her, Eloise. You don't know what she's capable of."

My heart aches at the torture in his voice, but I won't be made to feel guilty for trying to mend a broken family. "But she wants to be involved. Why can't you hear her side?"

"Her side?" He throws his arm out, his voice rising to a near shout. "Her side of the story is continually choosing drugs over her own daughter. Over our relationship. Goddamn, Eloise!" He turns in a tight circle, cursing before facing me again. "How fucking naive are you?"

The words burn, but I stand my ground. "I'm not naive. I just believe in second chances. You got one. She should too."

Roman leans in, his voice a low growl. "And what about your own family, Eloise? How many chances have you given them? How many times have you let them walk all over you?"

I jerk back, shocked by the sudden shift in the conversation. "What does that have to do with anything?"

"It has everything to do with it. You can't even stand up to your own parents. How the hell do you think you can tell me how to fix my family when you can't even fix your own?"

I think it would have hurt less if he'd tackled me to the ground.

For the way the air is knocked out of me, it feels like he has.

I stumble back a few steps, my breath lurching as I surrender the fight with my tears.

I've always struggled to assert myself with my family, to make them see me for who I am, rather than who they want me to be. But that doesn't mean I'm incapable of understanding the complexities of Roman's situation.

I sniff a few times, wiping my cheeks with the backs of my hands. "I may not have all the answers, but that doesn't mean I don't care. That doesn't mean I can't see the love you have for

Mazie, the sacrifices you've made." I take a deep breath, my voice cracking. "And I don't know why you'd punish me for trying to help. I'm sorry I didn't talk to you about it, but I didn't want to bring it up if nothing came of it. I was only trying to help, and I don't think..." I clear my throat, blink until my vision clears. "I didn't think you'd so easily believe I'd hurt you on purpose. I didn't think you'd throw what you know about *my* family back at me."

His expression softens for a moment, a flicker of regret in his eyes, but it's gone as quickly as it appeared. "Eloise—"

I hold up a hand, cutting him off. "You're not the only one who's allowed to be angry. You're not the only one who's allowed to feel betrayed."

Silence hangs heavy between us. He lets his chin dip, his attention on the pavement as his jaw works like he's chewing on his words, and I'm suddenly all out of fight. So I give him the last of my truth. "I thought I loved you. I thought you loved me. But I guess it was really fake after all."

I can see the impact it has on Roman, the way his face pales, his fists clench at his sides. But I can't take it back. I'm not sure I want to.

For a long moment, we stand there, watching each other. His shoulders rise and fall with every breath, unaffected by the bitter November chill even as I wear his coat. Meanwhile, I'm freezing, not from the cold but from the space between us. The hole opened up clear through my chest that's allowing the wind to whip around inside me.

The three feet that separate us might as well be three miles, and I can barely hear him when he speaks again. "I don't know what to say."

I bite my cheek, struggling to find my voice in the chaos of my emotion, and I have to clear my throat a few times before I can speak. "I don't know either."

Stupid.

This is all so stupid.

How we went from being on top of the world to being buried underneath it.

Or, at least, that's how it feels for me.

Like I'm clawing through six feet of dirt, losing my grip, gasping for air.

An eternity passes before Roman moves. He steps forward and extends his arm, his hand out toward me, and for a second, I think he's going to touch my chin. He's going to pinch it, his thumb and forefinger squeezing, his eyes caught on my lower lip.

I think that's what he's going to do, but he doesn't. His hand lands heavily on my shoulder. "You should go inside. It's cold out."

I breathe out a rough laugh at my assumptions. At my fantasies that seem so ridiculous now. Making more of what we had than there was.

And this feels like the end.

I start to take off his coat, though he doesn't remove his hand from my shoulder, almost like he wants me to keep it on.

The idea kills me.

Actually stops my heart.

My broken fucking heart.

"Here." I shrug, taking off his coat before I can think twice or he can stop me. I hold it out to him, and even though I have trouble keeping his gaze, I can feel it on me. He's slow to accept the coat, and I shake it at him. Silently begging him.

Please, don't make it hurt worse.

When he finally accepts it, his fingertips brush mine, and it's amazing how that tiny touch ricochets through me.

Maybe because I fear it's the last one I'll ever have.

"I think..." His voice is rough, and he pauses for a second

before continuing. "I think maybe we need some time. To think."

I nod even as my heart cracks further. He's right. We both need space to process this. But the idea of not seeing him, not talking to him, feels unbearable.

Still, I force myself to say, "Yeah. That's probably for the best."

Another endless moment passes, and I force my eyes up to his. They're red-rimmed. He seems to be on the verge of speaking, his lips parting then pressing together again. But whatever it is remains locked away.

Better for it. I'm not sure I'd be able to handle it without completely crumbling.

I gesture vaguely behind me. "I've, uh...gotta get back."

He nods but keeps quiet, and it takes me much longer than I'd like to admit to turn away from him. At the back door to Sweet Cheeks, I chance a glance over my shoulder to find him glaring at the ground, mouth moving in words I can't hear, and there is one part of me that wants to go back to him, comfort him.

Yet there is another, bigger part of me that's finally breaking through the wall of keeping the peace. That voice is telling me to stop being a doormat. To hold my ground and speak up for what I want and demand to be treated with respect.

I just hate the voice only showed up now. When it came with a cost.

Chapter 28
Roman

I've been avoiding Aster Street for the last three days, but Mazie was invited to a birthday party, and she insisted we go to Chapter and Verse because the birthday girl loves unicorns and we *have* to buy her a Kitty-Corn book. So, like the total coward I am, I park on the opposite side of Sweet Cheeks and drag Mazie into the bookstore, hoping I don't run into anyone.

Of course, that could never happen.

Nicole isn't behind the counter, but Clara and Marianne are there, browsing around the bookshop, and as soon as my daughter runs inside, they light up, opening their arms for hugs. They might not be biologically related, but they are part of the extended Stone family, regardless, and Mazie has become the apple of everyone's eye. Including Taryn's best friend and her irritatingly nosy wife.

"Hello, handsome," Clara says, gazing at me like I'm a kicked dog. "How ya doing?"

"Fine," I grumble, and she places her hand on my arm.

"Are you?"

"Yes."

She laughs at me as Marianne slips her arm around Clara's shoulders. "We heard what happened with you and Eloise."

I wrench back. "What do you mean, you heard what happened with me and Eloise?"

"That you two got into a fight."

I scrub my hand over my face. "How? How do you know?"

Clara tips her head, in the direction of Sweet Cheeks, sitting right on the other side of Stone Ink. "She's been an absolute bear."

I huff. No way. That's not Eloise. "I'm sure that's not true."

Marianne lifts a shoulder. "She's been a tad cranky."

Clara snorts a laugh. "A lot cranky. A pretty good impression of you, actually."

I roll my eyes. "I don't know why you even care. Why does anyone in this town care?"

They both smile at me like I'm an idiot. Which only annoys me more.

"You're the prodigal brother," Clara supplies. "Everyone's favorite mystery. And Eloise is a popular woman. Of course there will be whispers about you two when you go out to Tabby Cat together, when people spot you kissing and holding hands." She presses her hand to her chest. "Sets my little romantic heart on fire. The grumpy bad boy returning home and the sweet sunshine girl? I mean…"

Marianne shakes her head in amusement at her wife then turns to me. "What she means to say is, we care about you. We care about your well-being. Your whole family, your friends—whether you believe you have them or not—we want to see you happy, and it was clear Eloise made you happy."

As Mazie sprawls out on the floor with a book, the shop cat

next to her, I rub at my neck, tense from not sleeping well the past few nights. The exhaustion has been wearing on me, the anger I thought would make me feel better doing nothing to stem the pain at not having Eloise. Not being with her.

She is my panacea. But I don't know how to undo what I've said. How to move on from what she did.

With my mind on the relationship I've ruined with the apparent bear of a baker, I don't notice the owner of Chapter and Verse until she's almost right next to me, looking suspiciously...unkempt. Tangled hair, flushed cheeks, and the buttons of her top are mismatched.

Clara and Marianne break out in laughter, and Nicole realizes she's wearing her shirt all wonky and quickly fixes it, her face glowing even more red.

"Nice little lunch break you had?" Clara asks.

Nicole pointedly does not answer. Instead, she moves behind the counter, pulling two books off a shelf. "I have your orders here."

Marianne smothers a grin as she hands over a card to pay, and I remember that conversation I was forced to endure last week about Ian and Nicole's...proclivities.

"Where's Ian?" I ask Nicole, and she gestures upstairs.

"The apartment."

"You mind watching Mazie for a few minutes?"

She shakes her head, and I offer Clara and Marianne a wave as I head over to Stone Ink, silently greeting Riley and Jaybird on my way to the back, so I can take the stairs to the second floor.

I knock twice before opening the door to find my brother lounging in the living room, and he looks up from the paperback copy of *Persuasion* he's reading and lowers the glasses he only wears when he's working or reading.

"Am I interrupting your postcoital quiet time?"

Ian rubs his hand over his mouth and beard, a self-satisfied smile gracing his face. "Ah, you run into Nic?"

"Yep."

He nods and motions for me to take a seat, so I do, but he waits me out. Not bothering to ask what's wrong. Probably because he already knows. *Everyone* knows.

I last all of one minute before I let it all fly. I tell him about how I first met Eloise the night I moved back and that nothing felt more right than being with her at the wedding. Like I was supposed to be at her side, like I'm *always* supposed to be at her side. I explain how it feels like every bad thing I've ever experienced in life is all worth it if she's my reward on the other side.

It's when I come to the more recent events with Eloise and Amy that I need to pace the room. I've felt like clawing out of my skin every day since we had our confrontation out back, and the one thing that's been keeping me sane is staying in motion. Without Eloise's constant energy and chatter surrounding me, I feel like I've been standing still. And I miss it.

I miss her.

And yet...

"I know she was just trying to help, but it hurt. I don't want Amy in Mazie's life. Not yet, at least."

"Understandable."

It is understandable, which makes me angrier. More confused.

Like I need to defend myself and my choices.

"I'm pissed. She went behind my back. Never even asked or had one conversation about her idea. It's not okay."

Ian nods. "I can see why you'd be pissed."

His nonjudgmental tone sends me further into a spiral.

I complete another lap. "I know Eloise would never deliberately hurt anyone, especially Mazie."

"And definitely not you," Ian agrees.

"But it's hard to know what the right thing to do is in my situation, and I have to follow my gut to protect my daughter."

"And yourself," Ian adds.

"Yeah, exactly. I'm protecting myself." Blowing out a breath, I slow my steps. "I guess that's why I got so mad. I've spent so many years trying to build up this safety net, and in that moment, it felt like she tore it all down. Whether she meant to or not, she took something that I fought so hard to make and broke it."

I spin around to face Ian, with his even stare and placid features, listening intently. I let the last of it go. "Because I love her, it hurts more. I don't expect it from anyone, especially Eloise, but I thought..."

"You don't expect what?"

"Love." It's difficult, but I force the one word out, knowing I'm admitting to a particular issue that's bigger than Eloise and me.

She is pure happiness and sunshine and loves with her whole heart. How could I possibly be good enough for her? I don't deserve her love. I don't deserve anyone's.

This has Ian shifting on the couch, his even tone spiking, "You still don't think you deserve it, huh?"

I slant my gaze away, unable to hold his. Then I shake my head.

Ian stands up, not even a yard between us. "Look at me, Roman."

When I do, it hurts, the amount of kindness and understanding in his eyes. I may not have known my father, but I've known my brother. Rough around the edges, yet all c heart on the inside. He reaches out to grip my shoulders, squeezing. "There is nothing you can do that would make me stop loving you. *Nothing*. All the shit you did, all the mistakes you made, it means nothing to me. And you may blame yourself for any number of things, but no one else does. Your past is exactly that, *past*, and I'm only gonna tell you this one time, okay? Mom would be disappointed in you—not because of your past, but because of what you're doing now. How you've worked so hard and come so far and still you think you don't deserve love."

He yanks me into him, holding me tight. "I love you. *We* love you. But until you accept you're worthy of it, you're going to keep fucking up."

I wrap my arms around him, my palms flat against his back, eyes closed tight against the sting in them, and Ian pats the side of my head like I'm a child.

At the moment, it feels like I am.

"One argument isn't worth throwing away your entire relationship with Eloise, because *you* are worth it," he says, and I duck my head to his shoulder, embarrassed by the lump in my throat and threatening tears. He merely runs his hand over my head. "You are so much more than your addiction. You are the father of a funny and smart little girl. You are the grandson of an immigrant and the son of a single mother who wanted nothing more than for you to succeed. You have gone through hell and come out the other side. Don't keep punishing yourself for your past, because you deserve to be happy, and you are worthy of love."

He tugs me away from him, holding my head in his hands so I can't look away and ignore him when he says, "I love you. Griffin, Taryn, the kids, they all love you. It's up to you to decide to accept it or not."

Then he lets me go with a shrug and steps back. "You came home, so you might as well accept the rest. We're family—all of us—and no matter how long it takes for you to understand, none of us are going anywhere."

I swipe my clammy palm over my face and nod a few times, although I can't seem to find my voice. But he clearly doesn't expect me to respond because he slaps his hand hard on my shoulder. "Now, go make me proud and get your girl. She's scaring all her customers away."

If I weren't so overwhelmed with emotion, I might find it humorous, but I can't do much else besides shake his hand and see myself out, taking a few deep breaths before slipping back inside Chapter and Verse, where Mazie greets me with a piece of paper. "Look at this! I drew it!"

"What is it?" I ask, taking it from her hands.

"Us. Our family."

"Good job on giving me blue hair."

She giggles. "Thank you."

"You drew our family? Who's that?"

She points to each figure in her crayon drawing. "That's you and me and Steve and Eloise."

Of course. Who else would have yellow hair and a pink dress with brown...spots all over it. "What are those?"

"Cimanin rolls," she says like I should've known, and I guess I should have.

My throat tightens, and I scoop Mazie up into a hug. "I love it."

She smacks my shoulder a few times. "Can you hang it up?"

"Yeah."

"In a frame?"

"If that's what you want."

"Can we go see Eloise now? I want a cimanin roll."

"Not today. You have your friend's party." And I have some groveling to do.

"Oh yeah! Well, let's go! Hurry up."

I purchase the book Mazie picked out for her present then choose to carry her to the car because I feel torn in two, and my daughter is a good Band-Aid. She takes the picture back and tells me, "We hafta hang it up because we don't have any pictures of us in the house, and we're supposed to have family photos in our house."

"Eloise isn't technically a part of our family."

My daughter shrugs. "She should be. Sadie's mommy came in to be the surprise reader the other day, and Eloise is a lot prettier than her. And I want Eloise to come and be a surprise reader, but she has to be my mommy to do that."

A lightning strike would have surprised me less.

"You like Eloise that much?" I ask, buckling her into her car seat.

"I love her. You do too, right? How comes she hasn't been to our house in a long time? Like a whole year!"

"It's been a few days," I correct and close the door, feeling suddenly hot.

I crack my window when I settle behind the wheel. "I think she'll come over again. Hopefully."

"And she can be my mommy?"

I eye Mazie's reflection in the rearview mirror, unsure of what to say. She has a mother, although Mazie hasn't seen her in over a year, and not too often before that. But hearing her desire to be a family with Eloise is hard for me to ignore when it's what I want too.

I turn to face Mazie. "I don't know about her being your mommy. We'll have to talk to her about that."

"Today?"

"No, not today."

"Tomorrow?"

I heave out a sigh. "Probably not tomorrow either."

"When?"

"I'm not sure, Maze. That's a big conversation, and me and Eloise need to talk about adult stuff before that."

She huffs and folds her arms. "Don't take too long. We have to ask her before somebody else does."

I start the ignition. My daughter's right. Can't wait too long. Can't let Eloise slip through our fingers.

Chapter 29
Eloise

Things for Sloane have been moving at lightning speed, while I feel as if I've been walking in mud ever since everything went down with Roman, so it's weird to walk into Sloane's house to find her on the floor of her living room, completely frozen.

It unsettles me, and I go into hyperactive mode, while she stares blankly at the tablet in her lap. "You're freaking me out a bit, Sloanie," I say, straightening up, folding blankets, and putting pillows back on couches. "What's going on?"

She doesn't answer until I'm right next to her, a tiny purple sweatshirt in my lap that belongs to Livie. "We're selling the house."

I blow out a breath. "That's... Full steam ahead."

She holds out the tablet to me. "I've been looking at apartments."

I take the device from her, scrolling on it for a few seconds, then hand it back to her. She looks like she hasn't slept in days. Probably hasn't.

"Trevor's pissed because I want to wait until after the holidays to tell the kids," she says, and I don't know what to do or how to fix this.

Her life is being turned upside down. Micah's and Olivia's lives will be turned upside down, and all *he* can think about is that they're not moving along fast enough?

"I think you're right to wait. I don't know anything about real estate, but I feel like putting a house on the market right now isn't the best time."

She sighs, rolling her head side to side as if she's got a kink in her neck. "That's what I said, but he knows best."

"He knows shit."

She huffs a sad sort of laugh. Progress. "I'm not even sure what I'm supposed to tell my parents. You know how they feel about him. What am I gonna say when he doesn't show up on Christmas? Sorry, Trevor can't come, he's fucking his girlfriend."

I shrug. "Might as well."

She bends her knees and sets her elbows on them to hold her head in her hands. "This is a mess."

I rub her back. Sloane's good with messes, but this one is a little too big to clean up, and I offer what I can. "It is a mess, and I hate that he's not helping you clean it up, but I will." I lean my head on her shoulder. "I love you."

I feel her cheek settle on my head. "Love you too."

After a minute passes, she sits up and blinks a few times, clearing the glassiness from her eyes and stands, taking Livie's sweatshirt from my hands. "Tell me about something else. Distract me."

I follow her to the kitchen, where she fills up the dishwasher. "I decided I'm making chocolate pecan pie and pumpkin tarts for Thanksgiving."

She snatches away the dish towel I'm playing with to toss it into a basket along with other dirty cloth napkins and towels. "Riveting stuff."

"There's not much else to tell," I lie as I trail her to the laundry room, and it's such a shame they're selling this house. Well, it's a shame Trevor's a cheater, and the least he could do is let Sloane stay in the house. My best friend was the one who made this house a home. It could be featured on HGTV. A fever dream of Joanna Gaines, all farmhouse chic in the middle of a college town in a Philly suburb.

"You're such a liar," my best friend says, tossing the kitchen towels into the washer. "You look like shit."

"Oh, real nice." I open the dryer to remove the clothes from it. "Why the hell are you still doing Trevor's laundry?"

"I don't know," she mumbles, grabbing a thick plastic hanger from the bar on the wall like she might use it as a weapon. "I don't know what the fuck I'm doing anymore."

I throw Trevor's white undershirt on the floor. "Well, don't do his laundry should be number one on the list. Don't do anything for him."

She stabs the hanger into one of his button-down shirts. "I just need to make it through to the end of the year." She tosses the shirt and hanger to the floor before jamming her fingers into her hair. "I found a lawyer, and she said I'll be able to receive alimony, but you know how much I make. It's not a lot, and I'm worried about staying afloat with the kids."

"Has he said anything about custody?" I ask carefully, and she shakes her head a few times then bends to pick up the clean clothes from the floor. Because my best friend doesn't throw tantrums.

I wish she would.

I think she'd feel better.

Once everything is in the basket, she takes it in her arms

and turns to me. "Please, I don't want to talk about it. Tell me what's going on with you."

I bite my lip, afraid to pile my drama onto her when she has so much stuff going on, but as if she can read my mind, she says, "I need to focus on something else, so give it to me. Why do you look like a feral prairie dog?"

"I'll take that as a compliment. Prairie dogs are adorable."

"Also Micah's latest fascination. They can run up to thirty-five miles per hour and have complex communication like dolphins and chimps."

I make squeaky noises, and Sloane pauses mid-stride. At her confusion, I tell her, "I'm a prairie dog."

She coughs a laugh. "That is not what prairie dogs sound like."

I trail her back to the living room. "Then what *do* they sound like?"

"Not like that."

I roll my eyes. "You don't know." I proceed to search YouTube on my cell phone for a video and turn the volume all the way up. I wasn't too far off from their barking call. "See?"

"See how you're changing the subject? Yeah, I do."

I flop on the couch and take two of Micah's socks out of the basket to continuously roll up into a ball, only to unroll. "I don't want to tell you."

She folds one of Olivia's T-shirts. "Why not?"

I set down the folded-up socks. "Because you have your own stuff going on, and I'm not gonna pile on my stress."

"Why not?

"Why are you so obsessed with me?" I ask in an imitation of Regina George.

She throws a pair of superhero underwear at me, and I laugh, tossing them on the growing pile of folded clothes. I reach for another pair of socks, these purple and belonging to Livie, and I heave out a sigh. "I don't even know where to start."

I take a deep breath, trying to find the right words to explain the mess I've found myself in. "So, Roman and I... You know it was getting intense there, and the other night I told you we were gonna go out, but when he showed up at my house, we..."

Sloane raises her brows when I trail off then fills in the blank. "You fucked instead?"

"Yes!" I throw myself to the side. "But it wasn't just fucking, it was making love."

"Making love," she teases in a high-pitched voice. "Roman with the anaconda dick makes looooooove."

I giggle because, of course, I already filled in my best friend on the important details. Like length and girth and how he likes his nipple piercings played with.

"It was amazing," I say, covering my flaming face with my hands. "Like, never ever, *ever* felt that way before."

Recalling that night, remembering how confident and safe he made me feel, and how I thought he loved me the same way I love him, I start to lose all my good humor. It takes me a long time to recover, and Sloane waits patiently as I gather myself. She's always been a good listener, and I'm grateful for that now more than ever.

"I told you that I reached out to Amy," I say quietly, and she nods. "But I didn't ever tell Roman."

Sloane stops folding the laundry. "Oh, Ellie."

I sniff. "I know. I know. I just... I didn't want to bring it up if nothing ever came from it."

She shakes her head, clearly reiterating what I already know—wrong decision.

"So what happened?" she asks, sitting down next to me so I

can put my head in her lap. While I stretch out, she plays with my hair. "I'm assuming he found out?"

"We missed our reservation, so he went out to my kitchen to order food, and he saw my mail. I didn't even know Amy had written me back. He didn't say anything about it, didn't tell me he saw it or read it or anything. He just left. Walked out."

"Walked out of your apartment?"

I toy with my necklace. "Mm-hmm. I guess it serves me right for reading his mail. Getting into his business." I take a deep breath that hiccups in my throat, and I'm close to losing it again. "He didn't respond to any of my texts or calls, and then when he finally talked to me the next day, it all blew up."

"Blew up like an argument?"

"Kinda." I rub at the stinging in my nose. "But not really. He was angry, and I got angry, and..." I blink a lot, attempting to stop the tears before they start. "He basically threw my family back in my face. Said I shouldn't be trying to fix his family when I have problems with my own."

Sloane sucks in an audible breath. "Ouch."

"I'm a big girl," I say between sniffles. "I can take it. I know I have stuff to deal with, and I know he was lashing out at me because I hurt him, but..."

"It's hard to hear it said out loud," she fills in, and I nod.

"Yeah, and even more because I love him." I force myself up, repeating to my best friend what I'd told Roman. "I love him."

And then I break down, crying into her shoulder. It takes me a minute to pull myself together enough to apologize to her. "I'm sorry. I didn't want to burden you with this. You've got enough on your plate."

She shakes her head. "You're my best friend. You could never be a burden to me." She takes my hand in hers. "I'll always be here for you, like you're always here for me. I'll help carry your load, like you help to carry mine."

Her words make me cry even harder, and she hands me the tissue box before standing back up to finish folding the kids' laundry. "So, what are you going to do?"

I rub at my wet eyes. "I don't know. I want to be with him, but I don't know how to prove that to him."

Once she's finished her task, she eyes me carefully. "Maybe you can start by proving him *wrong*." When I frown at her, she flicks her hand out toward my cell phone on the coffee table. "You told me you loved how he stood up for you at the wedding. Maybe it's time to stand up for yourself. Stand up for him."

My stomach churns at the idea of confronting my mother in a real way. Finally telling her what I've always wanted to but have been too afraid to rock the boat. I think about what Roman said, about how he never cares what people think about him... except for me.

He cared about me, and if I do this, it wouldn't only be for me, but for us too. I psych myself up with a few deep breaths and stand, shaking my hands out before pressing my mom's contact on my cell phone. I put it on speaker so Sloane can listen.

Mom answers on the third ring. "Eloise, hello. Haven't heard from you in a while."

"I've been busy," I say, and she makes a dubious noise on her end.

"So what do you need?"

"There's something I've wanted to tell you for a long time."

"Finally. I'm glad you came to your senses—"

I cut her off because I know she's still expecting an apology, but she's not going to get one. "You hurt my feelings."

"What?" She screeches the word. She can't even comprehend it.

"You hurt my feelings a lot with the way you speak to me. You talk down to me, and it makes me feel bad, and that's why I have a difficult time being around you."

"Eloise. How dare you."

"No, Mom, how dare *you*. It's funny that you're acting so surprised, when you literally do it every time you speak to me or see me."

"Do what?"

"Condescend to me. You say backhanded things about what I look like or how I act. You've never tried to understand my diagnosis, and you act like it's not real."

"You're being dramatic now. I've always been supportive of you."

Sloane rolls her eyes and sticks her middle finger up at the phone, and her being here for this makes me stronger. Bolder. Braver.

"It doesn't feel like it for me. That's what I'm trying to tell you. Your version of being supportive is not. It's always been a competition between you and your sister, and if you're not pitting me against Lily, you're tearing me down so that I become closer to the version of the daughter you want, and it's not okay. It's not right."

"This is..." She huffs. "I can't believe you've been keeping this from me."

"Because you don't ever listen to what I have to say. It's not easy to be your daughter when you're so critical of me, and I'm afraid to bring anything up to you because you'll either ignore it or tell me I'm making it up."

She stays quiet, so I take that as my sign to go on. Maybe she's finally getting it.

"I dread going to family events because of what you might say to me. It's not a fun way to live."

An eternity passes before she finally speaks, proving she does *not* get it. "Well, I'm a horrible mother, aren't I? Raising you, keeping you fed and clothed, and *supporting* you when you dropped out of college. How terrible to have parents who give you money to open your bakery. What an awful mother I am."

I squeeze my eyes shut. "This is exactly what I'm talking about. You're not listening to me. I never said I'm not grateful for you and Dad, but you speak to me as if I'm a piece of shit. That's how you make me feel, and I'm done taking it. Because I know what it feels like to be loved for all of my faults, and it doesn't feel like that with you."

"What are you talking about, Eloise? You're my daughter. Of course I love you."

"Then please start being kinder to me. Stop judging me. Because I can't be around you. And I especially don't want to bring my boyfriend around you. Not when I know what you think of him."

"You're still with him?" She scoffs. "Good lord, Eloise. He is not the man you—"

"He's everything I want. I love him, and if you can't deal with that, then you can fuck right off."

There's a stunned silence on the other end of the line, and I glance over at Sloane, who smiles and nods, silently clapping. I smile too. I think of how Roman would be proud, and like him, I don't have much else to say. "That's it. That's all I called to tell you, that I'm done being your punching bag. So, I guess I'll talk to you later, if you want. But only if you can have a good conversation with me. Otherwise... Bye."

I hang up on her and fall onto the couch. Sloane hugs me. "That was so fucking awesome. I'm so proud of you."

I exhale a relieved breath. A weight off my shoulder. "That felt good."

"One down, one to go. Just gotta work it out with Roman next."

I roll my head to the back of the cushions. "Actually feels easier now that I told my mother off. I might go complete a triathlon or something while I'm at it."

"You're on your own for that one," she says and checks the time. "The bus will be coming in a few minutes. You want to stay for dinner?"

"Obviously."

As we head outside to walk down to the bus stop, I throw my arm around her slim shoulders. "Thanks for being my best friend."

She slings her arm around my waist. "Thanks for being *my* best friend. And I wouldn't worry too much about Roman. I don't know him as well as you do, but I've been around those Stone boys long enough to know he fits right in. They all love hard. This is a rough patch. You can work through it."

I accept her wisdom with a sad smile because while it will hopefully work out for me, it won't work out for her.

But I've got her back.

And she's got mine.

Chapter 30
Roman

"Slow down, Maze."

She briefly stops her galloping at the corner of the sidewalk to wave at me to hurry up. I picked her up from school, a change in our regular schedule, but this couldn't wait.

And neither could my daughter.

I hold out my hand for her so we can cross the street, heading straight toward Sweet Cheeks. I texted Eloise to see where she was earlier this afternoon, and it made me nervous that she didn't text back right away, but when she eventually did, she informed me she was working, so here I am.

Ready to lay it all on the line.

As I stand outside the door, my heart thuds in my chest, and I wipe my palms on my jeans before pushing on the handle. Mazie races in, jumping up and down at the counter, while I slowly step inside, my gaze sweeping around the place for my woman. But she's nowhere in sight.

"Hey there," Mio says from her place behind the counter.

"Hi!" My kid points at the cinnamon rolls behind the glass. "Daddy said I could have one."

Mio laughs. "Lucky girl." Then, as if she's been expecting me, she motions to the curtain. "Elle's in the back."

Well, then.

With Mazie settled at a table with one of Eloise's gigantic cinnamon buns, I make my way to meet the baker herself. She's faced away from me, and I can't see what she's doing, but I assume whisking something by the way she's moving infinitesimally and the sounds of metal scraping. Her hair's pulled up in a knot at the back of her head with her usual headband keeping loose locks away. She's dressed in high-waisted leggings and a short pink shirt, her round hips and ass on display, a sliver of skin visible that my fingers tingle to touch. The memory of her thighs around my waist and the feel of her belly under my hand ransack my brain, hurling all the words I'd practiced from my head.

I watch as she steps over to one of the ovens and slips on mitts to pull out a pan that makes my mouth water with the scents of sugar and cinnamon wafting my way. I'll never not think of Eloise when I smell it.

She pours the icing she'd been mixing over it then places the bowl in the sink, but not before running a spoon along the inside and popping it into her mouth. She nods to herself then turns to wash her hands, and that's when I close the distance between us. I snatch a folded towel from the counter near me and hold it out toward her as I step up to her side.

When she sees me, she stumbles back, one wet hand planting on her chest, the other ripping out her AirPod. "Oh my god."

"Sorry."

She droops, taking the towel from my hands, and wipes them off before setting it down along with both of her AirPods.

She lifts her gaze, and all the air whooshes out of my lungs. Like the first time I laid my eyes on her, it's that same punch in my chest—strong, overwhelming, undeniable.

I love her.

I loved her from that first moment.

And I still love her.

I plant my feet and anchor myself to the moment, breathing her name like a prayer and apology all in one. "Eloise."

She blinks, her lips parted in an inhale, and then blinks again. Her pretty green eyes fill with water, and I bend immediately, catching the first tear on her cheek with a kiss. "Don't cry."

She sniffles, leaning into my touch. It's been a few days since we've seen each other, but it might as well have been years for the magnitude of how it feels to be reunited with her. I know I said I was the one who needed time, and that was a self-inflicted wound.

I didn't need time to know I loved Eloise. I needed time to realize I can't do what I've done before and run away. There is no running away from Eloise.

It would be like losing a limb. An organ.

My heart.

I wait until her eyes are dry, but I keep my hands on her face, sweeping my thumbs over her cheeks. "I'm sorry. I'm sorry for walking out of your apartment that night and not answering you, and I'm really sorry for what I said about your family. It was way out of line."

She nods, curling her hands around my wrists. "And I'm sorry for going behind your back to contact Amy. I shouldn't have overstepped like that."

"I know you did it because you thought it was the right thing," I say, holding her gaze, "but I wish you would have talked to me first. I want you in my life. You're the one and only person I actually want up in my business, but—"

"But only if you know I'm up in your business," she finishes, and I pinch her chin.

"I promise I'll tell you everything and be open with you. I want you to know everything about me. No secrets."

"No secrets," she agrees, and then I kiss her because I can. Because I can't wait any longer. She tastes familiar and new all at the same time, but before I can get sidetracked by the taste of her tongue, she backs away slightly and crinkles her nose. "I... Reading Amy's letter..."

"It's okay." I slide my hands down to her throat, her pulse beating rapidly behind my fingers, and she licks her lips.

"I don't want this to come off in a type of way..."

I shake my head. I won't ever judge her, and I feel her swallow under my palm. She clears her throat. "Amy seems like, maybe, she still needs to work through things."

"Yeah."

"I didn't like what she said about you."

I shrug.

"I understand why you're so hesitant, and I'm really sorry."

I lean down to kiss her again, but she stops me with two fingers against my lips.

"I also had a conversation with my mother."

My brows shoot up in interest.

"I told her that she had to stop speaking to me the way she does, making me feel bad." I don't have time to ask more questions, because Eloise goes right on. "She tried to make me feel bad about that, but you were right in that I had to stop letting her rule me. I had to stand up to her. I told her how she constantly makes me feel like shit, and she was quiet at first. I think because she must've realized what I was saying, how much she's hurt me, but then she tried to turn it around on me."

She flicks her hand. "So now I have a new list of things to talk about with my therapist. I'm just done being her punching bag. I can't have her in my life if she's going to continue to treat me the way she does. And you, too. She has to be nice to you. I told her that I love you, and if she can't accept us being together, then she can fuck right off."

Pride swells in my chest. Not only because she did something really difficult and stood her ground, but that she claimed me.

"There's my girl," I murmur and cover her mouth with mine. I pour everything I feel for her into that kiss—my pride, my love, my devotion. Pressing my forehead to hers, I tell her, "I'm so fucking proud of you. You're strong and brave, and I love you. I love you so much."

She gasps at my declaration, her smile as bright as the sun.

My sunshine.

"Say it again," she orders, and I will tell her as many times as she wants to hear it.

"I love you, Eloise, and I want to be with you. You're mine."

She speaks her answer against my lips. "You're mine too."

"Look," I say, swiveling my head to show her the new ink on the side of my neck.

"Oh my god," she whispers. "Is that..."

I nod. "For you."

"Are they..."

I nod again. "Your lips."

"How?"

I face her again, but all of her attention is on the hot-pink lips I had tattooed by Ian. A perfect replica of her mouth. "The night we went to dinner before the wedding." I mime how she patted her lips after she put her lipstick on. "I kept the tissue."

She stares at me with wide-eyed wonder. "I can't believe

you did that. Kept a tissue." Then she drags her fingertips over her permanent mark. "I can't believe you did this."

"I've always got you with me. It's not the only one either." I take off my coat so I can lift the sleeve of my T-shirt to show her the one Cash inked on my triceps. The small prairie dog with bright, rainbow-colored fur, holding a cinnamon roll.

"Oh my god! I was just talking with Sloane about prairie dogs. They're Micah's latest obsession, and now I'm kind of obsessed with them too. Did you know they have tight-knit family units called coteries and those coteries form little neighborhoods?" She presses her fingers together in front of her face as if she's becoming a prairie dog in front of me. "Isn't that adorable? There are whole prairie dog towns."

I love anything she loves, so I nod, extraordinarily happy at the coincidence of having a perfect tattoo to represent her.

"When did you get that?" she asks, tracing her fingertips over the tiny rodent on my arm.

"Before our fight. I lost a bet and had to get something by one of the guys."

"That's why I didn't notice." She frowns, touching it, opening her mouth like she might apologize again, but like Ian said, the past is in the past.

"It's over. We don't need to keep rehashing it. Just tell me you love me and keep moving forward, okay?"

"I love you." She loops her arms around my neck, ducking her face so her nose skims my throat. "You're a big softy, aren't you? My giant refrigerator is actually quite ooey, gooey underneath."

I'm about to argue, but she presses her lips to my neck, right over *her* lips, sucking at the spot. Goddamn, this woman drives me wild.

Unable to resist any longer, I sweep her up, her legs wrapping around my waist. Our lips meet again, hot and urgent. We lick into each other's mouths, a little sloppy, a lot desperate, and I tighten my grip on her ass as she tunnels her fingers into my hair. I'm about to lift her onto the stainless-steel counter when the sound of the curtain swishing open makes us both freeze.

Eloise and I both whip our heads around to see Mio's eyes go wide. She immediately spins on her heel to march right back out, and Eloise bursts into giggles against my neck. I let a smile loose too.

I reluctantly set her back down and smooth my hands over her hips, silently cursing that I hadn't thought ahead about how I'd want to strip her naked and fuck her as soon as possible. But we're in her kitchen, and my kid's right out front.

"I brought Mazie with me," I say, linking my fingers with Eloise's, tugging her toward the curtain, but she stops me.

"Wait. Wait. I have something for you." She pulls me toward the other end of the counter, where the pan she took out of the oven sits on a cooling rack. Sitting front and center is an enormous cinnamon bun, drizzled with so much icing it's spilling over the edges.

"I made this for you. And Mazie." She bumps my hip with hers. "My own way of apologizing."

"She's gonna sleep at your place after she eats this. You can deal with her sugar high."

"Nothing I can't handle."

I don't doubt it, and we make our way out to the front of the bakery, hand in hand. I immediately spot Mazie, perched on a chair with cinnamon bun carnage covering the table in front of her. She's managed to coat her cheeks and chin in icing. But the second she sees Eloise, she jumps down and charges over.

"Ellie!"

She crashes into her legs, and Eloise doesn't hesitate to sweep her up into a hug, getting icing smeared all over her shirt in the process. She doesn't even flinch, merely laughs and wipes at Mazie's mouth with her hand, something so natural and maternal about the action, and I know she was meant for this. Meant for us.

"I have something for you," Mazie practically screams at Eloise, and I blow out a breath.

"Volume, Maze."

She ignores me—of course—too intent on retrieving the paper bag from her table. She holds it out eagerly. "For you!"

Eloise takes it, peering inside. When she pulls out the framed drawing, her smile falters. I watch emotions flicker across her face as she takes in the picture Mazie drew of us— her family. The same one she'd drawn of me with blue hair, Eloise as a pink stick figure, Mazie in a pink dress, and Steve. All of us holding hands. Even the rabbit.

I did frame it, like she asked.

Tears fill Eloise's eyes, and Mazie's forehead crinkles with concern. "Why are you crying? Are you sad?"

Eloise is quick to assure her. "No, babe. I love it. I just got a little choked up because I'm so happy." She kneels down to Mazie's level. "This is the most special gift anyone has ever given me."

My daughter beams, throwing her arms around Eloise's neck. "I love you."

"I love you too. So much."

Eloise meets my gaze over Mazie's shoulder before picking her up and leaning against my chest, so I can wrap my arms around both of them. And I know without a doubt, we're going to be a family.

Me and my two girls.

Chapter 31
Eloise

In the two weeks since Roman and I reunited, I've rarely stayed at my own apartment. So much so that he bought me my own toothbrush and toiletries, making sure I have my shampoo and conditioner. In return, I convinced him to start wearing moisturizer and stop using a three-in-one body and hair wash.

Soon, I'll have those luscious locks of his shining and healthy. I comb my fingers through the nearly black strands as he rests his head on my chest, one arm slung around my waist, the other tucked up under me. My personal weighted blanket.

We spent the night with the entire extended Stone family at Griffin and Andi's house, where I ate way too many servings of Nicole's sweet potatoes fried in butter and cinnamon, and laughed so hard at Clara's impression of *Batman* during charades that my cheeks still ache.

There was more fun and love in this one night than I think I've experienced in my own family in all the years combined. My mother had called and left a voice mail about attending Thanksgiving dinner at her house, but didn't say anything else, didn't reference anything I told her when we previously spoke about how she treats me. So I ignored it.

And while it makes me uncomfortable to disappoint people, my chosen family more than makes up for it.

I trace my fingers along Roman's arm, over the dark ink of his forearms and up to his biceps then back to where he has his mother's tattoo next to mine. I smile to myself at the outrageously adorable animal then splay my palm over the balloon, thinking about Violet Stone and how she must be so proud of Roman. Of all her kids. Her entire family.

"I had a lot of fun tonight," I say, breaking the silence, and he shifts his weight so he can look at me while still lying on top of me.

"It was fun. I'm glad you came, that you're with me."

"I guess it's a good thing that your family already likes me. I don't have to impress anyone."

He levers up over me, his muscled arms holding himself up, and I wrap my hands around his thick shoulders, his hair falling like a curtain around us, as if giving us even more privacy. "Did you think you had to? Do we need to play our game again?"

"No, I don't need to name anything I'm good at." He arches his eyebrow dubiously, and I laugh. "I'm fine. I'm just thinking about things."

"Things like what?"

"Your mom, and what she would think of me."

"I think she'd love you."

"You think she'd be upset by how fast we're moving?"

Since my own mother disapproves of my choices, I would hope at least his mom would be okay with them. That she'd approve of Roman and me being together. That she'd want us to be happy.

"You think we're moving fast?" he asks, and when I shrug, he lowers himself back down to lie on me, his face against my throat, legs settled in the pocket of my thighs. "I've never done what is normal for society, so I've never considered it. But if we are moving too fast, we can slow down. We can go at whatever pace you want."

I focus on the ceiling of his bedroom. All the walls are white, and there is no personality anywhere to be seen. "You should paint in here."

"Okay," he agrees, lips ghosting over my earlobe.

"The only room you painted so far is Mazie's room, right? You need to do all of them. They're so sad. Like a hospital with all the white."

"You volunteering to pick out colors?"

"Yes."

He tucks my hair behind my ear, his beard scraping in the hollow behind it. "Not too fast, then?"

"My brain goes two thousand miles an hour. You could never keep up with me."

He leans up on his elbow, accepting the challenge with a cluck of his tongue. "No?"

"Pfft. I've thought about every possible scenario already."

"Like what?"

"A wedding."

He nods, eyes never leaving mine. "Laid-back, with no first dances or assigned seats. Outside, with comfort food and disposable cameras for everyone to take pictures."

I grin. "You remembered all of that."

"I told you. I remember everything you say. Like how I would be invited, but I'd have to bring a date."

"I did say that," I murmur, as he strokes his index finger across my cheekbone and down to my lips.

"Too bad for you, you're my forever date."

"You want to get married?"

"Definitely," he replies without hesitation, toying with my

bottom lip, rubbing the pad of his finger back and forth across it.

"What about more kids?"

"I'm forty. Seems a little old for a baby."

I shrug. "I'm thirty, and that biological clock is almost out of battery."

He pinches my chin, holding my gaze. "So you want some?"

"I'd like to. If you want more."

He ducks down, speaking his words into my mouth. "Only with you."

Then he wraps his hand around my throat, angling my head to kiss me, unhurried and almost lazy. For a conversation about how fast we're moving, we're at a glacial pace now.

My limbs are heavy, my body weighed down by the holiday dinner. I didn't plan on having sex tonight, but I don't try to stop Roman when he tugs my sleep T-shirt off, revealing my breasts to his hungry attention. He uses his hands and mouth to love them, squeeze and kiss and suck until my hips are bucking off the bed, and then he shucks my pants, leaving me naked and on display. He kneels between my legs, licking his lips as he admires me, and I've never felt so beautiful as I do under his dark gaze.

He reverently strokes his hand over the roundness of my stomach and down to my thigh, running the backs of his fingers along the sensitive inner flesh, inching closer and closer to where I want him with every pass but never meeting.

I squirm, reaching out for him, but he shakes his head. "Hands down. Let me enjoy."

It's difficult to stay still, but I try my best as his mouth follows the same path his hand did, his hot breath wafting over me, his tongue wet, lips soft. His beard tickles, and he inten-tionally rubs it over certain spots since we both like seeing the red reminders there later, before finally backing up to kneel on the floor, tugging me to the edge of the bed so he can give the aching flesh between my legs the same treatment. Soft licks of his tongue, too-tender kisses that send shivers down my spine. Blood pools low in my belly, his quiet hums echoing in my bones.

I'm hot and on edge by the time he leans over me, his lips shiny and swollen. "On your side," he directs roughly before digging into the nightstand drawer for lube and a small silicone plug that makes my insides flutter with anticipation. He strips then settles on the bed in front of me, drawing me close with my leg over his hip, leaving just enough room for me to slip my hand between us to fist his erection. He grunts quietly when I squeeze it, whispering, "Daddy."

"Careful, sunshine. I want to go slow with you tonight."

And my already overinflated heart grows another three sizes, practically bursting out of my chest. "I love you."

"I love you too," he says, then carefully squeezes out the jelly, working it between my legs and up to the back, prodding and circling until I'm begging him for more. That's when he slips the plug in and drives his length inside me.

I don't think I'll ever get used to the feeling, the bite of pain and the rush of pleasure. He fills up every part of me, careful with each inch.

The man who looks like he could kill, brought low by a bit of sugar and a whole lot of pink.

Chapter 32
Roman

The vague smell of paint and fresh carpet lingers in the air as Ian, Griffin, and Taryn take a look around the house. In the past five months, I've renovated every single room, installed a new garage door, repaved the drive and the cracked sidewalk, and torn out the dead tree in the backyard, making room for a swing set.

Dante helped a lot, but Ian and Griffin took turns on weekends, when they could, helping me paint and spackle. It was important for me and them that they were here. As we worked, they told me stories about the house, memories they had—good and bad—some about Dad, but mostly all about Mom. It healed all of us to fix up the house. When we finished the kitchen, we all measured ourselves against the doorway, marking it with our names and year.

Mazie's looking forward to seeing how she grows. I am too.

"A smidge over," Taryn says, and I barely move the frame before glancing over my shoulder at my sister. She nods. "Perfect."

I settle the photo and stand back, folding my arms over my chest.

"It's perfect there," Ian says, gesturing to the windows on either side of it, the sunshine pouring into the room, mimicking the light in the photo behind our mother.

"Thanks for holding on to it for me," I tell Griffin. "I told you I'd come for it."

He grips my shoulder tightly. "You did, and I'm real glad."

Silence descends between the four of us as we admire Mom. Her long, dark hair around her shoulders, her big smile, a book open in front of her. We can't be sure, but we estimate she was in her early twenties when it was taken. Andi found the photo in Griffin's closet, and she blew it up, framing copies for each of us.

When Griffin texted me to tell me, it was in the middle of a bad day with Mazie. At that point, we hadn't seen Amy in a few weeks—this was before she was even arrested—and I'd finally soothed Mazie to sleep after a crying jag. Then the message came through with a picture of the photo, and I had chills all over.

A voice in the back of my head that sounded suspiciously like my mother, telling me it was time to go home.

Three years later, I finally did it.

Home.

With my family.

Taryn clears her throat and sniffs. "You did a wonderful job, Rome. Everything, the house, Mazie... Be proud of yourself."

I manage a tight smile, feeling like there is a balloon in my chest. "Thanks."

Ian points to the custom shelves Dante installed. "Is that the pillow?"

For The Weekend

When I nod, he crosses over to the wall to pick it up. After Mom passed away, we all chose some of her personal effects to keep. Taryn took the *I Love Lucy* collectibles, Griffin picked a box of pictures, and Ian brought home the few pieces of jewelry she wore. I chose the pillow. Mom taught high school English her whole career, and one year, her graduating seniors made her a pillow, signing their names and messages about how much they loved and appreciated her with a big *#1 Teacher* in the middle. I'm not sure why, but at the time, it felt like it was evidence she was important not only to me but to the world. She was beloved.

"And the blanket," Ian notes with a laugh.

I also chose the baby blanket, the one she supposedly used to wrap all of us in to bring us home from the hospital. It's a thin scrap of material now, with so many holes it is unusable, but I could never let it go.

Especially now.

Even though it's purely sentimental, it's a reminder of why I called my siblings over in the first place.

With a deep breath, I face them and let it rip. "Eloise is pregnant."

Like they did months ago, they stare at me, eyes like saucers, and then shout, "What the fuck?"

But this time, Mazie is out of the house, at the park with Eloise, so there is no foulmouthed little girl to repeat it.

When they come back to their senses, they converge on me in one big group.

"Congratulations!"

"When's the due date?"

"Does Mazie know?"

"You did good, kid. You did real good."

"I guess my lessons on birth control never stuck."

I give in to a laugh that's rough with emotion and lift my head, turning to look at Mom.
Smiling at all of us.

Epilogue
Roman

Just as I place the frame with the ultrasound picture of "Blob" —the nickname Eloise gave our future baby—on my desk, Shawn sprints into the office. "Yo, boss, Camden fucking Long is out there."

"Oh yeah."

"Oh yeah?" He tosses his arms out to the sides. "Oh fucking yeah? You knew he was coming?"

"He's the owner of the Camaro."

"Shit." Shawn settles back on his heels. "No wonder you kept it under wraps."

I nod and step around the excited twenty-year-old. "Take your lunch."

"Yeah, okay. But you think he'll sign something for me?"

I arch my brows. I doubt it. "You want his signature?"

Shawn grins. "He might be a dick, but he's still Camden fucking Long, you know?"

"Take lunch," I say with a roll of my eyes before heading out to meet Camden fucking Long.

He's in the lobby, dressed casually in jeans and a T-shirt,

aviators over his eyes. I reach out my hand to introduce myself. "Hey, I'm Roman Stone."

Camden dips his chin, clearly taking me in over the rim of his sunglasses. "Didn't expect you to be such a big mother-fucker."

I shrug. We're about the same height, though he's leaner than I am. He's in peak physical condition, at the top of his game. Too bad he's a dick, like Shawn said. "Didn't expect you to lose the Bowl for us."

At that, his arrogant mask slips, his jaw tight as the man next to him coughs into his fist. When I turn to him, he offers me a smile. "I'm Malcolm."

"My babysitter," Long grits out.

"Assistant," Malcolm corrects.

Long whips his head to the side. "You're fired."

"You don't sign my paychecks. You can't fire me."

"Oh my fucking god," Long grumbles then blows out a breath before gesturing to the garage. "Can I see my car now?"

I wave for him to follow me to the back, where I tug off the sheet I had covering it to reveal the bright-blue 1978 Camaro LZ1. He finally removes his sunglasses, whistling through his teeth as he bends to glide his fingers along the hood. I explain how I modified the engine, converted the fuel injection, and put in the new seats to accommodate his size, as he requested, and Camden Long actually smiles at me. "Beautiful work, Stone. You take checks, right?"

At my nod, he slides a checkbook out of his back pocket and steals a pen from his assistant's hand.

"This is a terrible idea," the assistant-babysitter says, but Long shakes his head.

"Don't go running your mouth about it back to Rosenstein."

"That's literally my job," Malcolm mumbles so only I can hear as Long finishes signing the check with a flourish.

Epilogue

He hands it over to me with a pat to my shoulder. "For keeping it on the down-low for me. Thanks."

The paper in my hand has an extra zero on the end of the number we agreed upon, and he might be an arrogant prick, but at least he's a generous one.

I shake his hand with a warning. "I used to play ball. I was at Penn State and threw it all away. Don't be like me."

He slides his shades back on, but not before I catch the slight tension around his eyes. He catches the keys I toss to him and hops behind the wheel as I open the garage door for him to drive out. Malcolm stands next to me as we watch him take off down the street, engine firing loud enough to hear from a few blocks away.

"Work in public relations, you'll be great at it, they said." He snorts and tips his head up to meet my gaze. "Professional sports, it'll be fun, they said." Then he sighs and turns away from me with a quiet, "Nice meeting you."

I walk out with him in time to see Eloise sashaying toward me, pink box in hand. She waves to Malcolm, asking, "Hey, how are ya?" as if she knows him. Then she throws herself at me, smelling of sugar and spice and everything nice. "Thought you might want to try my new cherry tarts."

I grab her ass, lifting her slightly. "After."

"After?"

Shawn will be back from his lunch break in twenty minutes, so I need as much sunshine as I can get before he returns. I tilt my head, silently directing her to the office. "*After*."

"Yes, after," she agrees with a smile, one hand on her stomach, over our Blob, the other reaching for me, tugging me forward. Where she leads, I follow.

* * *

What's Next?

If you want more Roman and Eloise content, use the QR code to have it delivered straight to your inbox!

To stay up to date with all things Sophie Andrews, use the QR code on the next page to stay in touch!

What's Next?

Acknowledgments

In the summer of 2024, I wrote a version of Roman and Eloise's story that I thought was going to be book one in a series about a tattoo shop. But after attending Romance Author Mastermind, put together by Skye Warren, and being coached through new plans by some really amazing authors, the Stone Siblings were born. While Roman and Eloise's story has changed a little bit since that first draft, I believe they are all the better for it.

Thank you to Lily Bear for the amazing covers. As always, Libby and Lisa have turned my brain vomit into a pretty decent novel, which is always a miracle.

Biggest thank you to all of my readers. Thank you for your DMs and for your early reviews and for making all of this worth it. Without you, I'd literally just be writing these books and reading them out loud to myself like I used to do when I was a kid. And while that's fun, it's so much more fun to know people love these silly little books. I am forever grateful for you.

And if you'd like more information about me, you can find it at https://sophieandrewsauthor.com/

About the Author

Sophie Andrews is a contemporary romance author who writes steamy books that will leave you smiling. As a millennial, she's obsessed with boybands, late 90s rom-coms, and will always be team Pacey. When she's not writing, she's most likely trying to wrangle her children or drinking red wine. Or both at the same time.

Also by Sophie Andrews

Stone Family

Under One Roof

Just This Once

Right Next Door

For The Weekend

Single Dads' Club

The Rehearsal Fling

The Nanny Tenure

The Dating Pact

The Bartender's Baby

Tangled Series

Tangled Up

Tangled Want

Tangled Hearts

Tangled Beginning

Tangled Expectations

Tangled Chances

Tangled Ambition

Stand-Alones

How to Ruin a Wedding

Love at a Funeral and Other Awkward Conversations

* 9 7 8 1 9 5 7 5 8 0 7 6 0 *